DEADLY BY
NATURE

*For Serkay & Benny
with much love,
Murdin*

DEADLY BY
NATURE

Meredith Andrew

A *Midnight Original* MURDER MYSTERY

THE MERCURY PRESS

The publisher gratefully acknowledges the financial assistance of the Canada Council and the Ontario Arts Council, as well as that of the Government of Ontario through the Ontario Publishing Centre.

AUTHOR'S ACKNOWLEDGEMENTS

For my puzzle solver, A.S.

The author would like to thank Jeff Richardson for his trusty friendship and advice.

The quote from "Don't Fence Me In," by Cole Porter, is copyright © 1944 WARNER BROS. INC. All rights reserved. Used by permission.
The quote from "The Blackfly Song," words and music by Wade Hemsworth, is copyright © 1957 by Southern Music Publishing Company (Canada) Ltd., copyright renewed, international copyright secured, all rights reserved. Used by permission.

Edited by Beverley Daurio
Cover design by Scott McKowen
Composition and page design by TASK
Proofreading by Dan Bortolotti
Author photo by Tony Fouhse
Printed and bound in Canada by Metropole Litho
Printed on acid-free paper
First Edition
1 2 3 4 5 99 98 97 96 95

Canadian Cataloguing in Publication Data
Andrew, Meredith
Deadly by nature
ISBN 1-55128-022-1
I. Title
PS85551.N47D43 1995   C813'.54   C95-932322-8
PR9199.3.A74D43 1995

The Mercury Press
137 Birmingham Street
Stratford, Ontario
Canada   N5A 2T1

CHAPTER 1

The river was desperate. It rushed its overflow down and down, over huge, lichened rocks, over torn and tugged-at tree roots, over its own banks, furious in its resolve to lighten itself. It was a furious river but a foolhardy one, for the sky had it beaten.

The rain was still falling hard, as it had since Monday. It splattered and clattered on the river in a mess— there was no complex pattern like what's formed by rain needling down on a still lake or city pavement. All of that was lost in the force of the rain's attack on the river and in the river's frantic bailing out.

At the edge of the Speller River on Wednesday there was nothing to hear but water. Further up the boulders and smooth shield banks, where the Jack Falls hammered, you could easily go mad with hearing it. But back in the woods, along a path through the fern, trilliums and young birches, with the red pine, budding oaks and maples overhead condensing the rain into fat drips and splotches, there was near silence and a shy veery fluting— its voice like one of those hose-type kids' toys that swings in circles to make a round hollow sound.

The steep, hesitant path wound up for a hundred yards and ended at a clearing above the falls. In summer the long grasses there would be sparked with yellow hawkweed and devil's paintbrush. Now, in May, everything was a pale, fragile green.

In the middle of the clearing were the soggy ashes of a camp fire, a half-collapsed tent, and three men standing, with their hands on their hips, over a sodden shape on the ground.

The three men were Gamenagi natives from the reserve up river. The reserve was accessible by car from the highway, but only along a winding, wayward, and sometimes impassable corduroy road.

Some of the natives would leave their trucks in the provincial parking lot closer to town and travel the three miles upstream to the reserve by canoe— despite the tough paddling, the portage around the falls, and the sometimes dangerous state of the river. They figured the wear and tear it saved their trucks was worth the trip.

Angus Pender and his two nephews, Paul and Cyril, had been heading back down the overwrought river to get their truck from the lot. They'd been on their way into the town of Shallow Bay where they'd been planning to shop for a wood-splitter.

Friends had told them they were nuts, that they should wait until the weather settled. But this spring it looked like the weather never would, wood-splitters were on sale and Christ, after all, how many times had they done the trip? They knew the damn river, Angus especially. So.

They'd hauled out their canoe for the portage at a cautious spot for them. Normally they would have paddled closer to the falls. They'd seen the tent in the clearing and had gone over. When they'd gotten to the guy lying face down, with soaked clothes and putty coloured skin, they hadn't been crazy about touching him. Then Angus knelt down. When he rolled him over, the guy groaned.

"Shit," Angus said, stepping quickly back.

The guy's face and neck were poxy from black flies and he was all puffed out with moisture and venom. There was a ragged bar of mud across his forehead and a smudge of mud on his nose, like zinc oxide on a sunbather. As the rain fell on his face, the mud broke up, trickled down his temples and cheeks and dripped from the hair of his beard. His eyes were closed but his mouth continued to move a little, as if he were tracing out the syllables in a slightly disgusting book.

"We better get him somewhere," said Cyril. "We better take him down to the Bay." Cyril looked back and forth between his uncle and brother.

"No," said Angus. "That'd take a good two hours, at least. We better take him up home and call somebody. They can send out a helicopter and we can warm him up meanwhile." Angus stepped back over to the guy, leaned down and touched his forehead. "Jesus, he's freezing. It's okay, buddy," he said, "You're gonna be okay, right?" The guy shuddered.

"You two look in the tent for a dry blanket or something to wrap him up in. Then let's get the hell outa here."

In the drooping tent they found two sleeping bags that were only partly wet and wrapped the guy up in them both. They also found two half-unpacked backpacks, shoved clothes and odds and ends into them and loaded them and the guy into the canoe.

Paul stayed behind because there wasn't room.

"Since I'm fucking stuck out here, I'll look around for the other one," he called as Angus and Cyril began shoving their weight against the river. "Two bags, two packs. There's got to be another one around, eh?"

"Look for the boat, anyways," Angus yelled back. "They didn't walk all the way here."

It took the Penders almost an hour to get back home. It took almost another hour for the helicopter to come from Shallow Bay Memorial Hospital. On it were two paramedics and two cops from the OPP.

Angus and his wife Doreen had found the guy's wallet in his pants. Patrick Joseph Irving, his ID said. They'd undressed him and put him in their bed, piling all of the blankets in the house and a couple of winter coats on top of him. Cyril had tried to get Irving to drink some water but it had spilled down his bearded chin, and he had slid into a stillness that had all of them on edge.

"Dehydration and hypothermia," one of the paramedics yelled out over the rain and the whoomfing of the propeller. "And something else. He's been vomiting a lot." The helicopter dipped and swung off, taking away Irving, on a stretcher with an IV in his arm, and leaving the cops and the Penders standing in the rain looking at each other.

"Let's go inside," said Angus. "You probably want to ask some questions, eh?" The cops said yeah and they walked the few steps to Angus' house.

"You want us to take off our boots?" the older cop asked Doreen, who was taking their slick coats and hanging them over chairs in the kitchen.

"That's okay," said Doreen, uncomfortably, "the place is already soaked."

"Suit yourself," replied the cop and dropped down on to the sofa, while the younger one stayed standing with a notebook and pencil, peering around at the room.

The cops asked their questions. The Penders answered. The story got told.

"Okay, so let's take a look at those packs," said the older cop. "We know about Mr. Irving thanks to your nosing around in his wallet."

"I recognized him," said the younger cop.

"So you said already," snapped the older. "Now let's see what we can do about the other one." They started to empty the first pack, an olive green Arc'teryx.

"Pricey," the younger cop commented.

"Okay. Here we got a lot of men's stuff and then we got some ladies' underwear," the older cop said. "So either Mr. Irving was camping with a lady or he liked to dress up in ladies' underwear and came out here to the woods where nobody could see him do it..." The younger cop looked up from his notebook and laughed.

"Some things coulda got mixed up," Cyril said. "We just shoved in everything we saw."

"Ohhh, thank you, chief, for the clarification. I'd also like to thank you for touching everything you could get your hands on. Next time, use your brains, okay?"

Cyril lightly kicked the table next to where he was standing and whispered, "Fuck you."

The cops examined the other pack and found mostly women's clothes. At the very bottom they found a small leather pouch. In it was $180 cash, a couple of credit cards, and a driver's licence.

"Gina Ferrara," the older cop read. "Real flattering shot. Jesus. She looks like she just got told her goddamn dog died." He turned to Angus. Throughout the interview, he had been watching the rain through the window. "So, okay. You leave anything out?"

Angus glanced at him and then went back to the rain. "Now what's supposed to happen? My nephew's still out there getting pissed on."

"Well, he's gonna get a lot worse than that if he's been making mud pies outa that campsite. God, don't you people know any better? You get TV. You know you're not supposed to touch anything in a situation like this."

Angus looked at him again, this time hard. "We didn't know it was a 'situation,' mister. We just found a guy that was pretty sick. We coulda left him, right? Now if you two are done you can go wait for your ride in the rec hall over there. There's a pop machine and everything. You'll be real comfortable."

The two cops got their coats and went back out into the rain, without ever having told the Penders their names.

CHAPTER 2

Lucy Shepherd was tired. She'd been awake half the night, spiffing up her nine o'clock lecture— at the last minute, as usual. At about four in the morning she ran out of cigarettes and dashed through the rain, without a coat, to the 24-hour corner store which was, at that hour, closed. She peered through the streaming plate glass door into the freezer-lit greyness. The only life inside was a cat which whisked its tail and stared back at her dryly.

"You little catty creep," she whispered, tapping her finger on the glass. "You little kitty shit."

She then reasoned herself out of the need to buy cigarettes, figuring she'd only be up another hour. There'd been a time, after all, when she *hadn't* smoked. Life had gone on normally and her brain had worked okay. So surely now she could handle it. Surely she had the strength for that. And so, she went back home.

When she left the apartment again, twenty minutes later, she was wearing a man's dark green wool overcoat that she'd bought second hand, and was carrying an umbrella with a broken spoke. Back on Dundas Street, several cabs slowed down as they drove past her, and one of the drivers swore at her when she shook her head no. A police car cruised by and also slowed down, then inexplicably accelerated, squealing its tires as it took the corner at the light.

Two hookers with wet, lanky hair were sheltered under a dry cleaner's awning, wearing open-toed high heels and tiny dresses under short bomber jackets. Lucy kept her eyes down as she passed them. A red-faced toothless man at the donut store door asked her for money as she went in.

The donut store was a swirl of stale smoke and she felt disgusted for making herself go through this. The fluorescent light, the orange walls, the crazy old woman making faces in the corner, the two drunks talking loudly and incoherently, with one untouched coffee between them, about "Gus and that fuckin' broad," the grim Chinese girl at the counter— this stuff made her sick and sad. She bought a half-pack of Export A to get her through the night and a cherry danish that she didn't even want to look at. She gave the toothless man a loonie on her way out. He said, "God bless yer."

It was after five when she finally got to bed, and at eight the coffee didn't do much good. Her head felt like a styrofoam cup filled with sand.

But she made it to the university with ten minutes to spare, dumped some papers in her office, flattened her short brown hair and headed for Room 41, where she was about to deliver a third-year lecture on the physiology of the land leech.

Halfway there she met Cheryl Popywich, one of her grad students, a bit of a keener but brainy and efficient.

"Cheryl," Lucy said, "how're you doing?"

"Pretty good, Lucy, but I've got way too much to do today," Cheryl replied. She lowered her voice, and put her hand on Lucy's arm complicitously. Lucy hated being touched like that and gritted her teeth.

"I read about Patrick Irving," Cheryl was saying. "I was really upset. I hope he's going to be all right."

"What?" Lucy said, looking at Cheryl in surprise. "What happened to him?"

Cheryl dropped her hand from Lucy's arm.

"Oh, I just assumed you knew. Nobody phoned you or anything? It was in the *Toronto Post* this morning. I'm really sorry. I assumed you knew," Cheryl rambled on in confusion.

"What happened?" said Lucy with exasperation and alarm.

"He was in some kind of accident up north. He was with Gina Ferrara who wrote for the *Post*..." Cheryl looked grave but talked with a tingle.

Lucy had known that Patrick was going camping, fifty miles east of North Bay. He'd told her the week before that he was thinking about going with Gina Ferrara. But even if he hadn't told her, she would have known. The trip— including a map of the white-water sections of the Speller River, running north out of Lake Ganemag into Lake Nipissing— had been described in the weekend edition of the *Toronto Post*, a paper which Lucy would pick up if she went to the store, but then usually ended up reading with rolling eyes.

Gina Ferrara was a Saturday columnist for the paper. She wrote about "The Ontario Outdoors," a subject which Lucy, as a "resident of the urban interior," found pretty dull. She'd met Gina Ferrara, though, and so felt vaguely obliged to be a little bit interested.

That past Saturday, Gina had written about her planned camping trip on Monday with "the controversial environmentalist, Patrick Irving" to a site that was one of her all-time favourites— near Jack Falls on the Speller, fifteen miles outside the little town of Shallow Bay on Lake Ganemag. They were going up to collect "wild foods," which Patrick, as the expert, would cook up into some "wild gourmet meals." Gina had joked about not wanting to give away her secrets, but Gina's map had pinpointed the site with such detail that even Lucy, who could lose her way in an elevator, would've been able to find it.

Lucy's eyes unfocused and she mentally shook herself back. Students streamed past them in both directions. Her class was due to begin.

"Do they know what happened?" she asked Cheryl, quietly. "Did they say what kind of accident?"

"The paper just said Patrick Irving was found unconscious at their campsite." Cheryl watched as the last of the students disappeared into the rooms off the hall. "Are you going to be all right? Maybe you should get someone to take your class. Want me to go tell them you're sick?"

"I'm kind of stunned," Lucy said. "I didn't get much sleep last night. But I'm fine. I should get going. Thanks."

She turned away from Cheryl and mentally snagged the number of her classroom as it floated by her brain. She held onto the number tightly until she got to the room. She opened the door and saw twenty faces turn towards her, and then she released "41" and reeled in "land leech" to take its place.

CHAPTER 3

The police found Gina Ferrara on Thursday, the day after the Penders had found Patrick Irving. They discovered her a good half mile down river from the Jack Falls, lodged against a tree trunk that had toppled into the water. She was battered and bashed, blue and purple. And she was dead.

"Well, I wouldn't have believed it," said the older cop, Detective Freeman, as he eyed the body with disgust, "but she looks *worse*."

"What's that, sir?" asked P.C. de Freitas, the younger cop, who was scribbling on his pad.

"She looks worse. Worse than the picture on her driver's licence." He curled his lip slightly at de Freitas who continued to write conscientiously. "You done, de Freitas? Or are you working on your grocery list?"

P.C. de Freitas slapped shut his spiral-bound pad and followed Freeman along the bank to where the doctor stood under a paisley umbrella, miserably stamping his feet. The doctor— who'd come out that morning from Shallow Bay– had thought to put on rubbers over his brown loafers, but a rude rush of the Speller had surged over his feet and soaked him up past his ankles.

"So?" Freeman asked.

"Numerous contusions, Detective," said the doctor, his teeth chattering. "The pattern of bruising seems to indicate that some were received before death, some after."

"Yeah?"

"Yes." He paused and Freeman crossed his arms, waiting. The doctor glanced longingly at the police launch which was taking on the men in the Crime Scene Unit and the body of Gina Ferrara, wrapped in black plastic. Then he looked back at Freeman, who seemed oblivious to both the rain and the threat of being left out in it. "I can't say with complete assurance at this point," the doctor resumed, "but I would speculate that death was by drowning. The force of the river..." A chill shook him from head to toe, "the force of the river, Detective," he began again.

"Yeah, yeah, okay," Freeman said. "I get the idea. You know when she died?"

"Again, I can't say with complete..."

"So say it with flowers, then. Gimme a real rough estimate."

De Freitas, taking notes, laughed.

"Two or three days ago, perhaps."

"Like on Monday?"

The doctor mouthed the days of the week backward from Thursday.

"Yes. Possibly on Monday."

"Thank you, doctor. Your cookies and hot chocolate are waiting for you back at the station."

The doctor sped off toward the launch.

"Okay, de Freitas. Let's go," Freeman said. "I want you to call the next-of-kin when we get back. The mother in Toronto."

De Freitas stared at Freeman, aghast.

"Yeah, you, de Freitas. Sound sorry."

"I *am* sorry," de Freitas stammered.

"Good. It'll be easy, then. I'm gonna phone the hospital and check up on our friend, Mr. Irving. About time he woke up." Freeman started to walk. "C'mon."

P.C. de Freitas followed, anxiously chewing his pen.

The police launch chugged off downstream, towing Patrick Irving's canoe, which the police had discovered half submerged and twirling slowly in an eddy formed by a depression in the solid rock bank. There was a splintered gash in the canoe's bow. Like Gina Ferrara, it too had felt the frenzied force of the river.

CHAPTER 4

On the third floor of Shallow Bay Memorial Hospital, Patrick Irving lay propped up looking at a grainy photograph of Gina in the *Post*. In the picture, her eyes were open.

The curtains were drawn around Patrick's bed. His lank blond hair curled around his ears and his beard was thin and wispy. The whites of his blue eyes were marbled with blood. His face was still swollen, especially around the mouth. It gave him a petulant, pouty look.

They'd put him into a semi-private room. He'd still been unconscious when, two days before, they'd moved him from Intensive Care. He vaguely remembered some doctor peering at him from behind a chart and announcing that Gina Ferrara was dead.

The goddamned doctor had then left the room, without saying a single thing about Patrick's own condition. These things pissed Patrick off. Everyone was treating him like shit.

Patrick's stomach hurt. They'd apparently pumped it. There couldn't have been much in there, he thought. He remembered throwing up like crazy. He also remembered an incredible pain, as if someone had been scaling his stomach with a grapple and crampons.

He wondered where the hell Lucy was. I almost fucking died, he thought, and all I get from her is a two-minute phone call, and half of that is about Gina. He punched the newspaper in vexation. "I've got to get out of here," he said aloud.

He heard the tapping of heels on the linoleum and recognized the steps of the older nurse. All of the younger ones wore running shoes and would creep up and surprise you with some disgusting "procedure" before you could even think to ask for chrissakes why. These younger nurses wore pastel outfits that made them look like goddamned after-dinner mints.

The older nurse wore white. She even wore an old-fashioned starched cap. She liked to give Patrick a hard time.

"Mr. Irving," she said reprovingly, swishing back the curtains. "Please stop closing these. We need to keep an eye on you."

"I need my own space," Patrick grumbled.

"You *have* your own space," she said gesturing around the room. "You've got this whole room to yourself!"

Patrick looked down and made a face. There wasn't anyone else in the room. There was one other bed and it was empty. But just the possibility that someone could be wheeled in at any moment—some boring bandaged kid or some old coot with a kidney problem—was enough reason for Patrick to want to keep himself draped.

"There's a Detective Freeman here to see you," the nurse

continued. "He wants to speak to you about the death of your friend." As she spoke, a middle-aged man in a brown suit appeared in the doorway. He had a grim mouth, scant dark hair and dark eyes that were set too close together. He slid into the room and grabbed a blue vinyl armchair which he dragged behind him up to the side of the bed. The nurse went out. Patrick set down the newspaper and stared at the cop. Freeman leaned toward Patrick and stuck out his hand. Patrick gave him a dead fish to shake. He didn't like cops.

"Well, Mr. Patrick Irving," said Freeman with a thin smile. "Welcome back to Shallow Bay. We love to have you, we always have such fun when you come. But for some reason— I just don't know why— by the time you leave we're always feeling real cranky and hung over."

"Have we met?" asked Patrick, with a long-suffering roll of his eyes.

"Oh, I feel as if I know you like a son. A very naughty son. A bad boy who gets into other people's business and does nasty little things to them, like making them lose their jobs. Oh, you can be a bad, bad boy, Master Patrick."

"Knock it off," said Patrick with irritation. "Get on with it. You're very amusing but I'm really not in the mood."

"You bet. Yes, sir," said Freeman, leaning back into his chair. "Now, tell me all about it. How did Master Patrick get so sick to his tummy-wums? How did his lady friend get so wet?"

"Jesus Christ. No wonder you're stuck working out here in the middle of the woods. You've got a great bedside manner. Really charming."

"The sight of suffering just chokes me up. I wanted to be a nurse but they said I was too sensitive."

"Yeah, right," said Patrick.

"So let's give the nice detective the whole story. There's gonna be an inquest and the nice detective needs to know."

Freeman opened the briefcase he'd brought in and took out a tape recorder which he placed on his knees. He flicked it on to record and muttered into the microphone. He then adjusted the volume and said, "You and Gina Ferrara knew each other how."

Patrick reached over to the bedside table and picked up the green plastic water glass. It was empty. He glanced at the pitcher, which was too far away for him to reach, and looked briefly at Freeman, who was watching him. Freeman smiled thinly and didn't make a move. Patrick set the empty glass down and leaned back in the bed.

"I met her at a party about a year ago," Patrick said into the air.

"You were romantically involved?"

"No."

"Then why were you sharing a sleeping bag out on the Speller River?"

"Jesus Christ," Patrick said, looking at Freeman with distaste. "We weren't sharing a sleeping bag. We were sharing a tent. We were friends. It was platonic, if you know what that means. Do you have to be obnoxious all the way through this? Is this how you scare all the lousy drunk lumberjacks?"

"Just asking, Mr. Irving. Now. You left your car in the parking lot on Monday morning and you got in your canoe and dipped-dipped-and-swung. Then what?"

"We canoed up to the base of the rapids and portaged to the top. Then we unloaded our stuff by the river and took the trail up to the campsite."

"What did you do with the canoe?"

"We rolled it over and left it near some trees. Stuck the paddles and stuff underneath."

"That was very trusting of you, Mr. Irving. Weren't you afraid someone might come along and steal it?"

"Hardly anyone goes camping this time of year. The black flies are too bad, for one thing."

"Oh, yeah, black flies. Of course. Thanks. I hadn't noticed them," said Freeman sarcastically. Patrick twisted around in the bed and shoved down a pillow.

"Any time you want me to shut up, just let me know." Patrick leaned back and made a face. "Christ, what do they stuff these pillows with? Straw?"

"So you left the canoe there and then what?"

"We went up the trail to the campsite and we camped."

"Why didn't you just leave the canoe below the rapids? Wouldn't you have to portage it back down there later?"

"We wanted to shoot the rapids on the way back. That was part of the trip."

"Uh-huh. Fun. You said you camped. Maybe you'd like to give me some details."

"We hiked around, collected some food, caught some fish, made dinner and ate it. A while later I started to feel sick."

"From something you ate?"

"I doubt it. Nothing we ate would have made me sick."

"Uh-huh. So?"

"So I started to throw up and I had this pain in my stomach that I thought would kill me. We wanted to get back to the canoe but I could hardly stand. I collapsed. Gina was freaking out. She dragged me into the tent. She told me she was going to get help."

"And this was Monday night."

"Yeah, it was just starting to get dark."

"And she had to get down those rapids."

"Well, she would have figured she could do it. She wouldn't have wanted to waste time on a portage, anyway."

"Getting back to what you ate."

"Yeah."

"Why don't you tell me what you had for dinner."

"God. Okay." Patrick scratched his beard with both hands. "We had trout. Fiddleheads."

"Fiddleheads?"

"You've never heard of fiddleheads? Jesus. They're young ferns."

"Young ferns. Sounds yummy. What else?"

"Some bread Gina brought. Early mushrooms."

"What does that mean, early mushrooms?"

"Mushrooms that come up early. Morels. I collected them. Gina told me that it was a great place for them. That's one of the reasons I went up with her."

"Mushrooms, eh? Did Gina Ferrara eat any of these mushrooms?"

"Look. It wasn't the mushrooms. I'm an expert on mushrooms. I probably know more about them than just about anybody in the province. I don't eat poisonous mushrooms. Take my word for it." Patrick shifted his weight in the bed. There was a pause.

"Did Gina Ferrara eat any of these mushrooms?" Freeman repeated.

"She hated mushrooms," Patrick said. "Look, Freeman..."

"I know," said Freeman, smirking. "It wasn't the mushrooms. Well, we'll find out when we analyze your blood and the contents of your stomach, which we've kept, by the way, in a pretty little bottle this big." He stretched his thumb from his forefinger.

"Christ."

"You were found about ten feet outside the tent. How did that happen?"

Patrick considered. "I must've crawled out there. After Gina left, I started to feel a bit better. I was dying of thirst and she didn't leave me any water. Then the pain got really bad again. I guess I passed out." He looked at Freeman. "So, who found me, anyway?"

Freeman muttered into the tape recorder again and then switched it off.

"A couple of Indians. They felt real sorry for you and brought you home to their wigwam. You looked very handsome, Master Patrick. Like grey meat."

"I'm sure. You finished?" Patrick picked up the newspaper and flicked it smooth.

"The way I see it is you ate something bad for your tummy and your lady friend had an accident and drowned trying to get help. She should have got a Purple Heart. Huh," he laughed in one syllable. "She sure got purple all right."

Patrick clicked his tongue in disgust.

"Sorry," said Freeman. "Sorry. I'm just an ignorant guy. But then you don't seem too broken up about Ferrara, so it's easy to forget to be warm and fuzzy. Anyways, we'll let the inquest decide what's what."

"Let's do that, shall we?"

"I'll probably be back to visit you again, Master Patrick," said Freeman, standing up. "In the meantime, you take good care of yourself. You're a real special person. Everybody here in Shallow Bay wants to see you feeling good enough to go home real soon."

Freeman tucked the tape recorder back into his briefcase. He stood gazing down at Patrick who'd picked up the paper and was reading it ostentatiously.

"Seen your good friend, Mr. Bantam, lately? How's he enjoying his little holiday in Kingston?"

"Bye, Freeman. You're a real special person, too. A real asshole, in fact," said Patrick, without looking up.

"Huh," Freeman laughed again. He patted Patrick's shoulder and then turned and left the room.

CHAPTER 5

It was one of those iffy spring days that some call partly sunny and others partly cloudy, when some put on their sandals and sunglasses and others carry parkas and umbrellas under their arms, just in case. The weather, with blank indifference, had improved in time for Gina's funeral.

Stan O'Keefe stood alone in the sunshine well away from the front door of the church. He held his hands clasped in front of him to keep them from wandering into his pockets. He often had to fight his tendency to look too casual and this morning he'd shaved, clipped his hair and put on a tie. The tie was too narrow, and too festive, but it was the only one he had that wasn't way too wide. It was tough, he thought, keeping up with the ebb and flow of the tie.

Stan thought of himself as fifty-fifty. He was average height, average weight and took an average shoe size. When he went out to shop for clothes, which he tried to do very seldom, his size was almost always sold out, or dwindled to a tumbled heap of the out-and-out outlandish. And that seemed to him just another thing that implied his mediocrity: he wanted the same things as everybody else, only everybody else got there first.

Stan had curly black hair, melancholy blue eyes, and a fine but slightly crooked nose. His teeth were crooked too and they made him self-conscious— he'd try to keep his mouth closed when he smiled. But it didn't usually work. When something struck him as wondrous or absurd, his coupled lips would curve apart and he'd end up grinning, his sad eyes dancing like a poet on vacation.

When Stan had left his farmhouse that morning to drive to the city for the funeral, the dogs had watched from the window, stricken. Dogs have a keen sense of mortality, he thought. Each time you leave them they mourn for you in advance. And then when you come home they celebrate your survival.

Stan nodded gravely at Elizabeth Atkins, his and Gina's editor at the *Post*, as she came out of the church. Elizabeth nodded back and went over to the small group standing around Gina's mother and sister.

Lucy Shepherd came out of the church. Had Stan himself been a dog, he would have stood stock-still and pointed. He'd seen Lucy sitting a few pews ahead of him, with her head bowed. Every now and then she had suddenly looked up towards Gina's sister as she delivered the eulogy. Stan, too, had listened harder at those moments, trying to figure out their significance.

Stan had met Lucy for the first time several weeks before when they'd sat together with Patrick Irving on a CBC radio panel. The issue had been the naturalization of urban parks. All three of them had been in favour and the show had been a bit of a wash.

Whoever had chosen the three of them to talk must have been desperate or dippy, thought Stan. Stan was the wildlife expert, Patrick the authority on trees and plants and Lucy the expert on life below ground. She was a zoologist in the Department of Environmental Studies at the University of Toronto. She specialized in the Annelida, and that day she'd talked a lot about earthworms. She was the only real scientist among them, in Stan's view. He automatically discounted himself and felt that Irving's prejudices discounted Irving as well. Not that Irving would agree.

Patrick Irving. After Lucy Shepherd, what Stan remembered most from that panel was something Patrick Irving had said. He had gratuitously compared Stan's recent *Post* column on encouraging back yard wildlife to the city's "Be nice, clear your ice" campaign on TV. Both, Irving had implied, were cute, well-meaning and utterly Mickey Mouse.

Stan had been mortified. But, lying in bed that night, staring at a fly bouncing around on the ceiling, he'd found himself agreeing more and more with Irving. Stan's columns weren't earth-shattering. They were Saturday morning columns, meant to interest, not to jar. But they *were* supposed to be serious, and that's what really depressed him. If Irving didn't take him seriously– Irving, who seemed to have seriousness like a disease– how many others were reacting to Stan's columns with a snort? Was Lucy Shepherd one of them?

Lucy came out of the church with a man Stan had never seen before– a man in his early fifties, tall, tanned and coughing. Lucy was wearing a black short-sleeved cotton sweater with a pleated skirt and was carrying a very large shoulder bag. The man had on a dark overcoat and a scarf around his neck. He was pulling on gloves as they walked along towards the group with Gina's family.

Lucy spotted Stan and Stan waved discreetly. Lucy said something to the man and left him to come over to Stan.

"I saw you in the church," Stan said to her, "and I was trying to figure out how you knew Gina."

"Oh," Lucy answered, running her hand back through her hair. "I didn't know Gina that well. I met her through Patrick Irving."

Shit, thought Stan, with a rush of mortification.

"Oh, right, Patrick Irving," he forced himself to say casually. "Have you heard how he's doing?"

"Well, I spoke to the hospital yesterday and they said he's going to be fine. He's conscious and he's off the IV. I'm going to try to get up to see him next weekend."

She's going to go to see him, thought Stan. How well does she know him, then? Stan wished he could stand on his toes without Lucy noticing. She was about an inch taller than he was.

"Give him my best wishes," Stan said. The bastard, he thought. He jammed his hands into his pockets. "How have *you* been? I was thinking about you the other day when I was walking down Jarvis

Street with all the worms out on the sidewalk."

"Great!" Lucy laughed. "*I'll be looking at the worms /But I'll be seeing you.* Earthworms aren't the only thing I study, you know, Stan."

"I know." Stan's teeth showed. "But I did want to ask you what they're doing out there on the sidewalk in the rain. I've always wondered."

"When the ground gets too soggy to hold enough oxygen for them, they have to come to the surface to find it. And if the surface itself is really wet, then they keep moving until they get to a drier place where they can breathe. That sometimes means a sidewalk. But they often die there because they can't handle the sun's ultraviolet rays, and of course they can't get away from the sun because they can't burrow through cement. So there you go."

"There you go."

The last of the people had come out of the church and other small groups had formed. Stan saw some people he knew from the *Post.* The tall man who'd come out with Lucy was walking back towards them, coughing and miserable. His face, though tanned, had a dull, pasty quality to it. His features lacked detail, somehow—there weren't enough lines or shadows around his mouth and eyes.

The two funeral directors in their sober suits were hovering halfway between the main circle of mourners and the hearse parked by the curb. They wore reverent expressions, often whispered to one another and shifted their weight from foot to foot. They looked a little impatient.

"I don't think I will go to the cemetery, Lucy. I really don't feel at all well," the tall man said as he came up.

"You don't look very well," Lucy answered. "Do you think you're going to be all right to go to the conference? Oh, I'm sorry, Stan," she said, seeing Stan begin to step away, "I do this all the time. Stan, this is Robert Milliken, Professor of Entomology in

Environmental Studies. Gina was a cousin of his wife's. Robert, this is Stanley O'Keefe, a writer and naturalist and a colleague of Gina's at the *Toronto Post*. There," she said, smiling, "a really succinct intro."

"Yes, Mr. O'Keefe, I've read your column. It can be very enjoyable," said Milliken. Stan winced. "It's terrible what's happened to Gina, isn't it? Just terrible." Stan murmured yes. Milliken turned toward Lucy. "Would you like me to drop you off at the school, Lucy?"

"You go ahead, Robert. I should speak to Mrs. Ferrara, too, although she won't know who I am probably. Go on and get some rest. I can take the TTC. "

"I can give you a lift," said Stan, quickly. "I want to speak to Gina's mother myself and then we can go... If you want, I mean, " he added, going a bit pink.

"Great, Stan, thanks."

"I'll see you tomorrow, then, Lucy. I'm headed home to bed," said Milliken. Smiling vaguely in Stan's direction, he walked away toward the street.

Mrs. Ferrara seemed to be running on nervous energy. She couldn't stop saying how much Gina would have appreciated their coming. Stan knew, however, that Gina would have told them all to go screw themselves. She would have preferred to have been put out with the garbage for Tuesday morning pick-up. She would have liked her friends to drink themselves sick.

By the time Stan and Lucy got to Stan's truck, the sky was more cloudy than not and the wind had begun to get gusty.

"Jeez, I'm freezing," said Lucy, wrapping her arms around herself and looking up at the clouds. "I always do this. The first sign of warmer weather and I completely underdress. Nice truck."

"It's a real mess inside. Let me just get rid of some of this junk," Stan said, opening the passenger door and leaning in to clear away the scattered papers, unpaid parking tickets, empty take-out coffee cups and candy wrappers covering the front seat. He'd been meaning and meaning to clean the truck out. She'll think I'm a real slob, he thought ruefully. And I'm not. I'm not at all.

"Sort of reminds me of my apartment," Lucy commented.

"I've got a pullover in the back, if you want. It's pretty clean. A few dog hairs, maybe," Stan said, climbing into the driver's seat and glancing over at Lucy, whose teeth were chattering. God, she's superb, he thought.

Lucy's short hair was a disaster. Her nervous habit of running her hands through it meant that it usually stood on end in all different directions. She had heavy dark brows that were often furrowed, and green eyes that wavered between gently sane and wacky.

"I'll be okay," Lucy said, "As long as you can get some heat going. You've got a dog, do you?" Stan jerked his black Ford truck into the traffic on St. Clair and immediately got stuck behind a streetcar.

"I've got two dogs. They keep each other company. I'm away from home a lot."

"Oh, yes," Lucy said vaguely and then suddenly, "Stan, would you mind if I had a cigarette? I'll blow it out the window. I've been dying for one but I couldn't very well at the funeral... You probably don't want it in your car." Lucy looked at Stan like a little kid who knows for sure that the answer is no.

"Oh, yes, sure, go ahead," Stan laughed, pleased that he could please her this way. "It doesn't bother me a bit. I like the smell," he added.

"Thanks a lot," Lucy said with relief. She grabbed a cigarette from the pack in her bag and lit it up with a green Bic lighter. "I've got to get serious about quitting. You wouldn't believe how these things control your life."

"I didn't realize you smoked. You managed pretty well at the radio thing. You seemed relaxed and everything."

"God, if you only knew. I was going up the wall... I felt really bad, you know, Stan," she added quietly. "About what Patrick said to you. He can be such an asshole."

Stan was edging his truck up alongside of the streetcar as it closed its doors at a stop. He stepped hard on the gas but couldn't make it around in front before the next line of parked cars. He was forced back in behind the streetcar again.

"Shit," he said, meaning both the streetcar and Patrick. He glanced at Lucy, who was looking at him curiously.

"He was right, though, you know. I was thinking about it afterwards. My stuff is pretty infantile. That friend of yours at the funeral obviously thought so too."

"Robert? What did he say?"

"He called my stuff 'enjoyable.' Very diplomatic, I thought."

"Oh, he didn't mean anything bad, Stan. He always talks like that. Though he is a diplomatic type, all right." She flicked some ash out the window.

"Who did you say he was?" Stan asked, happy to change the subject. "A colleague of yours?"

"Yes. He's done some amazing work on tree parasites. Published a lot in *Science* and *Nature*. But right now he's in the running for a pretty big job. Head of the National Science Commission. I don't know what his lab will do if that happens. He sort of *is* the lab."

"And he was a cousin of Gina's? I've got to get off this street." Stan turned right, on to a side street. As he did, drops of rain began to patter on the windshield.

"More rain. I can't believe it. Actually, Robert's wife, Kelly Hanlan, was Gina's cousin. Kelly died a couple of months ago. Breast cancer. Do you have an ashtray in here?"

"Yup." Stan pulled it open. "Kelly, yeah. I remember her. Gina used to mention her sometimes."

Lucy stubbed out the second half of her cigarette, settled back into the seat, and sighed. Stan glanced at her again and wished the university wasn't so damn close. Another couple of minutes and they'd be there. Just another couple of minutes to find out what he really wanted to know.

"So, Lucy," he began, seeing half a dozen ways to get the information and, because time was short, choosing, with nervous reluctance, the most direct one, "I was wondering if there's anybody you're going out with or anything right now. I mean," he felt his hands tightening on the steering wheel, "I mean, I'm not involved with anybody and I was wondering..."

He felt Lucy looking at him but couldn't meet her look. She wasn't saying anything. He had turned on to Harbord Street and was wishing now that the university was closer than it was. He started to feel sick.

"I'm actually sort of involved with Patrick," she said, finally, staring straight ahead.

I knew it, thought Stan. I knew it. The light ahead turned from yellow to red. Lucy reached into her bag for another cigarette.

CHAPTER 6

The daffodils in Shallow Bay were a week away from blooming and the grass would soon be needing its first spring cutting. Ray Clifford surveyed the front of his white bungalow as he drove up the driveway in his company car, the green Ford van with "Clifford Plumbing" on the side.

The house needed some work; new eavestroughs, new paint on

the porch. The driveway needed resurfacing but that could wait another year. Ray wanted to recap the chimney, but that would have to wait as well. It was this damn recession. During the boom, he'd had the money for stuff but not the time. Now he didn't have the money, and he didn't have the time, either, since he was forced to bid for and take on jobs miles away from home.

Like today, Saturday, for instance. All the way down to Muskoka for a half-day's work to finish a job. Huge new monster cottage, Jacuzzi, sauna, air. Brass lanterns on stone pillars at the entrance, three-car garage. They'd cut down the old trees and then they'd planted new ones. Ray had driven longer than he'd worked and he wasn't getting paid for driving.

At least somebody's still got money, he thought, as he slammed the door of the van behind him. And that's lucky for me. That's lucky for us.

Susan was at the door as he opened it. Her greying blond hair was back in a hairband but a few strands had unravelled down over her brow. Up till a few years ago, she'd gained and lost weight seasonally— on in winter, off in summer. Then came last summer and the thing with Jamie. Last summer, there was no leafy rabbit food for supper, no weight chart stuck up on the fridge, no groaning from the bathroom as she looked at the scales. After Jamie's accident, she'd stopped dieting and she was getting kind of fat.

Ray could tell from her look that she'd had a bad day, but so had he and he didn't want to hear about it. He knew she had it rough. He could get away from it more than her. And even when she did get away, to her part-time work as a nurse, she was surrounded with sick people like their son, buzzing their buzzers and whining like babies.

Not that Jamie ever whined. Ha. Ray wished he would. He wished Jamie would do anything. Anything to show them there was something going on. Any goddamned thing at all.

"You're home early," Susan said to him.

"Yeah," said Ray, twisting out of his jacket. "I just had to finish up the one bathroom. God, five bathrooms," he added scornfully. "In a cottage." He hung his jacket up in the front hall closet. This is where he tried to be helpful, by keeping things neat and in control.

"At least you're working," said Susan automatically, turning to the kitchen. "I was just going to get something to drink. Jamie's asleep."

"I'll have a beer," Ray said, following her. He sat down on the bench at the kitchen table where she'd spread out the newspaper. Susan got a can of beer from the fridge and put it on the table.

"Patrick Irving's conscious," she said. "There's an article in the paper."

"Where?" Ray said shortly, picking up the front section and turning the pages.

"Third page, I think." Susan leaned against the kitchen counter and crossed her arms. She watched Ray as he read.

Ray scanned the short article quickly, looked up at Susan, and grunted. He read the article again.

"It figures," he said, finally. "God, it figures." He closed the paper and opened his beer, took a long drink and leaned back on the bench. "The goddamned guy leads a charmed life."

"You'd rather he died, eh, Ray?" asked Susan calmly. "You wish he was dead."

"Nah," said Ray, taking another swig of beer. "What I wish is that he was stuck in a bed, staring up at the ceiling, for the rest of his goddamned life. And I'd want him to know it, too. That he'd never get better. That he was gonna be that way for good."

Ray stood up and brushed past Susan to the fridge. He opened the door, looked inside for a moment and then closed it again.

"Didn't you have lunch?" Susan asked, moving out of his way as he headed back to his beer.

"Yeah, I did. I was just hoping you'd got in some cyanide. I was thinking I could use some."

"Good idea. I'll pick up a six-pack. Maybe I'll join you," Susan replied steadily. She sat down across from Ray and rubbed her eyes.

"Shit!" Ray shouted suddenly, banging his fist on the paper on the table. "I can't believe that goddamned Irving! His girlfriend kicks it and he's gonna be just fine! Jesus Christ!"

"Ray, you've got to stop this," Susan said, "or you're going to drive me crazy. You're getting obsessed. You don't even know for sure if Patrick Irving was involved."

"Oh, he was involved, all right. This thing was his baby. That Bantam guy just did what he was told. You saw Bantam in court. He wilted like a little flower. Just like a little pansy." Ray laughed harshly.

Terry Bantam was a tree hugger who was now serving two years in prison. The year before, he'd taken over from Irving as director of Earth for Earth's Sake, an anti-logging group that had been screaming and yelling to have a large area of forest, north of Shallow Bay and abutting the Gamenagi reserve, made into a park. The forest was mainly old growth and the trees were big and valuable. Lambert Forestry, a local Shallow Bay company, had the contract to cut them. Lambert had been fighting protests, assessments, commissions, and God knows what else for well over five years. It had not yet managed to cut down a tree.

It had gotten close, though. The previous spring, Lambert had got so close as to start building a road. Irving's group, EES, hadn't made it easy. They'd blockaded the road for several months.

Somewhere around this time, Irving had left the group and Bantam had taken over. Two weeks later, Jamie Clifford's life had pretty well ended.

There'd been an explosion on the road. Jamie, who'd been working for Lambert for a year and had just barely turned nineteen, was hit by debris and ended up brain damaged. Terry Bantam and two others had been charged with attempted murder, but were convicted of almost shit. Bantam was sentenced to only two years. Ray had been livid.

To Ray, the light sentence was bad enough. But worse was Patrick Irving's escape. Ray had lived with Jamie's bitching about Irving from the day that Jamie had started working for Lambert. The delays and uncertainty had all been blamed on Irving, and if things had stayed hung up much longer, Jamie's getting laid off would have been blamed on Irving, too. They'd joked about it, then: the only thing that was gonna get cut in *that* forest was Jamie's nice new job.

Ray Clifford finished his beer and took the empty can over to the sink. He opened the fridge and took out another.

"I'll have one of those," Susan said. She didn't usually drink during the day, especially when she had to work at night and tonight she had to go in for seven o'clock. Maybe she'd get to lie down for an hour. There was spaghetti sauce in the freezer that they could take out for dinner. Broccoli in the fridge.

"Jamie okay?" Ray asked, putting the beer down in front of her. Why do I bother to ask, he thought. Since the explosion, when was Jamie ever okay?

"Mm-hmm," said Susan, getting up and taking a glass from the cupboard over the sink. Ray never remembered she liked a glass.

"When's the therapist in next?" Ray asked. Who really cares about the therapist, he thought. How could Jamie get anywhere from nowhere? Ray took another beer from the fridge.

"Next Tuesday," Susan replied.

Ray grunted and walked to the kitchen door. There were still chips in the moulding from when they'd moved the hospital bed into the house. They hadn't been able to get it around the corner in the front hall and so they'd had to lug it in through the back. Then Ray's friend, Tony, who had been in front, had jammed it into the moulding and chipped off the paint.

What a day *that* had been. The night before, Susan had worked a twelve-hour shift and hadn't got home till eight in the morning. Ray's van had been in for some repairs and he'd had to pick it up before getting over to the hospital supply. He'd driven it only halfway there when it overheated out on the highway. God, had he been pissed.

CAA had towed the van back to the garage where the mechanic had refused to accept the blame. Ray had yelled and the mechanic had yelled, but in the end Ray had been forced to ditch the van and rent another from a nearby Budget. Ray had told the mechanic he'd deduct the cost from his bill. The mechanic had said, "Good luck."

When he and Tony had got home with the bed, Susan was throwing up in the bathroom. Her job was supposed to have been to get to the hospital and arrange Jamie's discharge. Jamie was being brought home in an ambulance and Susan was going to ride back with him. But Susan had the flu. So Ray'd had to go instead, and of course, when he got there, Jamie's doctor was nowhere around and they wouldn't let Jamie go till he was.

Three hours later, the ambulance men had carried in Jamie. He was as limp as a kid asleep, his arms and head dangling as they lifted him on to the bed. After they'd got him settled, Ray'd stood by his bed and talked for a while. Then Susan had come in, white as winter, and had sat and rubbed Jamie's hands with her own.

"Anybody call today?" Ray asked, pausing at the kitchen door.

"Just George Robitaille to ask about Jamie," Susan said.

"He sure stays in touch, that guy. You'd think he'd have better things to do with his time. Maybe he's still worried that we might sue."

"You're a real cynic, aren't you?" Susan replied, pinching a dead leaf off the geranium on the table. "Maybe he's just a nice guy."

"Yeah, maybe, but I wish he'd knock it off. Gets kinda tiring telling him the same thing over and over. And he's always so goddamned cheerful, drives me up the wall. What's he got to be so cheerful about? Lambert must be losing money like nuts." Ray walked out through the door.

"He just liked Jamie, I guess," said Susan, yawning and closing her eyes.

CHAPTER 7

'Twas black fly, black fly everywhere
A-crawlin' in your whiskers,
A-crawlin' in your hair,
A-swimmin' in the soup and
A-swimmin' in the tea,
Oh the devil take the black fly
And let me be.

"Oh, God," said Stan, abruptly standing up from the desk in his upstairs office. His two startled dogs scrambled to their feet.

"You alarmists," he chided them. "Just lie down. Nothing's happening. No," he repeated quietly, walking to the window, "nothing sure is happening."

Folly, his old black lab, turned a circle and settled back down with a grunt. His pointer cross, Slim, watched him with lifted ears. Stan squatted by the low window and leaned his arms on the sill. Slim came over and stuck his nose into his armpit. Stan shifted his weight and stroked Slim's head.

The view out the window was of a field of new hay. Beyond the fence at the back of the field, Stan could see his neighbour's beef cattle grazing. The white one with the brown head wasn't there. It had been taken to market, Stan figured, one of the series he'd noticed and then noticed gone.

Sometimes when Stan worked at his desk late at night he would hear the cattle lowing in the darkness. On windy nights, they sheltered in the woods and their voices would gust desolately across the fields. Stan would be tempted to go out to look for them and imagined them always retreating just as he was getting near, leading him, like some fairy tale spell, deeper into the woods.

This morning, as he gazed out the open window, he could hear the clink of the bobolinks that had marked out their territory. They perched on last year's weed stalks, now and then taking off with rippling flight and song. Nearer the house, three gleaming grackles arced down to the ground by the bird feeder and lurched and jerked after the fallen seed.

Stan had been living alone in this old farmhouse for over a year and a half. He used to share it with his girlfriend, Cath, until she met a fireman and took off. Cath and her fireman were married now and had a kid. Cath used to tell Stan she'd never get married, and that she'd never have kids. She'd told him that for five years.

Stan stood up and sighed. He glanced over at the computer which, with a beep, had reminded him to "save." He wished that computers offered an option equivalent to crumpling up, throwing to the floor, and crushing with your foot.

He moved back to the computer and stared at the screen. Slim crawled under the desk and flattened out over Stan's feet. The phone rang. Slim jumped up and bashed against the edge of Stan's chair which rolled back three feet on its castors so that Stan had to stretch forward to reach the phone with one hand while pulling his chair back towards the desk with the other.

"Slim, you idiot!" Stan said sternly as he lifted the receiver. "Hello."

"Stan. It's Elizabeth."

"Oh, great, hi, Elizabeth," Stan said, mentally moaning. He'd been working all morning on his Saturday column but all he'd got down so far was a verse from this goofy Stompin' Tom song. Elizabeth liked to have the copy as early as she could and often would call like this, several days in advance of the deadline, just to be sure that Stan wasn't doing anything that he shouldn't— like going out with women or flying down to Rio— before she got her stuff.

"How's it coming along? It's black flies this week, isn't it?" Elizabeth asked. Stan knew she had his list of topics for the next two months right in front of her. They always went through the same stupid exercise.

"Yup. Black flies. It's coming along just great," Stan replied. "I'll have it for you by Thursday at the latest."

"Well, if you could get it in a little earlier, Stan, I'd really appreciate it. What with organizing this obituary for Gina's space and everything, I'd really appreciate knowing you were taken care of."

"Uh-huh," Stan said. Right. Gina was at least well out of this routine with Elizabeth. It certainly gave Stan a routine pain. It had given Gina one, too. "I'll see, Elizabeth. You'll have it by Thursday for sure. Okay?"

"Okay, Stan. But try. I'll talk to you." I bet you will, thought Stan. Probably in about ten minutes. "It was a nice funeral, wasn't it?" Elizabeth added. "I thought Gina's sister's eulogy was very touching. Her mother seemed good."

"Yeah, she was holding up well. I'm planning to get over and see her in the next little while. Anyway, I'd better get back to work, okay? If you want this and everything," Stan said.

"Good. Bye-bye."

"See you, Elizabeth." Stan put down the receiver and looked at the clock on the wall. Eleven-fifteen. Time for coffee.

He went downstairs to the kitchen with the dogs clacking along behind him. The kitchen was huge and cold. Stan hadn't started the fire in the wood stove yet. He'd been hoping that the weather would finally start warming up the way they'd forecasted it on the radio. Except for Saturday, the day of Gina's funeral, there hadn't been any decent sun since fall. The cluster flies, which doted on these in-between days, buzzed and tapped against the inside of the windows and left their little yellowish specks of fluid on the panes. They drove Stan crazy. He had to get out with the ladder and caulk the gaps in the fascia where they were crawling into the walls. He'd been meaning to do it for ages but other work always got in the way.

Stan put on the kettle and thought about Lucy.

When she'd told him about Patrick he'd finally forced a laugh and said, "Damn." He'd then been stuck with her in traffic for what seemed like hours. He remembered asking her lamely what she was working on. He couldn't remember what she'd told him.

She'd managed well when he'd dropped her off. She'd said they should meet for coffee. She said he was really great. She said she'd give him a call. *That* he remembered.

"Yeah, right," Stan now said to himself. "Almost forty years old and I still grasp at straws."

The phone rang again as he was watching the kettle. He ran into the living room to grab it before the machine went on.

"Hello, Stan? This is Lucy Shepherd. Are you busy?"

"No. Not at all," Stan said with a catch in his throat that he swallowed quickly away. "How're you doing? I was actually just thinking about you," he said and immediately wished he hadn't.

"Why? Did you see a centipede or something?"

"No," Stan laughed, relieved that she'd taken it lightly. "Nothing like that. Though if you could tell me how to get rid of these flies I've got, that would be okay."

"Flies. Not really my area."

"Cluster flies."

"Cluster flies," Lucy repeated gravely. "Well, they're parasitic in earthworms."

"Earthworms," Stan said. "There you go."

"There you go," Lucy laughed. There was a pause and Stan could tell she was inhaling cigarette smoke.

"Stan, I've got something ridiculous to ask you and if it's a problem you just tell me to go screw myself or something, okay?"

"Hmm." Stan sat down on the "S" chair from his grand-mother's house. It was incredibly uncomfortable— half of the stuffing was gone, leaving lumps and indentations that had no reflection in human anatomy. It really belonged at the dump.

"I was talking to Patrick earlier," Lucy continued. "He's feeling pretty good, he says, but he had a detective come in and interview him. They're having an inquest."

"I know," Stan said. "I heard it through the paper."

"Yes, I guess you would. Anyway. This detective apparently gave Patrick a really hard time. Made some comment about Terry Bantam. Earth for Earth's Sake. The explosion, you know?"

"The explosion up on the logging road. Yeah." Stan remembered it very well. The *Post* had covered the whole story in detail. Terry Bantam's testimony had been quite sensational.

At the trial, Bantam had insisted that the bomb shouldn't have gone off when it did. He'd said EES would never have deliberately hurt anyone— that was against their philosophy as "deep ecologists." They'd only intended to damage the road. As far as EES was concerned, the explosion that hurt Jamie Clifford was an accident. Or possibly, just possibly, sabotage.

Nobody had followed up on this suggestion, though Bantam did manage to convince the jury that he and the others weren't murderous. Sabotage of sabotage, Stan had thought at the time. Downright Byzantine.

"I guess this detective was generally obnoxious," Lucy was saying. "But what Patrick's really upset about is that the cop seemed to think that Patrick poisoned himself with some bad mushrooms."

"Hmm," said Stan. "Did he pick some up there?"

"Well, he did. But he's sure that he didn't pick anything bad. Patrick is sure of himself a lot of the time," Lucy added quickly. "I know that. But mushrooms are one thing he really does know about."

"Hmm," Stan said, again noncommittally. He wasn't sure where this was going. He wasn't sure why Lucy was calling *him* about it. "I don't know a thing about mushrooms, Lucy. Did you want me to look something up?"

"Oh, no, Stan," Lucy said. "*I* could do that." There was another pause. "Look, I'm really sorry I'm calling you about this. But I know you work freelance. I thought you might have time."

Stan wished she didn't think she had to give so many excuses for calling him. Simple attraction would have suited him fine. Folly came into the room and sat square in front of Stan, staring. He stretched out his leg and scratched her with his foot.

"What did you need me to do?"

"Oh, God. Patrick's made up his mind that he wants to go back to the campsite to look around. They're letting him out of the hospital on Friday. But the thing is," Lucy continued with exasperation, "he's weak as hell. He won't admit it, of course. They're only letting him out Friday because he insisted. They wanted to keep him in over the weekend. You can't get to the campsite by car. You have to canoe and then you have to carry the canoe past some rapids."

"Portage." Stan uncrossed his scratching leg and Folly collapsed to the floor.

"Yes, portage. He can't do it himself. He says he can, but it would be a really bad idea."

"Doesn't *he* have any friends?" Stan wouldn't be surprised.

"He won't ask anybody. But he wants me to bring him up a book he needs and wait for him. I can't let him go out there alone, Stan, I just can't. But I've never canoed in my life. All the camping I've ever done is in parking lots in my parents' Winnebago. I can't even swim."

"Hmm," Stan said.

"I know, Stan. I know you don't like him. I'm such a creep to call you about this."

The kettle started to whistle.

"Just a second, Lucy, okay?" Stan set the receiver on the table and heaved himself out of the chair. I can't believe this, he thought, going into the kitchen. She wants me to go camping with her boyfriend. He slid the kettle off the burner. Slim started barking out the window at a squirrel. "Knock it off!" Stan yelled at him. He walked back to the living room and dropped down into the hellish chair. He picked up the phone.

"So. You want me to go with Patrick," Stan said flatly. "I don't know, Lucy. I'll have to give it some thought." Some very cursory thought. Talk about a pointless exercise.

"*I'd* still go up, you know. I didn't want you to go by yourself. I was thinking we could drive up Friday morning. I mean, I could drive with you. I don't have a driver's licence."

"You don't? You're kidding. Lucy, you need to learn more about life *above* ground. You've had your head in the humus too long."

Lucy laughed again. She has an odd laugh, Stan thought, like a meadowlark crossed with a donkey.

"I'm hopeless, Stan. Sorry. Anyway, you'll think about it? We'd need to rent a canoe and stuff. The police still have Patrick's."

"He just wants to go out there and head back? He doesn't want to stay overnight or anything?"

"He says he remembers exactly where he went. It would only take a couple of hours, I think."

"Plus four hours there and four hours back. Would you need a ride back to Toronto? Or does he have a car?"

"His car's still up there. The police brought it into Shallow Bay."

"Okay, I'll think about it, Lucy. I actually *am* kind of busy right now. I don't know."

"Stan," said Lucy, hesitating, "I do think you're great, you know. And I'm not just saying that so I can push you around. I *would* like to see you. We could talk in the car. It might be nice."

Stan didn't say anything for a minute. He suddenly felt depressed. He sat holding the receiver while his gaze glanced off objects in the room: the "action" lamp with the fish on it, the bird's-eye maple shelves he'd made, the framed chart of animal prints, the pogo stick he'd bought Cath. He didn't know if Lucy really meant it and, if she did, if it mattered. He remembered a joke he'd heard years ago in a philosophy class at university: What's mind? No matter. What's matter? Never mind. Not that funny, actually. Well, sort of funny.

"Stan?" came Lucy's voice.

Outside his house, a chickadee slammed into a window. A breeze picked up. A cow mooed loud and long.

Stan reached down and picked a burr off his pant leg. "Yeah, Lucy," he said finally. "It might be nice."

CHAPTER 8

Lucy had just finished inspecting her lunch when Robert Milliken knocked on her office door. She'd decided that morning to pack a lunch, to try and do something about saving money. Her smoking habit was costing ten bucks a day, seventy bucks a week, three thousand and so on a year. It was idiotic.

She'd taken a can of tuna from the stack in the cupboard and had been pleased with herself for having bought so much— ten cans at once on her last stop at Loblaws. That's they way she liked to shop. She'd never make a list and she'd never be prepared. She'd wait until she was really hungry and then rush into the closest store, grabbing quantities of anything that she felt like eating right then. If she was hungry in the morning, she'd get loaded down with cereal. Later in the day, it'd be frozen pizzas, Kraft Dinner or ten cans of water-packed tuna.

The only problem with this system was that, though she always had full cupboards, she never remembered to buy the basics— like milk or mayonnaise or bread. So, on that Thursday morning, she'd had her cereal with a cigarette instead of milk. And she'd had nothing to use for a sandwich but tuna.

In the end, she'd mixed the tuna with a chopped-up pickle and, when it hadn't held together, had poured in some pickle juice. She'd then loaded the mixture into a rinsed out jar. She had four boxes of Triscuits in the cupboard so she'd packed one of those into her bag, along with the jar of tuna and a spoon and a few sheets of toilet paper. She couldn't quite picture herself chowing down on this but hoped that by lunch time she'd be hungry enough not to care.

Now, when Milliken knocked, she was considering heading out for a burger.

"How are you today, Lucy?" asked Robert, after Lucy had invited him in. Four days after the funeral, he looked a lot healthier. He was pretty good looking for fifty, Lucy thought, tall with short dark wavy hair and deep brown eyes. His mouth, though, wasn't that attractive. It was too stiff or something. Only rarely did it change expression, sliding slowly up into a smile or snapping suddenly down into a frown. Just below his right eye, he had a small L-shaped scar where a fish hook, he'd once told her, had lodged itself years before. His wife, Kelly, had been learning how to cast.

Milliken glanced at the jar of tuna on her desk. "What have you got there? A soil sample?" he asked.

"That's my lunch," Lucy lamented, sliding the tuna off to one side. "Real cordon bleu. Would you like to sit down, Robert? How are *you* feeling?"

"Oh, much better, thank you. But if you're having your lunch, I don't want to interrupt. I just wanted a few words with you about the Bordeaux conference. But I can call you this afternoon." Robert turned towards the door and put his hand on the knob.

"No, Robert, now's fine," Lucy stopped him. "I don't think I really want to eat this. I might go out for something later. Please sit down." Robert looked around the office. The second chair was half-hidden by papers, two sweaters, and an empty shopping bag. He hesitated, his hand still on the doorknob.

Lucy stared at him and then followed his gaze to the chair.

"I'm sorry," she said, jumping up. She stepped out from behind the desk and scooped up the junk, stuffing it into a corner on the floor. Robert pulled the chair forward and sat down. Lucy went back to her seat behind the desk. She coughed.

"So you are feeling better, then," said Lucy.

"Yes," said Milliken. "My throat's still a bit sore, but it's nothing to get in the way. I must say, though, that I didn't think I'd make it through Saturday. By the time I got home, I was running quite a fever."

"And you had that drive, too." Milliken lived an hour north of the city, near Barrie.

"Yes."

Lucy sat back in her chair and clasped her hands in front of her on the desk. She had a snap memory of how they'd had to sit in public school, back in Winnipeg when she was a little girl. Bodies straight as rulers, arms rigidly out in front, hands squeezed together into a nice neat ball with thumbs flattened out on top. The straightest row got to leave the class first.

"So," she said, self-consciously leaning forward on her elbows. "The conference."

"Yes. The conference. What I wanted to speak to you about was the schedule." He pronounced it "shed-yule." "I'm scheduled to speak late on Tuesday afternoon and you're on Wednesday morning. Am I right?"

"Uh," said Lucy, scratching through the papers on her desk. She had no idea yet when she was "shed-yuled." And she had no idea which of all these papers would tell her. "Uh, yes, I think that's right," she said, finally. Of course, Robert would know if anyone did.

"I've spoken to Cecil Ho about this, Lucy, and I hope it won't be inconvenient." Cecil was the head of the department, a nice man, quite brilliant. "What I'd like to do," Robert continued, "is change times with you. There's a dinner party on Tuesday at the home of Roland Goudreau. He was Dean of the Chemistry Department at Université Laval until he moved to France in the early eighties. Now he's Dean at Bordeaux. He lives in Marmande, a village near the city." Robert spoke the French names with a proudly elegant authenticity. His fluency in the language was a point in favour of his federal appointment.

"Perhaps you've heard of him," Robert said. Lucy nodded. "In any case," he continued, "the dinner party is on Tuesday evening and, as I'm not presenting until five, I'm bound to be terribly late. I have to confess, Lucy," he added, smiling one of his slow smiles, "it's a question of political expediency. The party is a very small one and it's a great compliment that both Ho and I have been invited. It's in honour of Geoffrey Stayner."

Lucy looked at Robert. She was getting a little tired of political expediency, but then probably no one in the whole university was as unambitious as she was. Geoffrey Stayner was federal Minister of the Environment. He was giving a keynote speech at the conference, and was flying in and out specially to attend. Apparently he was staying long enough for dinner.

"I guess it's okay, Robert," she said slowly, looking down. "But won't it sort of screw up the programming?" She couldn't believe the organizers would take kindly to so late a change, especially for a reason like Robert's. She also wasn't thrilled about having to talk on the same day she'd be arriving. She'd be bound to be glassy with jet lag.

"Oh, no need to worry about that," said Robert, still smiling. "Cecil and I will take care of it. Of course, you may still have the odd person who'll attend your talk expecting mine, but then the same thing is likely to happen to me. Anyone wanting to know about your fascinating work will be sorely disappointed."

Lucy wondered briefly if he was being sarcastic. But the expression on his face hadn't changed.

"How is the work going?" Robert asked, when Lucy hadn't replied.

"Oh, not bad," Lucy said, shuffling her feet under her desk, "though this week is going to be a bit rough. I'm working on my lecture for tomorrow and I still have some exams to mark. Plus I've got to go out of town tomorrow. And what with whipping my talk into shape for the conference, I don't seem to have much time left for the lab."

"Yes," said Milliken, "teaching eats up time. I was relieved when I finally escaped it, myself." He stood up and ran his hands down the front of his pants to smooth the material. "Thank you very much, Lucy. You're fine for Tuesday, then? I'll tell Cecil Ho."

"Okay, Robert. You're welcome." Lucy stood up, too. She felt annoyed and she badly wanted a cigarette. She wasn't allowed to smoke in the building, though when she worked in her office late at night, she took her chances.

"Where are you off to tomorrow?" Milliken asked, absently, examining a postcard of Rome she had tacked up on her bulletin board near the door. "Pleasure trip?"

"I'm actually going up to Shallow Bay to see Patrick Irving," Lucy said, taking her overcoat from the hook on the door.

"Yes," said Milliken, turning toward her. "I meant to ask you about him. How is he? I understand there's to be an inquest?"

"Apparently," Lucy replied, getting antsy for that cigarette. "Patrick's fine. He's being released from the hospital, so I'm going up to meet him."

"Well, give him my best," Milliken said, his hand on the doorknob. "He must be terribly upset about Gina."

"He is," replied Lucy, ambivalently. When she'd spoken to him, Patrick hadn't seemed that upset at all. That is, he *had* been upset, but mainly about the suggestion that it was his mistake that had led to Gina's death. Lucy didn't know if Patrick had even particularly liked Gina. She really wished Robert would open the door.

He finally did.

"Again, Lucy, my sincere thanks," Milliken said, stepping into the hall and offering Lucy his hand. Lucy took it, amused now by Robert's formality. She'd known him for over five years but he still behaved as though they'd just been introduced. But then that's how he treated everyone, from undergrads to Cecil Ho. "Perhaps," he added, "if you can possibly find the time, you'd like to have an early lunch before we leave on Monday."

"Oh!" Lucy exclaimed, taken aback. Robert had never asked her to lunch before. "Sure. If I can. That'd be good, Robert," she said, collecting herself.

"My treat, of course. To thank you for your trouble. And it will also save you from having to bring something from home." His expression had settled back to its usual solemnity, his mouth as straight as the thin stripes on his pants. Lucy didn't know whether he was joking or not. She didn't know whether to laugh. So she didn't.

"We'll talk, then," Milliken said, heading off down the hall towards the elevator.

"Okay," Lucy said, "Yes." She walked down the hallway in the other direction. Now for that cigarette, she thought, speeding up.

She took the stairs at the end of the hall two at a time, grabbing the banister. Three flights down she opened the fire door and emerged into a parking lot half-filled with cars and with bicycles locked to racks. Three students she didn't know were clustered by the doorway, talking and smoking. They smiled at her when she lit her cigarette and one of them said, "Another pariah." Lucy smiled back, then started off toward the street.

A woman she'd talked to once had met her husband that way, smoking in the cold outside their office building. They'd worked for the same insurance company for years but they hadn't known each other, hadn't even seen each other, among the staff of several hundred. Having the company in common had been important to them. But it wasn't nearly as important as their both smoking Winstons.

Patrick didn't approve of Lucy's smoking. When he was in a good mood he'd just click his tongue and grimace, but when he was bored or angry, he would lecture. He'd always start out at her health and end up at his health, with a varying route in between.

The two of them made a pretty bad pair but Patrick didn't want to notice and Lucy was no good at making him. It was a symptom of her passivity that she'd continued to see him as long as she had. At first, she'd found him attractive. She liked his intensity and his single-mindedness— his energetic activity. He was like a cold shower to her own lukewarm bath.

Lucy crossed St. George Street in the middle of the block, hugging her coat around her as the wind tried to tear it away. Today was a little bit warmer, but not much. She thought with worry about Friday and wondered when she'd hear back from Stan.

CHAPTER 9

Patrick didn't see Lucy and Stan when they walked into the hospital. That is, he saw them, but they didn't register— they weren't the "just Lucy" that he'd been expecting. He'd been sitting in the waiting room for almost an hour with nothing to read except *Chatelaine* magazine. The polyester armchair was making his skin crawl and the fluorescent light was hurting his eyes.

Lucy's bus got in at twelve-thirty-five. When Patrick had talked to her on Thursday night she said she'd be there by one, so he'd made sure he was ready good and early. The cops had dropped off his car, tent, paddle and knapsack. Patrick had been feeling like shit when the cops came and hadn't even opened his mouth. They'd only stayed a minute.

The cops were keeping the canoe for a while. It sounded like it was so bashed up it wouldn't float a feather. Patrick hoped he could get it repaired. It was a classic cedar-strip with webbed seats and hand-carved gunnels. He'd had it for a long time. He felt the same way about it as Gina had felt about her paddle. Gina's paddle was a beauty— black cherrywood, over fifty years old.

Patrick didn't notice Lucy until she was standing right in front of him, blocking his view of the front entrance.

"You're here," he said, standing up startled.

"Sorry I'm late, Patrick," said Lucy, kissing him on the cheek and then glancing over her shoulder at a guy who was standing, hands in his pockets, a few feet back. "You remember Stan O'Keefe, don't you?"

Stan stepped forward and stuck out his hand. "Hi, Patrick," he said.

Patrick looked at him. He didn't get why this guy was here, but he shook Stan's hand.

"I just ran into Stan outside the bus station, Patrick," Lucy began. "So he came along here to see you."

Stan had had a hard time deciding what to do about Lucy's call. He'd put off phoning her back. He'd talked to himself and he'd talked to the dogs. He'd talked to the crows perched up on the phone line. He'd tried to make it all straightforward.

He was lonely, he knew it. He also knew that he liked Lucy. But he didn't think he had the heart for the chase, the theft, the insinuation, that would come with wanting someone who was with someone else. He didn't have the heart for playing the game but he knew what could happen if he did. His feelings would start him off at a trot, gently tap him into a canter, and then he'd be flat out with his feet off the ground, going at a gallop, reason run amok.

In the end he'd decided he'd like to see the two of them— Lucy and Patrick— together. They seemed so unsuited to each other that there must be some mistake. And maybe Stan was the one making it. Either Patrick would turn out a better person or Lucy would turn out worse. Stan didn't know which he'd prefer.

He'd tried to reach Lucy on Thursday night but she wasn't home and she didn't have a machine. Of course. He'd tried her again that morning and there still was no answer. By then, he'd been so set on going that he couldn't just say, oh, well. He'd called the bus station and found out about the bus to Shallow Bay. It made half a dozen stops so he had time to get there before Lucy did.

He'd filled a thermos with coffee and had given some extra food to the dogs. He'd put them in the hayloft with a tub full of water and had sneaked away, leaving them contentedly gnawing on bones.

He'd reached Shallow Bay ten minutes before the bus and had waited in his truck outside the bus station door, suddenly sure that Lucy wouldn't be on it. But she was.

She'd turned red when she saw him waiting. He wished they'd had more time to talk.

"Stan offered to go with you out to the campsite," Lucy was explaining to Patrick who was watching her narrowly. "And I thought, with the two of you, I could come, too."

"Well, that's nice of you," said Patrick to Stan, "but I'll be fine on my own."

"But, really," Stan began.

"Why don't you let us come, Patrick? It'll be so much easier," Lucy interrupted, "and a lot faster."

"And the three of us can find a lot more mushrooms than you can by yourself," Stan said, feeling suddenly like an indulgent dad reasoning with a two-year-old. Feeling also, in his own increasing agitation, a bit like a two-year-old himself.

Patrick crossed his arms on his chest and stared at Stan, and continued to stare as he spoke, quietly and resentfully, to Lucy. "You really filled him in, didn't you, Lucy? This was supposed to be just you and me."

Lucy sighed. Stan edged away towards the gift shop window where a white-haired lady was arranging stuffed animals. "I'll be over here," he called back.

"Patrick," Lucy said as Stan walked off, "listen. You're just getting out of the hospital. You've been lying on your back for over a week. We're here, so why not just let us come?"

Patrick didn't answer for a moment. He stood and looked at Lucy, considering.

"You haven't asked me how I am, you know," he said finally, stepping towards her and putting his hands on her shoulders. "And I bet you didn't even miss me." He wrapped his arms around her and squeezed.

"Of course I did," Lucy said, squeezing him back and looking over his shoulder for Stan, who had disappeared among the nightgowns and knitted toilet-roll covers in the gift shop.

"I missed *you* like hell," Patrick said, unwrapping and kissing her. "Did you bring the book?" Patrick had asked her to bring him his *Audobon Field Guide to North American Mushrooms*. So, on Thursday, Lucy had taken the streetcar to his duplex in the beaches and had squinted her way through his white, white rooms into his study where bookshelves lined two walls. On one wall were books on natural science, on the other were politics and poetry. Lucy never understood about the poetry. Patrick never mentioned it.

"It's in my bag in Stan's truck," Lucy said.

"Okay. Then let's get the hell out of here," said Patrick, taking her arm.

They met again seven minutes later at Johnson's Outfitters, where they'd intended to rent a canoe. Johnson and company were gone to lunch, leaving a note that said they'd be back at two. They sat and waited in separate cars— Lucy and Patrick together and Stan with k.d. lang— and when, at two-thirty, they'd seen no one show up, Patrick said they should go to Allistair's, another outfitter, down on Highway 11.

"The middle of a recession," Patrick said, "and these guys are taking a two hour lunch."

"I can't think of a better time," Stan answered, and then stopped himself when Lucy sent a look that said, please.

By the time they got to Allistair's it was after three and, as they stood in the parking lot, Patrick said, "You two go in. I'll wait out here."

"But Patrick," Lucy said with surprise, taking the cigarette from her mouth. She'd planned on smoking while Patrick went inside. He didn't like her to smoke in his car. "Don't you think you should go in? You know what you want."

"Actually," Patrick replied, bending down to tighten a boot lace and talking into the gravel, "they won't serve me in there, the bastards. Somebody's related to somebody who works for Lambert Forestry or something. Christ," he continued, straightening up and glaring across the parking lot at the door, "you think of what's already happened to the environment in this country and I'm supposed to get all teary-eyed over a bunch of goddamned loggers. It's not my fault if they've gone and got themselves stuck in a bunch of dead-end jobs. It's got to stop somewhere."

"Okay," Stan said, blowing on his hands. He'd forgotten to bring any gloves, though he had remembered his warm hat with flaps. The flaps, folded up towards the crown but not tied, were wagging up and down in the wind. "I'll go in. But won't they be closed by the time we get back? How are we supposed to return the canoe?"

"You'd better rent it for the night," Patrick said, frowning in Lucy's direction as she cupped her hands to light her cigarette. "Get a couple more paddles. And you'd better pick up some cheap sleeping bags. There's no way we'll have enough daylight at this point. I've got my tent. We can stay overnight."

"Patrick, I can't!" Lucy cried. "I'm going to France next week! I've got about fifty things to get done!"

"I really can't either, Patrick," Stan replied, more calmly. "I have to get back tonight." Stan didn't have any important appointments. He was thinking of Slim and Folly, locked up in the barn. They liked to sleep in the hayloft when the weather warmed up but they were always impatient to get out in the morning. If he wasn't there they'd have a fit. Folly, especially, would bark her head off. Slim would start to howl.

Patrick ignored Lucy, eyeing Stan. "What are you doing up here, anyway? Shallow Bay isn't exactly a big attraction."

Stan put his hands in his pockets and did a sort of half-spin away from Patrick, pretending to be interested in a flatbed truck that was rumbling down the highway towards them. He was getting tired. This was making him sick and tired.

The truck had passed them and chugged up and over a hill before Stan turned back to face Patrick. But before he could say a word, Lucy got in ahead of him.

"Stan has some friends up here," she said. "He was supposed to have dinner with them." Stan glanced at Lucy, who was looking straight at Patrick. She was wearing black earmuffs over her ruffled hair and held her cigarette between her thumb and index finger. Her cheeks were rosy, maybe from the wind, and her eyes were oddly bright. She looked like a thirties radio operator receiving a signal from little green men.

"Christ. You came all the way up here for dinner?" Patrick said. But he seemed satisfied with the explanation. He sighed. "Well, there's no point standing around," he said. "You know, Lucy, if you'd just stuck with our original plan, I'd have been there by now."

"Sorry, Patrick." Lucy dropped and stomped out her cigarette.

Patrick nodded towards Stan. "Okay, then," he said. "You go in and rent the canoe and pick me up a sleeping bag. Then you can go have your dinner and take Lucy back to Toronto. I'll go out to the campsite by myself and drive back home tomorrow."

"Oh, Patrick. You *can't*," Lucy groaned.

Here we go again, Stan thought. Now, children. Let's all join hands.

CHAPTER 10

Stan's black truck swung around the asphalt curves as the windshield wipers swept the spray from puddles that had formed on the road. On straightaways he could see Patrick's old Volvo up ahead, the rented canoe roped to its roof-rack, the ends of the ropes snapping behind.

Stan had made a phone call to his neighbour, Zane, and asked him to go over to look after the dogs. Then, he'd made a fake call to his fake friends in Shallow Bay and had cancelled his fake dinner. Patrick had been leaning against the phone booth at the time, eating a slice of Shallow Bay pizza.

They'd got the canoe and the sleeping bags, using Stan's credit card, since Lucy didn't have one. Then they'd driven back into Shallow Bay to get something to eat. They'd bought a large can of Muskol bug repellent. Lucy had picked up a pack of cigarettes. Stan had gone for a mickey of Scotch. Now they could make it through the night. With enough Scotch, Stan figured, *he* could, anyway.

Stan slowed the truck as the road narrowed at the gates of the provincial park. No one was at the warden's booth. It was still too early in the season. The door was padlocked and the windows were shuttered. There was nothing posted behind the glass on the notice board except a faded, fly-specked sign announcing an Annual Labour Day Fish Fry put on by the Gamenagi Band Council, tickets five dollars.

In the parking lot beyond the park warden's booth there was an old brown Bronco truck and a late-seventies Chevrolet, spattered with mud. Patrick had pulled over. He got out of his car as Stan drove up, and walked over to talk to Stan through the window.

"There's a road up ahead that leads down to the river but it's too broken up to use," Patrick said. "Although," he added, considering, "your truck could probably do it..." Lucy got out of the car, smiled at Stan and lit a cigarette.

"Christ!" Patrick said suddenly, with annoyance. "That was stupid! Why didn't we put the canoe on your truck?"

"Too bad," Stan said. He knew why they hadn't. Canoe equalled control. Stan was lucky to be carrying the paddles. "How far is it to the river? Is it worth putting the canoe on the truck now?"

"Shit," Patrick said, taking off a glove and scratching his beard. "No. Not at this point. We might as well just walk it. Gina and I did it easily enough. And we had a lot more stuff."

They took turns fogging each other in Muskol and then sprayed their own hands and wiped their necks and faces. The dirt road to the river was mostly mud and they walked as much as they could on the shoulders, which were slightly higher and drier with grass. A gritty cloud of black flies kept its distance above them.

"Somebody's been through here," Stan commented from under the canoe, his voice loud and round to Patrick, underneath and ahead of him, and muffled to Lucy, who walked "outside" and behind. Between the stretches of water that flooded the road there were ridges of tire tracks, smoothed out by rain and, in places, smoothed away.

In about fifteen minutes they had reached the river— the road ran right up to, and into it. A crude wooden boat launch, grey with age, sloped down the bank. Patrick and Stan hoisted the canoe off their shoulders and on to the ground.

"The water level's really dropped," said Patrick, breathing hard, perspiration dewing on his forehead. He swung down the sleeping bags that he'd had looped over his shoulders. He'd carried two. Stan had the other.

"Let's rest a minute, okay?" said Lucy. She'd been carrying the paddles and Patrick's knapsack, half-emptied for the trip, but with the rolled-up tent strapped to its frame. She dropped the paddles, struggled out of the pack, unzipped her old grey parka, pulled off her earmuffs and unravelled her scarf from around her neck. And then she started to cough and couldn't stop.

"God, Lucy," Patrick said, thumping her hard between the shoulders.

"I don't think she's choking, Patrick," Stan said, dryly.

"I'm okay," Lucy gasped between coughs. She walked around in circles with her head down and gradually was able to get her breath.

As they paddled upstream, Stan in the bow and Lucy in the middle, the force of the current increased steadily. Small branches, slender green plants and brown lacy bits of lichen streamed toward them. To keep from noticing his freezing hands, Stan hummed an old canoeing song from Camp Minewoke where he'd been sent for a summer the year his parents got divorced. That was the summer he'd learned to love birds. And learned to doubt that his parents loved him.

> Land of the silver birch
> Home of the beaver
> Where still the mighty moose
> Wanders at will
> Blue lake and rocky shore
> I will return once more
> Hah-ah-yah, hah-ya
> Hah-ah-yah, hah-ya
> Hah-ah-yah, hah-ya
> Hah ah ah ah

Stan was kind of enjoying himself.

"We're getting close to the rapids so we're almost at the portage,"

Patrick called out. He'd been unusually quiet as they paddled up the river. He'd needled Lucy about her technique— she'd been using the paddle like a giant spoon, stirring the water like porridge— but he did it good-naturedly and now Lucy was doing fine, Stan thought, considering she was in the middle, wearing a bulky life jacket and shouldn't really have been paddling at all. She'd wanted to, though.

"This must be around where they found Gina," Patrick called.

"Oh, God," said Lucy, unconsciously lifting her paddle out of the water as a flutter of unnatural yellow came into view— the tape the police had tied to the submerged tree where Gina's drowned body had been discovered.

They paddled past the place in silence. A hundred yards further on, Patrick pointed out the rock that marked the start of the portage. It was on the opposite side of the river from where they'd started out. Patrick and Stan maneuvered the canoe to the bank.

"I wasn't 100 percent sure I'd remember this," Patrick said with satisfaction when they'd climbed from the wobbling canoe on to the bank. "Gina was the one who knew where we were going. Christ," he went on, "what a disaster. I didn't want to come up here, you know. I hadn't even agreed to come and then she went and said in her column that I was coming. Jesus, Gina could drive you up the wall." Stan and Patrick slid the canoe up the rock and flipped it over.

"But you liked her, Patrick, didn't you? I thought you did," Lucy said, doubtfully.

"Yeah, sure. But she could be a pain in the ass. Kind of manipulative. And she wasn't all that great at telling the truth. She said she'd heard on the radio that the weather was supposed to be great, but it rained so fucking hard that I gave up on getting morels after about ten minutes. That's one of the things that kills me about that cop saying I poisoned myself. How the hell am I not going to notice a false morel when I didn't have more than about ten mushrooms all together?"

"A false morel?" Stan asked, standing with his chin resting on his hands on the blade of the paddle.

"Yeah. I'll show you in the book later. The name makes them sound like they look like true morels but they don't really at all."

"Uh," began Stan, hesitating, glancing briefly at Lucy who was taking off her life jacket as she looked intently at Patrick, "why did you want to come out here today? I mean, if you're sure about it and everything." He'd asked Lucy the same thing in the truck on the way to the hospital. She'd said that Patrick had only told her he wanted "to check." She'd then shrugged her shoulders and said she was sorry.

Patrick bent down and picked up the knapsack that they'd unloaded onto the ground. He slipped an arm through one strap and rolled his back forward to reach for the other. He jerked the pack up to fit it securely. Then he turned and faced Stan.

"You may remember I didn't ask you to come out here," he said evenly. "Lucy did."

"Yeah, she did," Stan said, feeling absurdly like a buck with his antlers down.

"Yes, I did, Patrick," said Lucy, flaring. "And now you're stuck with him. And me. And I wouldn't mind knowing what you're looking for either." She struck out at the black flies hovering around her.

Stan relaxed. He noticed now how sick Patrick still was: his skin was pale and his eyelids looked like they were struggling against gravity. Patrick looked cold, despite the sweat. He looked exhausted. He looked like he was in pain. Patrick turned and walked a few feet to the edge of the river, gazing up and then down it.

"I want to look for some more morels," he said softly to the river, "and I want to look for anything that looks like a morel. And I want to check that nothing that looks like a morel could have done to me what something did to me. In other words," he said, raising his voice as he turned back towards them, "I want to make totally sure I didn't totally fuck up and fucking end up killing Gina."

Stan dropped his eyes from Patrick's face. He took his paddle and picked up the other two and put them and the life jackets under the overturned canoe.

"We hike from here, right?" he asked.

"Yeah," Patrick answered.

"Okay, let's go."

No one talked as they walked through the woods. Stan signed to Patrick that he was willing to carry the pack but Patrick shook his head no. It was getting very late in the afternoon but the sun had come out, hitting the green tops of trees with gold. There were deer tracks on the path, wedge-shaped holes in the soft, moist, pine-needled earth.

Patrick, who was leading the way, stopped at a place where a smaller path converged with theirs from the direction of the river.

"That," he said, "if you're interested, is the path that Gina and I took when we portaged the canoe up from where we left it today. It goes back to the river just below the falls. We left the canoe there so we could do the rapids on the way back."

They continued along the path as it began to climb up, snaking between boulders and past bulging grey walls of rock, mottled with mosses and veined with minerals, mint green and rust red. Dark brown water trickled down black crevices and disappeared into pockets of spongy soil.

"It's beautiful here," Lucy said breathlessly, stopping to look around her.

"Yeah," said Patrick. "We're almost there. In a minute you'll be able to hear the falls."

The path began to level out past one last gigantic piece of rock which jutted from the ground at 45 degrees, the dark entrance to a small cave at its base. Stan thought it looked like a good den for a bear, sheltered and solid and snug. They circled around the rock and, as they did, the sound of water hit them like a roaring engine.

"That's amazing," Stan yelled. He retraced his steps back around the rock to the silence on the other side and then came round again, stopping at the whack of sound. He grinned at Patrick and Lucy. Lucy was grinning back. "Amazing," he repeated.

"It's not as loud over at the campsite," Patrick yelled.

"Jesus, I hope not," Stan hollered. "It'd be like camping in the New York subway."

Patrick walked on and Lucy, after waiting for Stan to catch up, followed. Three minutes later they came to the clearing. It was high and grassy and, thankfully, dry.

"Just like I figured," Patrick said. "There's nothing here I could've made a mistake about." He'd been thumbing through his field guide with a flashlight as the three of them crouched around the puny fire.

"Look," Patrick continued, laying the open book on the ground. Lucy and Stan peered down, trying to make out the photographs. "See, there are basically two kinds of morel that grow around here— under Douglas fir and yellow pine. These morchella are what I found." The mushrooms in the photo looked like brown conical brains on fat pedestals. "Then there are a couple of possible false morels." He flipped forward a few pages. Stan could see some similarities, but they really were pretty different. The false morels had a stretched and floppy look, very irregular. They looked like someone had pulled them like taffy.

Stan wondered why they couldn't have looked at the book in the hospital waiting room where it was warm and there was something to sit on besides the backs of their heels. It would have saved them a trip. On second thought, it probably wouldn't have. Patrick would have still wanted to go out to the site and check.

"It's still worth having a look around tomorrow, though," Patrick now said, as if putting a tick beside Stan's last thought. The Jack Falls sounded like muted applause.

"Patrick," Lucy said, her feet cold and her teeth on the verge of chattering. The temperature had dropped with the sun. "Don't you think that maybe you were just sick? Maybe you got flu or gastritis or something."

"No way," Patrick replied. "If you knew the way I felt... Christ, I would have been glad to die just to make it stop. No. What I'm thinking now is that somebody must've poisoned me."

"Oh, Patrick," Lucy said. "You're kidding."

"No, Lucy, I'm not kidding," Patrick said peevishly. "Christ, why do you think I'd be kidding? I can think of a few people who might want to try it."

And I can think of one, too, Stan said to himself, watching Lucy shiver. He wanted to be chivalrous and courtly and kind. He wanted to give her his coat. But he knew she wouldn't take it and Patrick would make her pay for his offer. Lucy stood up and stamped her feet. Stan held out his bottle of Scotch.

"You shouldn't be drinking that," Patrick said, as Lucy took a gulp. "The alcohol will lower your body temperature. You'll just get colder."

"I know," replied Lucy, "but by then I won't care."

"Anyway," said Patrick, "I have a theory about this and it's a good one. When it's more than a theory, then you, Lucy," he glanced at Stan, "will be the first to know."

"If you really think you were poisoned, what about Gina?" Lucy asked. "You ate together, didn't you? She didn't get sick, did she?"

"No, she didn't, and that's what makes it complicated. We ate all the same stuff except for the mushrooms. Somehow or other, somebody must have poisoned the mushrooms."

"How?" Stan asked. "And when? When would they have had the chance?"

"I don't know how," Patrick said, "but I might know when." He tossed a small branch on to the fire.

"When?" Lucy asked. She crouched back down beside him. Patrick stood up. His face flushed in the firelight.

"I was going to tell you about this anyway, Lucy," he began slowly, "so I might as well tell you now." Stan could feel himself beginning to vanish. Patrick spoke only to Lucy.

"You knew Gina had been after me for months, ever since that Christmas party at the *Post*."

Stan hadn't gone to the Christmas party the previous year. He'd been working on some kitchen cabinets and, by the time he had finished, it was too late to go. Not that he'd really planned on it anyway. He didn't like parties of more than a couple of people and the *Post* parties were always crammed and loud. The sports writers always looked after the music and the music writers stood around making faces till, inevitably, and following tradition, the sports writers played Queen's "We Are the Champions" and everybody let out a protesting howl.

"Anyway," Patrick was saying, "when we got up here, she was all over me. I sort of gave in." He paused and looked at Lucy who was gazing at the fire. "It was cold and the black flies were fucking terrible so we went in the tent. Then we came out and made dinner and, a couple of hours later, I got sick."

Lucy stood up and lit a cigarette. Patrick stood up and put his arm around her.

"It just sort of happened, Lucy. It didn't mean anything," he said quietly.

"So someone could've poisoned the mushrooms while you were in the tent, is what you're saying," she said, looking straight ahead and inhaling deeply.

"Maybe."

"Maybe they were trying to poison Gina," Stan said, surprised at hearing his own voice. Patrick shot a look at Stan. He was surprised, too.

"Well, then, they must have known they'd get me, too. After all, mushrooms are the one thing I'd be sure to eat, right? They would have really goofed about Gina. She hated them."

They settled into the tent early, giving up on staying warm by the fire. From the woods around them they could hear small cracks and gentle scufflings. Soprano spring peepers called out for mates. The Jack Falls kept telling them all to shush.

Sometime late, Stan crawled out with the flashlight and stumbled off to pee at the edge of the clearing. When he got back to the tent, Lucy, who'd been in the middle, had taken his place. Stan pulled off his boots and slipped into his sleeping bag— between the softly breathing Patrick, and Lucy, lying rigid with her arm flung over her face.

CHAPTER 11

"They ain't bitin'," Paul Pender complained as he propped his fishing pole against the wall by the door. "The fucking flies are but the fish ain't." He put the rusty tackle box down on the floor. Angus had told him to go out and catch some fish. He'd been gone half an hour.

"Well, we still got some hamburgers frozen," said Doreen. She was sitting on the sofa watching TVOntario. A Mexican woman was explaining how to make Chicken Mole. "Garnish with plenty of fresh cilantro," the woman said.

"'Fresh cilantro.' Sure, lady," Doreen muttered to the TV. "I'll just pick up some 'fresh cilantro' down at the Shallow Bay Foodland." Doreen stood up, taking a cigarette from the pack on the coffee table and lighting it.

"So now what're you gonna do?" she said to Paul, who had flopped down into a chair facing the television and was reaching forward to change the channel. He wore unlaced work-boots, jeans, a blue and yellow ski jacket, and a red baseball cap with the Esso logo on it. He was sixteen and had just quit school. He'd quit on his sixteenth birthday, in fact.

"What the fuck am I *supposed* to do?" Paul said without looking at her. He turned up the volume on an Aerosmith video.

"You're not gonna sit around in front of that TV all day," Doreen said.

"That's all *you* do," snapped Paul, without taking his eyes off the screen. Doreen turned and walked into the kitchen, a tiny square room with just enough space for a two-burner stove, a half-size fridge and a small Formica table with three odd chairs crammed around it. She stubbed out her cigarette in a metal ashtray that had "Friendly Florida" and a palm tree etched into it. An old enamel sink with six inches of counter on either side was piled with the morning's dishes, which Doreen began to ferry to the table. There were a lot of dishes with three men to feed.

She dribbled some dish soap into the sink and turned on the hot water. At least the water heater was working. At least there was water. Often, in winter, the PVC pipes froze as the wind swept under their raised four-room bungalow, built by the government in the early sixties. They'd fill pots and pans with snow and melt it on top of the wood heater while they thawed out the pipes with a light bulb.

Angus had tried shoving some pink insulation up and around what he thought was the problem but it hadn't seemed to do much good. When the temperature dropped below minus 15, they had frozen pipes for sure.

Doreen didn't know what to do about Paul. Even before he'd quit school, she'd known he didn't go much. But at least, then, he'd had somewhere else he could go. Now he was either home in front of the TV, or over at the rec hall, where he and his other drop-out friends spent hours standing around out back, smoking dope.

Paul and his brother Cyril had been living with Angus and Doreen since they were kids. Their father John, Angus' younger brother, had taken off for Toronto and had never come back. Mary, his wife, had left a year or so later. They heard about Mary now and then— first that she was in the city, then that she was somewhere out west— but John had just disappeared. He drank. He might be dead for all they knew. They'd stopped even talking about him.

Doreen and Angus never managed to have kids, so Paul and Cyril had become pretty much their own. Cyril was doing okay. He wanted to go to the college over in Sudbury as soon as he got the money together, maybe even next fall. He worked during the summer for the parks department, cleaning up the campsites and maintaining the trails.

Doreen dried each dish as she washed it and stacked them all away in the cupboard above the sink. The frying pan she left to soak. She went back into the living room where Paul was still watching TV, his feet stretched out in front of him and his arms crossed over his chest.

"If you're planning to hang around you could take off your coat. It's not that cold in here."

"I'm goin' out again. Okay?" Paul said peevishly and turned back to the TV.

Doreen wondered what Angus was doing. He'd gone back to

the shed to work on the skidoo engine and he'd been out there for quite a while. She wished Paul would leave before he got back. Angus was going to be mad.

His theory was that Paul had no brains. At sixteen, all he had was balls. The only time Paul got interested was when they put on the fish fry for the tourists, and then he only wanted to lay the girls. He wouldn't do any work, he'd just hang around trying to look sexy. Yeah, real sexy, Angus once said. He looks about as sexy as a skinny mutt.

They did the fish fry every year and, though they made some good money, getting it ready was a pain in the ass. A dozen of the men would go out before dawn and empty the nets they'd set out for the fish. The women would spend the morning peeling potatoes which they'd later fry with the fish, deep in fat, over campfires down near the park. Every year there'd be more to do, because every year there were more and more tourists. But there'd be one less next year, Doreen thought, sitting down on the sofa.

She hadn't known Gina Ferrara at all, herself. Angus had. Gina had been coming to the fish fry for years and she'd always spent some time gabbing with Angus. The first couple of years he'd made a joke about her, said she was a "wannabe injun." But she kept coming back and seemed pretty smart. He started to look forward to seeing her. She was different from the other tourists.

Most of the first-timers had a hard time hiding their disappointment that Angus and the others weren't dressed in skins and feathers. They'd been expecting to get their food on birch bark instead of paper plates. The tourists that had been before had a know-all look and talked loudly to Angus as if they were old buddies. When some of the white women asked after the native women's families, it was like they were asking after a litter of puppies.

Gina Ferrara wasn't like that, and she didn't show off. Angus knew that she wrote for a newspaper, and that she was good with a paddle, but he didn't know much else, except that he'd kind of liked her.

Paul stood up and yawned.

"You can turn that off," Doreen said to him. Paul didn't even bother to look at her. He walked towards the door.

"You gonna be back for lunch?" she asked. His foot got caught in the old rag doormat and he swore as he kicked it away.

"Are you?" Doreen repeated.

"Shit, I don't know. Who cares?" he replied, opening the door and stepping out.

"Just a minute," Angus said, appearing at the door as Paul was heading out. "I wanna talk to you."

He took Paul by the sleeve and guided him back through the door. In his other hand, Angus was holding a paddle.

"What?" Paul said, defensively.

"Where'd this come from?" Angus asked, showing him the paddle. "I found it out behind the shed, under a sheet of that black plastic. Wouldn't wanta paddle to get wet, eh?"

"It's just a fucking paddle," Paul said. "I found it. Big deal."

"You shut up," Angus said, angrily pushing Paul down on to the sofa next to Doreen, who shifted over, watching Angus. Angus walked over and turned off the TV, then came back and stared down at Paul. "This belonged to the girl that died," he said to Paul, evenly. "She showed it to me last summer. Where'd you get it from?"

"I *found* it," Paul said again. "That day. You left me out in the fucking rain for about ten hours. I found it down the trail."

"So why didn't you tell anybody?" Doreen asked, standing up. She didn't want to be sitting there next to him. Paul was a big kid now and she was just a bit worried he might try and slug her. It could happen.

"Who? The fucking cops? Just like you told 'em everything *you* knew."

"How many of your friends you show this to?" Angus said, standing over Paul, dangerously.

"It's just a fucking paddle," Paul repeated. "I didn't show it to nobody. Who cares about a goddamn paddle?"

"Get outa here quick," Angus said to him quietly. Paul got up. He reached for the pack of cigarettes on the coffee table, opened it and pulled out half a dozen. He crammed them into his jacket pocket.

"You didn't even tell 'em you knew her," Paul tossed over his shoulder as he went out the door, slamming it behind him.

Angus went into their bedroom and came back without the paddle. He pulled his bulky sweater off over his head and threw it on the chair.

"That little son of a bitch," he said.

"What are you gonna do with it?" Doreen asked. "You gonna return it?"

"I don't know yet," Angus answered, looking out the window towards the rec hall where he could see Paul smoking with three other boys. Paul gestured back towards the house and said something that made the other boys laugh.

"That little son of a bitch," Angus said again.

CHAPTER 12

"Black flies breed in flowing water; in rivers, streams, and creeks. In the fifties, the Federal Department of Forestry recommended a fast, cheap means of controlling flies in areas about to be logged. Just bombard all of the local waterways with DDT at their source, it advised. That way, poison would be dispersed naturally and without effort— carried downstream several miles by the current.

"This approach went a long way to improving living and working conditions for loggers. As for the indigenous wildlife... well, the *dying* conditions were great."

Susan Clifford stopped reading and looked over at her son Jamie. She read aloud to him like this as often as she could, which wasn't as often as she'd like. Though today was already Thursday, she was just now going through Saturday's *Toronto Post*. Ray often bought the Toronto paper on the weekend to get the sports news and she'd usually read the baseball to Jamie. Today she'd started with an Expos trade and then had skipped over the Outdoors column, which had been replaced with an obituary for Gina Ferrara. Then she'd gone on to Nature, by Stan O'Keefe, a column that was normally harmless and funny, but had surprised her this week with a downbeat ending. Susan was annoyed. She always tried to avoid anything violent, pessimistic, or sad. She wanted to keep Jamie's attitude positive.

Ray criticized her censorship. He thought Jamie probably would like to hear the "juicy" stuff, just like he used to like watching cop shows and disaster movies back when he was a normal kid. But Ray didn't do the reading. Susan did. So he shouldn't bug her about it, Susan said.

Jamie was propped up in his bed at a 30 degree angle, with his arms laid out on his chest, his right hand downward on his up-facing left. This gave him a thoughtful, expectant look that was belied by the expression on his face, which was, in fact, no expression at all. His cheeks were flaccid and his mouth drooped open, saliva glistening on his lips. His blue eyes were open but unfocused. His blond hair was cropped short. A puckered pink-grey scar crept from behind his right ear and met another one that ran up across his cheek. Two plastic tubes snaked out from under the sheets at waist level, ending at sacks attached to a stand at the side of the bed.

A saffron beam of late afternoon sun lit up a section of wall and a bedside table holding a box of Kleenex, a cup and a syringe on a tray. The room was still except for the soft clack of new numbers flapping forward on the digital clock.

Susan stood up from the chair and laid the newspaper on the dresser. She reached down to the foot of the bed and drew out the crank.

"I'm going to lower the bed a bit, okay, Jamie? You don't look very comfortable."

She turned the crank and the top of the bed glided down a few inches. She then walked around and gently lifted her son's head while she shifted his pillows. She dabbed at his mouth with a Kleenex.

She stepped back and looked, for the thousandth time, for some sign in his eyes. And, for the thousandth time, she saw nothing. Jamie's eyes now gazed at a point near where the wall and ceiling met. Just below was a poster of the "World Champion Toronto Blue Jays." He'd been in a coma when the Jays had won the Series.

She and Jamie hadn't got along too well in the year before the accident. He hadn't wanted her around. He'd even sometimes left the room when she came in. Ray used to get pretty impatient with him.

It had been different, of course, when he was a little kid. Then he'd almost driven her crazy, following her everywhere as if the two of them were hitched. He used to pretend he was a baby elephant, stretching an arm out in front of his face and holding on to the hem of her dress. Susan smiled sadly. He had loved elephants when he was small.

"Would you like me to bring in the TV later?" she asked, again watching his eyes. "Not that there'll be anything to watch." She sighed and placed her hand on his forehead, slipping it down to his cheek. She walked back over to where she'd put the newspaper. As she picked it up, the doorbell rang.

"That might be Joyce. She was going to drop off the cake pan she borrowed." Susan went out of the room, leaving Jamie gazing.

She didn't recognize the tall bearded man who was standing with his hands in his pockets, staring at the door as if he would stare it down. Susan hesitated, examining him through the peep-hole, as he rang the bell again. She didn't know him but, after all, it was broad daylight and her next door neighbour was out working in her yard. At least he wasn't a Jehovah's Witness. They always came in pairs. She opened the door.

"Oh, you're here," the man said. "I thought maybe no one was home. I was just about to leave."

"Yes? What did you want?" Susan asked, warily. No, she was sure she didn't know him. Maybe someone Ray knew? "Were you looking for my husband?"

"No, I was actually hoping I could talk to you, Mrs. Clifford. About Jamie. I met him a little while before his accident. I used to work with the environmental group EES. I'm Patrick Irving."

Susan stared at him. He'd said it so casually.

When Irving was in the hospital, she'd been curious to get a look at him, but was always either too busy or too damn tired. Susan worked on the second floor and he'd been up in 3 West. Her friend Joyce was on that ward, though, and had told Susan that he'd been a rotten patient, sour and demanding. Joyce had also said that the police had been there a couple of times and that Irving was even sourer when they left.

"I thought you might recognize my name," Irving said when Susan didn't reply. "I wasn't with EES when the explosion happened. So I wasn't involved in the trial. That's why we never met." He smiled.

Susan thought she would choke. Never met! As if she and Ray had chatted pleasantly with Terry Bantam and the others. Did Irving think they'd all gone out for coffee together while waiting for the verdict? Never met. She put her hand on the door. She wanted to slam it.

Irving took a quick step forward.

"No, don't, Mrs. Clifford," he said. He reached out towards the door but, when Susan glared at him, he pulled his arm back.

"Sorry," he said. "But don't. Please."

Susan realized she'd been holding her breath. She told herself to stop being silly, to calm down. She took her hand off the door and folded her arms across her chest. She could feel her heart beating hard.

"All right, Mr. Irving," she said, as evenly as she could manage. "What is it exactly that you want? I don't want to talk to you and, if my husband were here, he'd probably have called the police by now."

"The police?" Irving repeated, astonished. "Why, for God's sake?"

"He isn't too crazy about you."

"He's never even met me!"

"Well, it doesn't matter," Susan said, impatiently. "What is it that you want?"

"I was wondering if you could tell me if anybody from Lambert has been in touch with Jamie. Does anyone visit him or call him or anything?"

"Why do you want to know that?"

Irving glanced over at Susan's neighbour, who was squatting down, digging in a flower bed near some cedars on the far side of the driveway.

"Do you think I could come inside?" he asked.

"No, I don't think so," Susan said.

"Oh, Christ," Irving said, with annoyance. "Okay. Could you

please just tell me if anybody Jamie worked with has tried to get hold of him lately? I need to know. It might have something to do with what happened to me up on the Speller River. You must have heard about that."

"Yes." Susan wanted to get back to Jamie. She considered. She didn't really see that it mattered if she helped Patrick Irving out a bit. God knows he probably wouldn't get much help from anyone else. She didn't have anything useful to tell him but at least she could answer his question. Ray would be mad at her, but it was against Susan's nature to be spiteful.

"Nobody special has been in touch lately," she told him, finally. "Mr. Robitaille, the manager, often calls to ask how Jamie is. Other than him, that's it."

"Robitaille. Uh-huh," Irving nodded, pensively. "But no letters or anything?"

"No."

"Has Jamie ever said anything about that day?"

"Said anything? Of course not!" Susan couldn't believe her ears. *Said* anything. She'd had enough. "Mr. Irving, I'm very busy," she said, putting her hand on the door again.

"Wait," Irving said.

"I really don't have time."

"Could I see Jamie, Mrs. Clifford? Could I just talk to him for a second?"

Susan looked at Irving with her mouth open. He looked back, expectantly, and, when she didn't answer, he smiled.

"I won't upset him or anything. I promise."

Susan shivered and cracked.

"You don't understand what Jamie's like, do you, Mr. Irving?" she said, with quietly fierce precision. "You just don't realize what happened to him in what you call that 'accident.' Jamie's mind is alive in a dead body, Mr. Irving. He can't *talk*," she spat the word out scornfully, "he can't whisper, he can't even move his mouth. I don't have any idea what he's thinking or even *if* he's thinking. I'd like you to leave now."

"I'm sorry, Mrs. Clifford," Irving said, looking honestly shocked. "I didn't know he was that bad. I really didn't know."

Susan glared at him a second longer in silence.

"Of course you didn't," she finally said, coldly and dismissively. "You never bothered to ask, did you?" She closed the door, took a deep breath and headed into the kitchen. Then she picked up the phone and called Ray's pager.

CHAPTER 13

On Friday morning, Stan was tacking through Toronto traffic on his way to Mrs. Ferrara's house. Stan had met Gina's mother only twice before the funeral, but he was well acquainted with her baking, on which he'd been grinding his teeth for years. Mrs. Ferrara had taken a liking to Stan and so had taken to sending him, via Gina, regular batches of rock-hard, desert-dry cookies. Gina would present these to Stan when he met her at the *Post*, holding up the plastic bag and jiggling it like a dinner bell. "Mmm-mmm, Stanley. Your favourites," she'd smirk, knowing Stan was too polite to say anything but thanks.

"Thanks. Tell your mother thanks," he'd say as Gina stood grinning at him.

"Why don't I just tell her you think they're really bad?" Gina had said to him once. "Because we both know they are."

"God, no. No, they're not," Stan had answered, panicking. "They're good... they're really good for dunking."

Gina had laughed. "Well, okay. Since you like them so much, I'll get her to send you more next time."

From then on, Stan got three dozen instead of two. Gina was highly amused. Patrick Irving was right: sometimes Gina could be a bitch.

Gina, of course, hadn't lived with her mother. Fat chance, she would have said to that. She'd had her own place in Kensington Market, a two-room apartment above a cheese store turned gourmet coffee shop, incurably ill with roaches. Gina would complain bitterly to Stan about them, as if his love for animals made him somehow responsible.

Stan squeezed his truck down the narrow downtown street where Mrs. Ferrara lived in a red brick duplex. Cars were parked on both sides of the street, despite the signs stating this side this month, that side that month, permits required regardless. He drove past the house and around the corner before he found a place to wedge in his truck. Took him a while to do it.

When she'd said goodbye to him in Shallow Bay on Saturday, Lucy had done a startling thing: she'd taken Stan's hand and put it to her lips just as she ducked into Patrick's car. She'd done it quickly. Surreptitiously. Softly. Like a whisper.

Stan smiled wistfully to himself and climbed down from his truck. He slammed the door and walked back towards Mrs. Ferrara's house, stepping off the curb to let a woman with a baby carriage by, and rubbing at a sooty smudge on the sleeve of his drab duffel coat.

That morning on the Speller had not been a good time. Because of a misting rain, they hadn't been able to make a campfire and the only thing they'd had to eat was one Oh Henry bar that Stan had brought, split between the three of them. Patrick had been feeling lousy, Lucy had been cold, and Stan had been desperate for a cup of coffee.

Pale and taciturn, Patrick had led them off to where he'd found the mushrooms almost two weeks before. He'd issued instructions wearily, like a burnt-out scout master, and they'd fanned out through the dripping undergrowth, losing each other in tatters of fog, silent except for a Morse code of twig-snapping.

Twice, Lucy had called Patrick to come have a look and Stan had heard Patrick's murmuring as he'd inspected what she'd found. Stan himself had found nothing of note. Just a shocking orange toadstool with a white worm inside, and a tough frill of fungus around a dying pine. No morels, though, true or false.

Patrick, of course, had found a baker's dozen of *morchella*— the true morels— which he offered to Lucy and which she turned down, saying she wouldn't have a free moment to cook them. Stan wouldn't have touched them, himself. Even if Patrick had offered them, which he hadn't.

Now Lucy was in France for her conference but she'd be coming back the next day.

Stan opened the wrought iron gate and walked up the path to Mrs. Ferrara's house. He was kind of hoping she wouldn't be home. She was a talker, and he might have a hard time getting away. He climbed the stairs to the concrete porch and rang the bell. A moment later he heard the slipping of a lock.

"Hi, Mrs. Ferrara," Stan said to the middle-aged woman who opened the door a crack and looked at him vacantly. Nothing happened for a moment and then she blinked her eyes and smiled. Stan saw a gold tooth. Better crooked than gold, he thought. Maybe.

"Stanley," she said, swinging the door open wider. "I'm sorry. I didn't know you. Come in."

"Are you busy, Mrs. Ferrara? I'm sorry, I should have called. I found myself in the city and I thought I'd drop by," Stan said, "to see how you are." Stan felt ashamed of himself. He hadn't called first because he hadn't wanted to turn it into a big deal— an invitation for lunch or something. He wanted to have time to drop by the *Post* this morning.

"Come in, come in, Stanley," Mrs. Ferrara said, as Stan stepped into the dark hallway. "I'm not busy. What do I got to be busy about? You come in and we'll have some coffee," she said, turning toward the kitchen. "You go in the living room and sit and I'll make some coffee."

"Only if it's no trouble," Stan called, his heart sinking an inch.

Stan went into the pale green living room, took off his coat and sat down on the cream and gold sofa. There was a pathetically bad landscape— river, trees, rocks— hanging on the wall opposite him. It almost looked like a paint-by-number. On a wood veneer table were photos of two little girls in communion dresses and a bridal portrait of Gina's sister, Linda, gazing out a window with what was supposed to be wistfulness.

Half a dozen flower arrangements were scattered around the room, the glads beginning to look papery and brown at the edges, the tulips blowzy and dropping their petals. They gave off a musty smell that made Stan's nose itch.

Mrs. Ferrara appeared with a tray which she put down on the low table in front of Stan.

"The coffee will be ready in just a minute," she said, sitting down on a brown La-Z-Boy chair. She was an angular woman in her early sixties, with short steely hair that was slightly poofed by a perm. She was wearing toeless pink slippers and a beige printed cotton house dress.

"I'm so happy to see you, Stanley. I always say to Gina what a nice young man you are." Stan groaned inwardly. Gina must have loved that.

"How are you doing, Mrs. Ferrara? How are you feeling?" Stan asked.

"Oh, I'm fine. I been staying home, you know, and Linda does shopping for me at the Miracle Mart. I get so many cards and phone calls and everyone is so nice. So many flowers, too. You see?"

She pointed over at a marbled plastic vase filled with drooping freesia and foliage.

"Those are from your newspaper," she said, and then pointed at a large fan of gladiolas and carnations. "And those are from Kelly's husband. So beautiful."

"Kelly was your niece?" asked Stan.

"Yes. She pass away last winter. When she was in the hospital— oh, she had such terrible pain— Gina use to visit her every day. And now Gina's gone, too." Her voice broke. Stan realized he'd been jiggling a foot and made himself stop.

"I'm so sorry about Gina, Mrs. Ferrara. I'll miss her a lot," he said, truthfully.

"Thank you, Stanley," she replied, touching her eyes with a Kleenex she took from a pocket and standing up. "The policemen were very nice," she said. "They bring Gina's things home and they put them in her room."

"The things they found up north," Stan said.

"Yes. I must go to Gina's apartment and move her other things, too. Or maybe Linda and Manny will do that. I don't know. So many things. Maybe there's something you like, Stanley. I'll go get the coffee."

Mrs. Ferrara got up again and went out to the kitchen.

Stan squirmed in his seat. He wouldn't want anything of Gina's even if he knew what there was. In the years he'd known her, she'd never once invited him over to her apartment. He could almost hear her hissing at him not to go near any of her stuff. She was a pretty tough cookie, he thought, looking at the plateful on the table.

Mrs. Ferrara came back with a Pyrex coffee pot.

"Do you think maybe there is something you would take of Gina's?" she asked him.

"Oh, no, thank you Mrs. Ferrara. I don't think so," Stan said quickly. "But thank you." He leaned forward and rubbed his hands on his knees.

Mrs. Ferrara poured him out a cup of coffee and asked him about milk and sugar. She passed him the plate of cookies.

"Your favourites," she said. Stan took two and smiled. Mrs. Ferrara sat towards the edge of the La-Z-Boy with her knees together, holding her cup with both hands.

"Stanley, there was one policeman here a few days ago," she began. "I think he said he was a detective. He ask me if I know if Gina was depressed or unhappy. He ask me if Gina take drugs." She raised her voice. "To ask these things about my girl! He ask me if Gina ever talk about killing herself. Stanley, you know Gina can never do such a thing. She can never kill herself!"

Distressed, Mrs. Ferrara stood up, sloshing coffee on to her saucer. She put the cup down on the table with the photos.

"I wish Gina got married," she continued, picking up one of the little girl photos and staring at it. "She was always all alone." She turned towards Stan and appealed to him. "I think Gina would be alive still if she had a family, Stanley! If she had a nice man like you and children!"

Yikes, Stan thought.

"Mrs. Ferrara," he said. "Everybody who knew Gina knows she would never commit suicide. But, you see, the police probably had to ask you about it because of the inquest. They probably had to rule it out no matter how unlikely it seems. As a formality."

"Yes, I know." She put the photo back on the table. "Linda said to me the same thing. But he didn't have to be like that," she replied more calmly. She sat down. "If I can be finish with this inquest tomorrow then I know everything will be better."

"Are you going to the inquest, Mrs. Ferrara?" Stan was surprised. He didn't know if he'd be able to handle hearing the grisly details of his daughter's death. But maybe Mrs. Ferrara was told to be there. He didn't know how these things worked.

"Yes," Mrs. Ferrara said with a sigh. "Linda will drive me. That policeman ask us to come."

Stan stayed another half hour and heard all about Gina's sister, Linda, and the baby that was due in a few months and about Manny's job at CNR where he did "something with controls." He then took Mrs. Ferrara's recycling box out for her and left her at the door with a promise to come again soon. He knew he probably wouldn't, though. He wanted to forget about everything for a while— forget about Gina and Patrick and poisonings. Stan wanted to be free to contemplate Lucy.

He headed back down the street towards the truck, stopping for a second to spot the cardinal he heard singing in a tree. He then walked on and met the same woman with the baby carriage, coming back. He stepped off the curb again and into a puddle, swearing softly as he shook the water from his canvas boot before it could soak in.

CHAPTER 14

After nine hours on the plane, Lucy felt as if her eyes had been blow-dried. After nine hours on the plane without a cigarette, she had deep dents in her palms from her fingernails, and a strange stiff, hollow feeling somewhere in the back of her jaw.

Lucy stood in the Immigration line at Pearson airport, ready to bite. There was Immigration, then there was waiting for luggage, then there was Customs, then through the lobby, and then there was outside— fresh air and heavenly smoke. Half an hour maximum.

Unless they stopped her at Customs. They'd better not. She might bite.

Behind her in line, Cecil Ho and Robert Milliken were still discussing the Bordeaux conference. Lucy herself had run out of steam somewhere off the west coast of Ireland.

The conference had been deemed a success. At least that's how Robert and Cecil saw it— they'd had good attendance at their talks and their research had been well received. As for Lucy, well. Shortly before five o'clock on Tuesday afternoon, she'd peeked into the seminar room where she had been rescheduled to talk and had been pleased, though slightly unnerved, to see every seat taken and about a dozen people standing at the back. But when she'd made her entrance and moved to the lectern, she'd immediately sensed confusion. People had started buzzing and then, in a heavy German accent, a woman had asked, if "it was not Dr. Milliken who was the talk to be giving."

Lucy had mentally kicked herself, as well as Robert. She'd then reminded the audience of the schedule change and was told, in turn, that there'd been no change announced. For the next few uncomfortable moments, she'd looked at them and they at her and finally an American guy had asked what was the subject of her paper. She'd told them, feeling sheepish, and pissed off at feeling so, that it was "The Effects of Soil Erosion on Terrestrial Annelida," and had added that no one should feel they had to stay and that Robert Milliken would be speaking the next morning at ten o'clock. After another few uneasy moments several people had stood up, mumbled apologies and left.

Of those who remained, possibly a handful had a shred of interest in her subject, and the rest were being polite. Lucy had petered along through her paper, completely abashed. No one had asked any questions. She hadn't felt so mortified since her grade ten

class voted unanimously for another kid as class president, after the
teacher had stupidly nominated Lucy as the only rival candidate. She
still had dreams about that day and now she'd probably start having
dreams about this one.

When it was all over, embarrassment had given way to anger
and anger to jet-lagged exhaustion. There were flowers in her hotel
room when she got back that night— someone had obviously
informed Robert Milliken. Robert, himself, she hadn't seen until
the next afternoon. He'd looked as contrite as his features would
allow, saying that something had gone wrong at the Bordeaux end
and would she please let him take her to dinner, especially as she
hadn't had time for the lunch he'd offered in Toronto.

At that point, Lucy had been in a better frame of mind. She'd
awakened from a ten-hour sleep feeling philosophical and, when
Robert had told her that a number of people had left his own talk,
having expected to hear hers, she'd been ready to forgive him. Lucy
forgave easily. She really had no use for someone else's eye or tooth.

She'd accepted Robert's invitation to dinner and they'd taken
a cab to a tiny restaurant with white curtains, dark walls and a long
zinc bar. Robert had ordered them both a steaming ragout of chicken
and vegetables with garlic mayonnaise, a salad of about ten different
leafy greens dressed with walnut oil, a bottle of red wine— Margaux
something or other— and then cheeses, fruit, Cognac. The place had
been recommended by some hot shot Robert had met the night
before. Lucy got fairly shellacked.

They gossiped a bit about the department and Robert told her
about the politics involved in a national appointment. She told him
about an experiment her grad student, Cheryl, was doing, and about
her own trip up north with Patrick and Stan.

Robert had been charming. Relaxed. Intelligent, of course.
And... very interested in her. *That*, Lucy thought, might be a

problem. Though by the end of the evening, Robert was again distant and subdued and said good night to her hurriedly in the hotel lobby.

They made it through Immigration all right, Lucy with the usual feeling that she'd pulled a fast one. Robert and Cecil stood beside her at the luggage carousel and Cecil laughed for the second time at her "suitcase"— a green duffel bag with US Army stencilled on it. She'd bought it in the mid-seventies, when she was a student and trying vaguely to be radical. She'd never got around to replacing it, though her things always got battered, or worse: she sometimes forgot to put the shampoo in her carry-on.

When they reached Customs, Cecil Ho got stopped— probably, Lucy thought with disgust, because he'd been born Chinese. The three of them were to share a cab, so she and Robert stood and waited while Ho was taken behind a partition. Yup, she sure would like to bite.

Lucy was glad she'd gone out with Robert. From something Cecil had later told her, Robert might have been needing some friendly companionship. His important dinner with Geoffrey Stayner had not gone without a hitch.

Before the dinner, during cocktails, Ho had seen their host introduce Robert to a woman academic from Israel. Within moments of their being left together, the woman had slapped Robert hard across the face and then had asked for her coat and left. Several people had seen it happen, including the surprised host and the Minister.

Robert had made his apologies, explaining that the woman had been nurturing resentment about a paper he'd published several years before which had critiqued some research done in her lab. There'd been understanding nods and Geoffrey Stayner had smiled and commented that these things happened in his sphere as well. Rivalries, he'd said, can flare up at any time. This unfortunate incident was just more dramatic than most.

Cecil had told Lucy that Robert had taken the whole thing in stride. But he must have felt pretty humiliated. He hadn't even mentioned it during Lucy's dinner with him.

Cecil was finally released from the grip of Customs and Lucy began to feel around for her cigarettes. Just a few puffs, she thought, before we get into the cab. She pushed open the frosted glass doors and stepped out into the terminal lobby. The first person she saw was Patrick.

"Lucy!" he called. He shoved past the crowd lined up against the metal barrier and followed her to the end, grabbing her bag with one hand and the back of her head with the other as he pulled her forward to kiss her. "Surprise. Christ, it took you long enough to get out of there. I've got stuff to tell you. My car's at a meter out front. I actually nabbed one of those spots. First time. Let's get outa here."

Lucy glanced over her shoulder at Robert and Cecil who were coming up behind her.

"Wait, Patrick," she said. She turned to the others, who were looking at her inquiringly. "I'll be right back. I'll just be a second," she said to them, and moved off, taking Patrick by the arm.

"We were supposed to share a taxi, Patrick. Would you mind dropping them off?" she asked.

"Shit, Lucy. You're always doing this," Patrick complained. "I really want to talk to you alone. The inquest was yesterday, remember?"

"I know. I really want to hear what happened. But you can still tell me about it, can't you? They'd probably be interested to hear about it, too. Robert was related to Gina Ferrara, after all. I can't just take off and leave them when we're all going right downtown. Robert is staying at Cecil Ho's for the night, so it's just one stop. Cecil lives in the Annex."

"Cecil Ho? Is that Cecil Ho? Christ, he's so hand-in-glove with the forestry industry they'll probably provide free wood for his coffin. I don't want to give him a ride home. God."

Lucy realized what Patrick was referring to. Not many years before, when Patrick was with EES, Ho had co-authored an environmental assessment of a logging proposal for a site up near the Manitoba border. Patrick had thought little of it, and had thought little of it publicly. Patrick wasn't big on most people's opinions, not when it came to trees. He did, however, take hers seriously—something that Lucy could never quite understand and found disconcerting.

"Patrick," Lucy now said, resolutely messing her hair with one hand, "I'm not going to go with you if you don't take them. Please. I mean it." She swallowed. The feeling in her jaw reminded her of sponge toffee.

Patrick sighed his acquiescence. "Okay. All right. You win," he said.

They walked back over to the others and Lucy made the introductions. Cecil raised his eyebrows but offered his hand. Robert looked grim but he shook Patrick's hand as well. No one seemed too enthusiastic.

"Patrick has his car here," Lucy explained, "so we'll drop you off. He was at the inquest yesterday," she added, looking at Robert.

"Of course," Milliken replied. "And was there a verdict?"

"Yeah," Patrick said.

"Which was?"

Patrick hoisted Lucy's bag over his shoulder and looked across the lobby towards the exit.

"Gina's death was accidental, but they're going to investigate my attempted murder."

Lucy let out a gasp of surprise. Patrick glanced at her with an ironic smile. Then he looked away and started walking.

"My car's just out here," he said.

CHAPTER 15

"What was it like?" Lucy asked. "Who was there?" As they merged onto Highway 427, Patrick began to shift lanes, checked over his left shoulder and jerked back to the right. Lucy unconsciously grabbed the armrest and knew again why she didn't drive.

"Christ, I hate this highway," Patrick said as a car that had been hidden in his blind spot slid by ahead of them. He changed lanes.

Milliken and Ho were sitting silently in the back. Cecil had valiantly tried to make small talk with Patrick but had gotten nowhere at all. Robert, meanwhile, had said very little, and Lucy had the prickly feeling that he was staring at the back of her head. She still hadn't had her cigarette. Patrick had parked so damned conveniently that there hadn't been a dozen steps between the terminal door and his car.

"Okay, who was there," Patrick repeated. "About ten people. Gina's mother and sister. Coroner. Pathologist. That asshole cop, Freeman. The courtroom looked like a throwback to Perry Mason, except there was a picture of the Queen on the wall. The coroner was about five thousand years old and kept pulling all these handkerchiefs out and honking his nose. Shallow Bay. God. What a hole."

"How were Gina's mother and sister?" Milliken's voice came from the back.

"Her sister was fine. Mrs. Ferrara started crying during the coroner's report. She ran out of Kleenex. The coroner gave her a handkerchief." Patrick stepped on the brakes after a car passed him on the right, moved over in front and then suddenly slowed down. "Christ."

"What did the coroner say?" Lucy asked, releasing the armrest for the second time.

"Death by drowning. Gina was pretty bashed up by the rocks. They figure she was unconscious when she died."

"Oh," Lucy said. She guessed that was a good thing. The idea of someone struggling for life in water appalled her. She should learn how to swim.

"The main thing is about me. They read the toxicologist's report and it said that my blood showed high levels of MMH."

"Monomethylhydrazine," Ho offered.

"Yeah," Patrick said, glancing over his shoulder with annoyance. "Monomethylhydrazine. It's a toxin found in a few kinds of false morel. But the report said that I would've had to have ingested a shitload of false morels to account for the levels they found. And as you know, Lucy, I didn't eat a shitload."

"Yes." She twisted around to speak to Robert and Cecil. "Patrick hardly found any mushrooms at all that day." She turned back to Patrick. "What did you call the good ones, Patrick?"

"*Morchella*," Patrick replied. "The best kind of true morel. The best eating. Though I don't know if I could ever face eating another at this point. Whoever the bastard was, if he didn't kill me, he sure killed my appetite for morels."

"Interesting," said Milliken. "Do they have any idea how it might have been done?"

"What? The poisoning?"

"Yes."

"They didn't go into any of that. But since they didn't find any MMH in Gina's system, it must have been the mushrooms that were tampered with. They were the only thing that she didn't eat, and I did."

"Will they keep using the same detective? The one you don't like?" Lucy asked. They were on the Gardiner Expressway now, passing the Exhibition grounds along the waterfront. Lucy always missed seeing the Bulova clock tower. It had been torn down in the early eighties. The Fullova Bulova clock, she used to call it. She didn't know why. As far as she knew, it had kept time well enough.

"Christ, I hope not. I hope they bring in someone from here. That creep Freeman's like something out of that Sidney Poitier movie. That one set in the South."

"*In the Heat of the Night,*" Lucy said. "Rod Steiger... If he asks you, Patrick, just tell him, 'They call me Mr. Irving.'" She looked at Patrick and made a face. She was getting punch drunk. She needed nicotine. In the back seat, Ho laughed softly.

"What?" Patrick said. He glanced at Lucy twice. "What are you talking about?"

"Never mind," Lucy replied. "It's really dumb."

"Oh, I get it," Patrick said, taking the exit off to Spadina. "Mr. Chips or something."

No one said anything for a few minutes. Lucy felt gloomy. They stopped and started up through the twilit city and she thought how basically ugly it was— as if slabs of brown and grey had been systematically dumped on the pure, primal green. European cities had been too long settled to provoke any feelings for what had gone before. But here, in Canada, where it was all so new... She thought about the Speller River.

Patrick pulled up at another stop light. He looked across the street at a darkened shop with a huge "For Lease" sign in the window. "Huh, Sussman finally closed his fur store," he said. "Good." He then peered into the rear view mirror, where the headlights of passing cars cast pale strips across the two dark figures in the back. "So where do you live exactly, Ho?" Patrick asked. Lucy winced. She wished Patrick had used the "Doctor." She glanced at the clock on the dashboard. Ten smokeless hours and counting.

They pulled up in front of a huge house on Walmer Road,

where Cecil Ho and his family had an apartment on the second and third floors. Lucy got out and lit a cigarette as Patrick unlocked and opened the trunk.

"Well, I'll see you both on Monday," she said, exhaling smoke with gratification.

"Yes," Robert replied with a smile. He still looked fresh and spruce, and his black wool overcoat wasn't even wrinkled. "It was very enjoyable, though, wasn't it? And our dinner together was a pleasure. We'll have to do it again some time."

"Yes," Lucy said, ignoring Patrick's quick look. "We should."

"Well, thank you, Mr. Irving," Cecil said.

"Yes, thank you," said Robert.

Patrick grunted.

As Patrick and Lucy silently headed west towards Parkdale, the crowds of students disappeared, the streets got darker and the shops got smaller and stranger. There were two extremes in Parkdale businesses. At one extreme were the absurdly specialized— "Toronto's Only Hand-Mixer Specialists" or "Sole Suppliers of Splicing and Bunning," whatever that was. At the other extreme were the catch-all businesses, like the one near Lucy's apartment that offered driver's ed, rat extermination, and income tax services, figuring, Lucy supposed, that they'd best succeed by casting a wide net.

Patrick finally said, "So you went out with Milliken, eh?"

"Yes," Lucy said carefully, "he wanted to apologize for a mix-up with the schedule. He felt responsible." She told Patrick what had happened.

"What an asshole," Patrick said. "He should have done more than take you for dinner."

"Like what?" Lucy asked.

"Like offered to let you give your talk again at the original time."

"But he didn't find out about it until it was too late," Lucy said. This wasn't exactly true, and she wondered why she was making excuses for Robert. "Plus I'd already told a bunch of people when he'd be speaking," she added more confidently. "They would have been really thrilled to turn up and see me again."

"Well, dinner doesn't seem like such a big deal. Unless," he glanced at her, "he was interested in more than apologizing."

"What am I going to do with you, Patrick?" Lucy sighed.

Lucy didn't feel like a glamour queen but now, for some reason, she seemed to be the target of three men at once. It was unprecedented. The closest she'd come to this in the past had been going out once with a dental student the night after she'd been dumped by an MA in English. The student had asked her back to his place for a drink and had spent the next hour explaining the antibiotic action of saliva. Somehow it had put her out of the mood for kissing.

Stan, Robert, Patrick. Patrick, Robert, Stan.

Robert's advances might mean zilch, she thought. Lucy pretty well hoped they did. He was an attractive man but he didn't make her tingle in mind or in body, and he wasn't the kind of man "to grow on you," at least not as sweet-smelling flowers. Lucy smiled. That wasn't how the expression was meant: to have someone "grow on you" like a skin disease or fungus. Though she was beginning to think of Patrick that way. She frowned. How mean. Patrick would be aghast. She stared out the window at a big dog with a small kid. Patrick kept silent, his eyes on the road.

Stan O'Keefe, she thought. Stan was... well, Stan was like she felt when she dreamt she was hovering— floating above the earth a few extraordinary feet.

She had to end it with Patrick.

"Patrick," she said, as he turned the car on to her street of tall, thin, duplexed houses.

"Yeah," Patrick answered.

"Did you ever tell the police about you and Gina being in the tent together?"

"No," Patrick replied, eyeing her. "Not yet." He slowed down and pulled the car up in front of Lucy's place.

Lucy didn't like what she was going to ask next.

"Didn't they see any signs of it? During the autopsy, I mean. Didn't they know you'd had sex?"

"God, Lucy," Patrick said severely. He turned off the engine. "What do you think? I'm not that big an idiot. You and I always use condoms, you think I wouldn't with somebody I hardly even knew?" He clicked his tongue. "I don't really want to talk about this, okay? I'll tell the cops. Don't worry."

"Who packed the condoms?" Lucy was making herself sick, badgering.

"She did." Patrick looked at her with a mixture of curiosity and impatience. "I didn't go up there to play sex games, if that's what you're wondering. I explained it to you." He reached over and took her hand from her lap. "She's dead, Lucy. Don't be jealous."

Lucy slowly removed her hand from his. She opened her door but then leaned back in the seat.

"I'm not jealous, Patrick," she said quietly. "I'm just worn out. You've got me all worn out."

She climbed out of the car. Patrick got out and took her bag from the trunk.

"Can I come in?" Patrick asked, dismally. "We can talk about it."

Lucy took her bag from him. She wavered. She set herself straight. She kissed him lightly and touched his cheek.

"I need you now, Lucy. Someone tried to kill me," he said.

"No, Patrick," she said. "Not now. Not tonight. I'm sorry."

CHAPTER 16

Detective Sergeant Francis Eliot reached into his briefcase and took out a jar of honey. He unscrewed the lid, stuck in a finger, counted aloud to three and described a short, quick, sweet parabola into his open mouth.

Francis Eliot was squat and round with small pudgy hands. He had a shiny domed head that was buttressed at the sides with stiff slaty hair. His eyes were dark and little and his mouth was rosy pink. He looked like the Pillsbury Dough Boy dressed up in a K-Mart suit.

He was fifty-four years old. He had a wife named Jo, triplet girls aged twelve, a Dodge Caravan, a house that was paid for, a cabin that wasn't, and a new case of attempted murder to solve that would have him working late and on weekends.

Eliot sucked his finger with his eyes closed and wondered if Freeman would ever forgive him. It didn't look good at the moment. Chris Freeman, the Area Detective, had figured that he'd get the Irving case. Freeman had done all the slog work in preparing for the inquest. But the guys upstairs— or rather down the road a hundred clicks at OPP Headquarters in Orillia— had decided differently.

Eliot knew all the Shallow Bay players from the work he'd done the previous year on the EES explosion. His partner in that investigation had been Detective Sergeant Morris Stern, and Morrie would have been a natural to join Eliot again now. But Morrie Stern had just retired— the party had been in April at Dooley's Roadhouse out near Highway 11— so Headquarters had come up with a "special arrangement." Francis Eliot would be in charge of the case and Chris Freeman would be there to assist, working with Eliot, but under him.

An uncomfortable situation, having Freeman under him.

Rather like having to cover ground with gravel in your shoe. Eliot glanced down at the file that had ended up on his borrowed desk. It had been thrown there from across the room by Freeman himself.

Eliot considered the first move to make, given the many moves possible. Probably a good million Canadian citizens had known where Irving was going to be that day. Probably a good five hundred Shallow Bay citizens read that Toronto paper. Probably fifty of the five hundred would like to see Irving unhealthy and maybe a dozen of the fifty would like to see him dead.

Eliot figured he might as well start off with the twelve in Shallow Bay, and then worry about the million minus twelve later on.

He screwed the lid back on the honey jar and put the jar into the top desk drawer. A single loud knock like the blow of a mallet made him jump. The door opened.

"So, you read it?" Freeman said, striding in and sitting on the edge of Eliot's desk, perilously close to the pink-flowered clay giraffe, which teetered but stayed on its feet. One of Eliot's daughters had made the giraffe for his birthday and he'd carefully wrapped it and brought it up north with him. He thought it'd be good to look at when he needed a focus. The centres of the flowers on the giraffe were happy faces.

"Yes, Chris, I read it," said Eliot, reaching forward and opening the file, which so far was the only object on the desk besides two pens, a phone, and the giraffe.

"Look okay?" asked Freeman shortly. "Everything there that you figure should be?"

"Looks fine. Very thorough." Eliot leaned back in his chair to get a better view of Freeman, who was looming over him and the file. "The day you picked up Irving at the reserve, the native officer wasn't there? What's his name? Saint something?"

"Just Saint," Freeman replied. "He was down here in court as a witness in a B and E. Me and de Freitas made the call." He smiled thinly, like a sliver of glass. "I bet you thought there was no crime up on the old reserve, eh, Francie? I bet you thought it was a real paradise of brotherly feeling. No Indian gonna steal from no Indian, right? Well, I'm sorry to say it happens, and it just breaks my heart." Freeman paused then began again, flatly. "Some doped-up kid broke into some shack and stole a chain saw and five gallons of gasoline. Saint was down here on that. You don't mind if I call you Francie, eh?" he added between his teeth. "I can't remember what you said before."

"Frank," Eliot said. His wife sometimes called him Francie and he'd made the mistake of telling Freeman, back during the EES investigation, on one of the rare days when they'd been getting along. He must have been out of his mind.

"Oh, right. Frank." Freeman stood up abruptly and Eliot stretched forward and grabbed the wobbling giraffe. Freeman looked at it. "Cute," he said. He walked to the door and turned.

"You know, of course, Detective Sergeant," he began with mock formality, "that I'm here to help you in any way I can. Phone calls, photocopies, coffee, honey— anything I can do for you, you just shout." He looked at Eliot with pursed lips.

Eliot looked back without expression. His honey habit— another thing Freeman had unfortunately found out about. They'd stopped once for Kentucky Fried Chicken and Freeman had caught Eliot tucking extra packets of honey into the pockets of his suit. For the rest of the day Freeman had called him "sweetie pie" and had threatened to run him in for petty theft.

Eliot knew that he should pull rank. He'd been patient with Freeman up till now because he understood the bitterness: it was tough on these guys to always lose control of the good cases— all the ones that lead to promotions and appearances on the news. But if Freeman was going to be this tiresome... Well, Eliot would give him another day or two and then he'd see.

"Thank you, Chris," he said finally. "I'm sure we'll have much to do."

"Huh," Freeman laughed. He crossed his arms and leaned against the door frame. "So, where you gonna start?" he said. "Lambert?"

"I thought I'd speak to Mr. Robitaille, yes."

"You talk to Irving yet?"

"Yes. Not too loquacious, is he?"

Freeman fixed Eliot with a gimlet stare, mixed with extra ice. "Loquacious. That means chatty, right? No, he's not too 'loquacious.' But then me and him didn't hit it off too good. Maybe he'll get more loquacious with you. When he sees what a nice guy you are." And Freeman turned and left.

Eliot's pink mouth quivered slightly like a new blossom in a dry wind. He puffed up his cheeks and leafed through the Irving file with a fat finger. Then he picked up the phone.

Eliot arrived at the cinder block offices of Lambert Forestry just after lunch. He'd stopped at the McDonald's on the edge of town and had Chicken McNuggets and a vanilla shake. The shake had left Eliot's face sore from having to suck so hard to get it up through the straw.

Robitaille came out from his office wearing a grey flannel track suit and an apologetic smile.

"I'm sorry, Detective, I'm a little behind schedule. I was just out for a short run. Been on a bit of a health kick since we met last. If you'll wait a minute, I'll go and change. Just be a second. Go in and make yourself comfortable."

Robitaille slipped through a door behind the secretary's desk and Eliot went ahead into the office, still breathing hard from the two flights of stairs. He stood, unbuttoning his overcoat, and took in the changes in the room. The walls, which used to be painted an institutional green, were now redone in pale blue. The overhead fluorescents had been replaced with track lighting and there was a Lawren Harris print hanging where there had been a photo of the now ex-Prime Minister. The cupboard where Robitaille had kept the rye had disappeared altogether.

Eliot walked over and looked out the window, down on a small fleet of flatbed trailers and a few men lounging by a canteen truck. A short blast of wind knocked a styrofoam coffee cup off the truck's counter and it rolled and leapt crazily across the paved yard. One man's baseball cap blew off and he lunged away to trap it.

Robitaille came in and closed the office door. He'd changed into a charcoal suit with a white shirt and a yellow tie. He wore square gold-framed glasses and had a neat brown mustache, a shade darker than his neat brown hair. Eliot noticed, with some satisfaction, that the hair was getting thin at the top. He guessed that Robitaille was about the same age as he was.

"Well, Detective Eliot," Robitaille said affably. "Let me take your coat." Eliot wriggled out of his overcoat which Robitaille took and hung on a hook on the back of the door. Then he motioned to a cushy blue and green striped armchair that was pulled up close to the front of the desk. "Please. Sit down."

Eliot thanked him and sank deep into the chair with a grunt. Robitaille walked around the desk and sat on his own chair, a wooden one with an Obus-form back cushion.

"Good holiday weekend?" Robitaille asked.

"Hectic," Eliot replied. "We took our girls down to Canada's Wonderland."

They went through the obligatory weather and family chit-chat and then Robitaille asked Eliot if he'd like some coffee.

"I'm afraid I can't offer you anything stronger," he said regretfully. "I've had to get it out of here. Had a couple of troubling talks with my doctor. But then I never was able to get you to join me, was I?"

"No," said Eliot. "I'm still not much of a drinker. And no coffee right now, thank you." Coffee in the afternoon interfered with his sleep, especially if he was alone in a strange hard bed, like the one in his room at the Comfort Inn.

"All right then," Robitaille began. "What can I do for you? I can guess why you're back in Shallow Bay."

"Yes, I imagine you can. I'm looking into the attempted murder of your old friend, Mr. Irving."

Robitaille laughed. Eliot smiled.

"Detective, that man visits me in my dreams. He's like my evil genius, the way he keeps turning up. You know, I don't mind saying that I'm sorry you didn't nail him along with Bantam." He looked at Eliot and waited while Eliot tried unsuccessfully to shift his weight. The armchair held him like a soft, persistent hug.

"You still think he was involved, then," Eliot said finally, settling back into his original position.

"No, I actually don't think that any more," Robitaille replied. "I don't blame him for the explosion. I do blame him for a lot of blasted lives. Excuse the pun." He leaned back in his chair and crossed his legs. "We've laid off a third of our work force over the past six months, mainly because of that group's interference. And it all started with Irving."

"Do you think that many of your workers hold him responsible?"

"Sure. You know that. You talked to some of them before Bantam's trial. But it's more than just the workers we're talking about. You know what EES has done to this town. They've got the whole country thinking we're a bunch of red-necks out to waste the environment for the sake of a buck. We're right up there on a par with acid rain. Detective," he smiled, "there's an awful lot of people around here with a grudge against Irving. I don't envy you your job one bit."

"Yes. Well," said Eliot a gentle sigh, "maybe you'll be all the more willing to give me your help."

"Of course."

"I need the names of all the employees you've laid off in, say, the last year. And if there's anyone on that list that you remember as being abnormally upset, anyone who made any pointed comments or threats, mentioned Irving by name, I'd like to know that as well."

"Hmm. Well, the list is no problem. But I don't remember hearing anything about Irving. I probably *wouldn't* hear anything, though, would I?"

"No. I suppose you wouldn't. But if you do think of anything," Eliot said, grasping the arms of the chair with determination and pushing himself up out of it, "let us know. We'll be making our inquiries, talking to some of your people." He yawned and caught it with his hand. "Excuse me," he said. "Maybe I should've taken you up on that coffee."

What Eliot really needed was a nap. He did his best thinking when he dozed. But he'd had a hard time convincing Inspector Sayles of it the one time Sayles had caught him snoring.

"Oh," he said, shaking Robitaille's hand at the door. "I meant to ask about the Clifford boy. I understand he's no better?"

"No," Robitaille answered, frowning. "Not a bit better. His parents are beside themselves. In fact, if you're looking for some angry people..." He stopped.

Eliot looked at him with his eyebrows raised.

"I didn't mean it like that, Detective," Robitaille said hurriedly. "They're very decent folks."

"I know they are. Very decent. Thank you, Mr. Robitaille."

"My secretary will call you about the list. I'll get her on it right away."

"That'll be fine. Thank you."

Eliot bumped slowly back down the stairs, considering the angry Cliffords and the jar of Billy Bee honey he had stashed in his glove compartment.

CHAPTER 17

"Just coffee right now, thanks. I'm waiting for someone."

The grey-haired waitress snorted. Stan sat back in his booth and watched the door. It was twelve-twenty-five on Tuesday and Stan was meeting Lucy for lunch.

The Bud had been Stan's choice and Lucy had laughed and said she knew it. It was an irascible old diner from the days before Queen Street fashion, a tough, tattered, unshaven place with bleary windows and walls of jaundice yellow. There was a rat-like dishwasher working out back and then the cook, cashier, and waitress.

The short-order cook was generally suspected of being an ex-con, and even if he wasn't, he played the part. He fried eggs like a fighter in rolled-up shirt sleeves, smoke snaking up into his flat-nosed face from the flaking cigarette he flicked around in his mouth.

The fat-lipped owner of The Bud was Buddy, though he wasn't anybody's friend. He worked the cash with an air of suspicion, watching for the day he finally got short-changed.

But Stan came to see the waitress. She'd worked at The Bud since five-and-dimes and seemed to be threatening immortality. Stan suspected that she was in the minds of many of the waiters along the street as they bitterly paced the cells of their sunless restaurants, like political prisoners clutching cappuccinos. Stan didn't know her name. He thought of her as The Fury, the one who stood by the tables of the damned and kept snatching away their food before they could eat it. He'd seen that happen here.

The Bud served good breakfasts with "fresh squeezed" orange juice and black bread toast. Breakfast was Stan's favourite meal of the day, though he didn't usually eat it until lunchtime. He never had an appetite before noon and subsisted on espresso until his stomach grumbled. It was grumbling now, but quietly, and the restaurant was loud.

In the booth behind him, he could hear two young guys gravely considering whether they should show a Popeye cartoon before the debut of their film that night. One of them felt they shouldn't because the long-nosed "goons" weren't really PC. The other felt they should for exactly the same reason.

A sudden, loud "Yes!" shifted Stan's attention to the counter across the aisle, where a middle-aged man with slicked-back hair was listening impatiently to a plump woman barely balanced on her stool. As Stan listened, still watching the door, he realized they were having an argument over who was king, Jesus or Elvis. The woman cited the Gospels and the man countered with a few lines from "Hound Dog." They got louder and louder, both talking at once. Finally, the woman grabbed the man by the arm.

"All right! So Elvis is the King of Rock and Roll but Jesus is the King of Heaven!" she howled.

Stan grinned. The waitress dropped the coffee on his table like a bomb.

"Thanks," Stan said.

"Uh-huh," said the waitress, without looking at him.

Lucy walked in and Stan carefully took a sip of his coffee, put his chin on his hand and watched her. Lucy ran her hand through her hair and then moved aside to let someone by. She took her bag off her shoulder, looked down at it with surprise and moved it to her other shoulder. Then she straightened up, as if she'd remembered where she was, and surveyed the length of the restaurant, starting at the back. When she got to Stan, he smiled. She quickly came over.

"Not fair," she said, pulling off her coat and rolling it into a ball. She shoved it into the corner of the booth and slipped in after it.

"I know," Stan said. "I shouldn't stare. Sorry."

"I'm glad I didn't trip up the waitress or something. I do that kind of thing."

"She'd have broken both your legs if you had," Stan said. Lucy was wearing lipstick. Her mouth was peachy. He smiled. "Hi."

"Hi."

"I like your lipstick."

She blushed.

"Stop it."

"Sorry."

The Fury came and scowled above them as if she were about ready to let loose.

"Uh," Stan said, glancing up at her, "do you want to look at the menu, Lucy?"

"You have a hot turkey sandwich, don't you?" Lucy asked. The waitress' look seared her to dust.

"Fries or mashed," the waitress lashed.

"Mashed."

"Green beans, carrots, peas," she shot.

"Please, peas." Lucy coughed. "Peas. Please. And a Coke."

"I'll have a cheese omelette with black toast. And a large orange juice," Stan said. The waitress moved off like a storm, thundering the order and flashing her apron. The Jesus woman was still howling.

"Real Zen kind of place you chose, Stan," Lucy said, lighting a cigarette.

"I don't know. I never have the energy to go to most of the places around here. I'm not cool enough so I get self-conscious and I never have the energy to relax."

Lucy laughed. There's that laugh, Stan thought, appreciatively.

"I think I know what you mean," she said. She leaned back and exhaled.

"So, are you over your jet lag? How was your conference?" Stan asked.

"Oh, okay. Not great. Patrick came and got me at the airport."

"Oh," Stan said. He didn't know what else to say. He wondered why she had told him. He didn't want to know. He did want to know. A glass of Coke fell from Olympus.

"He wanted to tell me about the inquest," Lucy continued.

"He must be tickled pink about it," Stan said, without enthusiasm. "He's been pretty well vindicated."

"Well, he *was* right, Stan. I guess he's glad about that. He called me the other night. He's really excited about this theory he has. He won't tell the police, though. He wants to work some things out first."

"Has he told *you* what it is yet?"

"No."

The waitress wrathfully dumped down their plates.

"Thanks," Stan said.

"Uh-huh." She vanished in a cloud of Lucy's smoke, until Jell-O or the Apocalypse, whichever came first.

"Stan."

Stan looked up from his plate. Lucy stubbed out her cigarette and laid her slender hand on the top of her glass. Her brow was furrowed.

"I'm trying to end it with Patrick. It's just that he makes it really hard."

Stan reached forward and touched her hand. It was warm and soft, like a newborn pup. She turned her hand over and gently took hold of his. She examined his face and smiled.

"You must have thought I was some kind of nut. When I kissed your hand," she said.

"No," Stan replied quietly. "I thought you were a peach."

"A peach?" she laughed.

"Yup." Stan grinned at her. "You wanna eat?" Their hands slipped apart. Lucy looked over the table at his plate.

"Your omelette appears kind of flat," she said.

"And your sandwich appears fleshy."

"You a vegetarian?"

"Pretty well. But I'm not as good a one as I ought to be."

"How good a one ought you to be?" she asked, sawing through the sandwich.

"Well, I shouldn't really eat dairy stuff or eggs. I mean, if I really want to act on my beliefs." He shook salt and pepper on his home fries and ate one.

"And what are your beliefs?"

"I guess that I should do my best to cause the least amount of suffering possible to other living things. That I should live in such a way that no animal has to die unnecessarily on my account."

"Cows and pigs and turkeys." Lucy looked at him with her fork in her food.

"And fish."

"And fish?" She raised her eyebrows. "Does it bother you to see other people eating it?"

"No. I ate meat myself until I was in my twenties. It tastes good. Your sandwich looks great. That's why I still eat cheese and eggs, even though I know what's involved in the production. I love it and I'm too big a weakling to give it up. I'm a hypocrite, I guess. It bugs me." He took a bite of omelette. He swallowed. "But I'm still eating, right?"

They finished their food and Lucy bravely asked for rice pudding. Stan beseeched another cup of coffee. They talked about Stan and Lucy, mostly, and also about Gina. Lucy wanted to know what she'd been like.

"Scary," Stan told her.

"Really?" Lucy said. "Why?"

"Well, not exactly scary. Intimidating. At least to me. But she was also pretty funny, in a weird way. She'd come up to my place occasionally to visit and she'd always bring what she called 'supplies,' things that she said I needed in the country. Like a bug zapper and a cattle prod."

"A cattle prod. That's right up your alley."

"Yeah. That's what I mean. It was funny but it wasn't." Stan finished the dregs of his coffee. "She was really involved in women's issues and I think she was a bit frustrated with having to write about sports stuff. She would have liked a political column but they wouldn't give her one."

The restaurant had emptied out. They'd been sitting there for nearly two hours and were at risk of annihilation. The waitress was standing at the end of the counter, watching them with baleful eyes while she squeezed the life out of a glass of water.

"I should go, Stan," Lucy said, wrinkling her nose with regret. "I have to get back to work."

"I wish I could give you a ride but I left the truck up at Islington station. There's never anywhere to park downtown. I mean, not if you're cheap." He smiled, self-effacingly.

"That's okay. It's only a ten-minute walk." She looked over her shoulder out the window. "It actually looks kind of nice out now."

"I'll walk with you then, okay?"

"Okay. Sure."

As the owner at the cash watched with his arms folded, Lucy insisted on paying the bill. Stan was worried that it was because of his comment about being cheap and so, when she agreed to let him leave the tip, he left a whopping one. The Fury would accept it with cool contempt.

They walked together along Queen Street and up past the hospitals on University Avenue under a sky swathed in strips of clouds like gauze bandages. The wind tore the clouds this way and that, a plastic surgery patient impatient to expose a better blue, while the last of the yellow tulips in the planters honked in place of the cars. No honking, Stan punned joyfully, was *aloud* near the hospitals.

When they reached the steps up to the Environmental Studies building, Lucy turned and looked at him, almost shyly, holding the strap of her shoulder bag with both hands.

"I'd like to see your lab some time," he said.

"Okay."

"I'd like to see you, too. *Really* see you, I mean."

"*Really* see me?" she repeated.

"Like for a whole day," he said. He put his hands in his pockets, looked down and added, "Or a night."

"Okay."

He looked up at her. "It's kind of a ridiculous date but I've got a party to go to on Friday at a farmer's down the road. You could come see my place and we could drop by the party, maybe. You could meet my dogs and stuff."

Lucy looked back at him with her bright eyes and a slow, crazy smile slid home. She took a step forward and Stan did, too. He tried not to stand on his toes. He ran his hands down her arms and then up and clasped them together at the back of her neck.

"Stan," she said, in a moment.

"Peach?"

She laughed softly and touched his cheek. She pushed some strands of hair back from his ear.

"I really like stuff," she whispered.

When she'd slipped inside, Stan sat down on the steps and closed his eyes. He stretched out his legs and curled his toes. He felt like a trout shimmering in a clear pool, or a garter snake sunning its new green skin, or a tree swallow sweeping down to its nest.

CHAPTER 18

When Eliot pulled up in the Cliffords' driveway, Ray Clifford came to the door of the garage. He had a monkey wrench in his hand and a tired, stubborn look, like a striking worker who was getting nowhere with management. As Eliot dredged himself slowly out of the seat of his car, Clifford walked out towards him, dropping the wrench into a pocket and wiping his hands on his faded blue coveralls.

"Car trouble?" Eliot asked, extending his own pink, well washed hand.

"The van's been acting up," Clifford replied. He took the hand and shook it. "We can go in through here. Susan's inside."

Eliot followed Clifford through the garage, squeezing between the van and a wooden work table. His coat sleeve buffed the side of the van, picking up oily dust. The van hood was open and tools were scattered on the concrete floor. Rakes and shovels were propped against the wall and there was a small outboard motor over in a corner.

They went through the door and into the kitchen where a kettle was boiling, a cloud of steam dissipating as it hit the underside of a cupboard. Along a window sill above the sink was a row of small plants with purple flowers. The same kind, Eliot thought, as Jo's got in the bathroom. He didn't know the name.

"Susan!" Ray called. "Hey, Susan!"

"Just a minute!" Susan Clifford's voice answered from another room.

"Eliot's here!"

"Okay, Ray. Just a minute. I'm coming!" Susan's voice sounded harassed.

Clifford sat down on a kitchen chair and watched as Eliot brushed tentatively at the dirt on his coat.

"You'll have a hell of a time getting that off. Grease and salt. I guess I should have brought you in through the front." Clifford slid a chair out towards Eliot with his foot. "You wanna sit down?"

"Thank you," Eliot said, with a last sad look at his sleeve. He hated being dirty. He sat.

"How is your son?" Eliot asked after a minute's silence. Ray Clifford had aged, he thought. Worry lines on his forehead and frown lines around his mouth. He hadn't shaved this morning. His eyes were bloodshot.

Clifford laughed. It was a short unpleasant laugh that reminded Eliot of the day in court when sentence had been passed on Terry Bantam. Eliot had tried to speak to him on the way out of the courthouse and Clifford had shrugged him off with the words, "Justice has been fucking served."

"How's my son?" Clifford now repeated. "He's just great. Coming right along. Should be out playing baseball in a week or two."

"Is there any hope for improvement at all?" Eliot asked with concern, ignoring Clifford's sarcasm. Clifford scratched his nose and then noticed his oily fingers.

"Well," he said, finally, "they said all along that he wouldn't get anywhere. The only way they knew he was conscious was that some tests— EEGs or something— showed that his brain was working. Plus, if they looked real close at his eyes, like with a magnifying glass, they could see his pupils moving a bit."

"With a magnifying glass?" Eliot repeated.

"Yeah," Clifford answered, grimacing. "Can you believe it? Anyway, he was really bad. One of the worst cases anybody had seen. They didn't think he'd ever get any better. But now... Now, they're saying that he might get back some control of his eyes so he can say things. Yes. No. Spell things out with some kinda board maybe." Clifford looked towards the kitchen door. "What the hell is taking Susan? Susan!" he yelled.

Susan Clifford came through the door, frowning at her husband. Eliot stood up and she shook his hand. She too had aged, Eliot thought. And gained weight. He noticed his own belt was feeling tight.

"Didn't you offer him any coffee?" she asked Ray, looking over at the steaming kettle.

"I was waiting for you."

"It's probably boiled away to nothing by now. My God, Ray." She walked over and unplugged the kettle.

"That's fine, Mrs. Clifford. I won't have any coffee, thanks." Eliot plunked back down in his seat.

"Would you like anything else? Tea, orange juice, a beer?"

"No, thank you. I won't keep you long. I just have a few questions about this Irving business. Routine, of course. I'm speaking to everyone who had any connection to him."

"Did you tell him?" Susan asked her husband, walking to the table and sitting down.

"No," Clifford repeated peevishly. "I was waiting for you."

Eliot watched them pass quick messages back and forth, silently, with their eyes. The messages seemed to be about their marriage and the news didn't look very good. He reminded himself to call Jo when he got back to the station. She was getting a root canal done that day and would probably be feeling peaky.

Susan Clifford stood up and walked to the sink. She filled a glass from the tap and began to water the purple-flowered plants.

"Irving was here," Clifford said to Eliot, watching his wife. "Susan had a real nice jaw session with him. Right, Susan?"

She ignored him.

"When was this?" Eliot asked Susan. He'd talked to Irving twice— once in person and once on the phone— and Irving hadn't mentioned the Cliffords. But then Irving wasn't being cooperative. He didn't want to talk about his public life and, as for his private life, well, there was supposed to be a girlfriend, though Irving hadn't told him so. Eliot had heard it from Freeman who'd heard it through the hospital.

"Late last week," Susan Clifford said, still fiddling with the plants. "Thursday."

"The day before that inquest," Clifford added. "He came when I was out, the bastard."

"What did he want?" Eliot asked, looking at Susan Clifford's back and then at Ray Clifford's scowling face and finally again at Susan, who had turned around.

Susan told him about Irving's visit.

"And he said it had to do with the attempt on his life?" Eliot asked, unfolding his stubby hands from where they'd rested on his paunch.

"That's what he implied," she answered.

"He didn't mention any names?"

"No. When I told him about Mr. Robitaille, he just nodded."

"You gonna be seeing him?" Ray Clifford broke in. He'd been silent throughout his wife's story, except for a contemptuous snort when she reached the part about Irving's asking to talk to Jamie. Clifford was now leaning back in his chair with his arms crossed over his chest, like a bully at a bar, spoiling for a fight.

"Yes." Eliot had had other plans for the next couple of days but it looked like he'd better see Irving again. It looked like the man was trying to paddle his own canoe— run his own investigation— and it was time to tow him back to the dock.

"Well, when you see him," Clifford hissed, "tell him to keep the fuck away from my house. Tell him I'll fucking kill him if he comes around again."

"Ray!" Susan said reproachfully.

Clifford suddenly laughed.

"My wife's afraid I'm gonna implicate myself. Right, Susan?" he said, smiling wryly at Eliot. "Don't worry. I didn't try to murder Patrick Irving. But I'd sure buy a beer for the guy who did. Hell, I'd buy him a couple."

Clifford looked at his wife and laughed again. She just stared at him.

Eliot ran his hand over his smooth bald head and got down to why he'd come.

"Mr. Clifford, I'm afraid I have to ask you where you were on May fifth," he said quietly, watching Clifford with his small black eyes.

"You're kidding," Ray said, no longer laughing or smiling, either.

"As I said, at this point it's just routine. But I do need to know, Mr. Clifford, if you're able to think back."

Susan Clifford suddenly stood up.

"Well, I'm going to have a beer. I think this calls for a beer. Join me, Ray? Detective Sergeant?"

"No thank you," Eliot said with a short rosy smile her way. Ray watched Susan silently as she went from the fridge to the cupboard and came back to the table.

"This is really stupid," Ray Clifford said, when Susan had sat down with her glass.

"You can't remember?" Eliot asked. "Were you working?"

"Yeah, I was working in Muskoka for a while around then. I just did the invoice for the job so I can check the date, I guess. Jesus," he said standing up, "I can't believe this. Wasn't he poisoned or something? As if I know anything about poison. If I was gonna kill him, I'd use something normal, like a gun or a baseball bat. I'll be right back. Where's that invoice, Susan?"

"On the dresser," she said.

He left the kitchen and Eliot looked at Susan Clifford who was staring down at the glass she was holding with both hands.

"I'd like to know where you were, too, Mrs. Clifford," he said.

"At the hospital. I always work on Mondays," she said wearily.

"When do you start?"

"Seven in the morning. It's a twelve-hour shift."

"All right. And someone was here with your son?"

"We have a VON come in." She sighed.

Clifford came back into the room and handed the invoice to Eliot. He sat down.

"I always itemize it by date. I was down there that day, working on the kitchen."

Eliot scrutinized the invoice. He read:

Monday, May 5- installed double kitchen
sink, faucets, electronic water filter,
pyrotechnic heating line- 10 hours @
$40.00... $400.00.

"This was down in Muskoka?" Eliot asked.

"Yeah. Fawn Lake. South of Huntsville."

"When did you arrive there?"

"Probably around nine."

"And you left ten hours later?"

"More or less. I usually round it off."

"And then where did you go?"

"I came home. No, wait." He screwed up his face. "No, that day I stopped in Huntsville, I think. I went to the Canadian Tire to get some stuff for the van because the one here would've been closed by the time I got back. Then I grabbed a hamburger and then I came home. Yeah."

"When did you get home?"

"God, I don't know. Must have been close to ten."

"It was," Susan Clifford said. "I remember because when you came in I was with Jamie watching a movie that was just about over. And the ten o'clock news was on after."

"And I imagine there were other men working at this cottage that day as well," Eliot said to Clifford. Clifford sat and thought about it.

"Shit," he said finally.

"What?" Susan asked with alarm.

"I was the only one there that day. The owners were up on the weekend but they left Sunday night. And the carpenters were off on another job. Shit. It figures."

"Well," said Eliot, soothingly. "No doubt someone saw you."

"Yeah. I hope so," Clifford said.

"What about the receipt from the Canadian Tire?" his wife asked. "If you have it, it probably has the date on it, at least. Maybe even the time."

"Huh. Yeah." He passed her the only friendly message Eliot had seen so far. "I'll look for it. I probably tossed it out, though."

"Well, if you do find it, let me know." Eliot stood up and straightened his coat, woefully fingering the mark on the sleeve.

"Sorry about your coat," Clifford said, standing up, too. "You can go out the front."

On the front porch, Eliot shook the Cliffords' hands and remarked on how beautiful the day was becoming. He then asked them if they owned a boat.

"I noticed the outboard motor in the garage," he said.

"That's my brother's. He's got a junky little aluminum job. He asked me to overhaul the motor for the summer."

"I see," Eliot said, taking two steps down the stairs and turning. "And where does he keep his boat?"

Clifford and Susan looked at each other, Susan shaking her head.

"At his cottage," Clifford said.

"And that is where?" Eliot mildly asked him.

"On the goddamn Speller River."

CHAPTER 19

The computer was gone. So was the fax machine. And papers were everywhere, like a badly tossed salad. Books were pulled from some of the shelves and politics and poetry lay scattered across the floor. A white screw-on lamp had been wrenched from the desk and dangled with a smashed bulb from the cord that was snagged on an open drawer. The venetian blind had been yanked from the window and the room looked whiter than ever, the pale light of the drab day casting no relieving shadows.

Patrick Irving threw down his suitcase and ran. He took the corner into the kitchen and kicked a can of chickpeas six feet. He yanked open the freezer door, rummaged frantically, pulled out a plastic bag and was jubilant.

"Ha! You bastards!" he shouted with glee. "You stupid goddamn bastards! Close but no fucking cigar!"

With his heart racing and his face flushed, he uprighted a chair and sat down on it. He barely noticed the devastated kitchen— bottles smashed, cupboards yawning, Cuisinart and coffee maker no longer there. He fingered the plastic bag and stared, beaming, into space.

"Man!" he said. He hadn't felt this good since the Conservatives got crushed in the last election. "Man!"

He tapped his feet in a quick little jig and jumped up from the chair. Still holding the plastic bag, he ran back into the office and looked for the phone. He found it in a corner. It had been torn from the outlet and thrown against the wall. The plastic connector was broken off. The answering machine was gone.

He went down the hallway and into his bedroom, stepping over the clothing and pillows on the floor. The phone was still there on the bedside table, the old black rotary he'd had for fifteen years. He lifted the receiver and heard the dial tone, then he put down the plastic bag and cleared a hole in the heap on the bed. He sank into the hole and, with excited fingers, dialled the number.

After six rings he was about to hang up when Lucy's voice said a breathless, "Hello."

"Ask me how I am, Lucy."

"Patrick?"

"Ask me how I am. You always used to say I never said I felt fine."

"Patrick. Okay. How are you?"

"Fucking great!" Patrick laughed. He tucked the receiver under his chin and swung his legs up on to the bed, over the piled up sheets. He reached across to the table and picked up the plastic bag. "Ask me why."

"Patrick," Lucy answered. "Stop being weird."

"Just ask me."

There was silence.

"C'mon, Lucy."

"Okay. Why do you feel so fucking great?"

Patrick lifted his legs up in the air and dropped them with a bounce. He laughed again, giddily.

"Well, Lucy, since you're so damn insistent, I'll tell you. Are you alone? You don't have Milliken or Stanley there on your lap..."

"I'm going to hang up on you, Patrick."

"No, don't," Patrick said, putting the bag down beside him and shifting the phone to his other ear. "I'll be serious now. I promise." He traced a cross out over his heart. "I just got home and my apartment's been torn to shit," he said solemnly.

"What?" Lucy exclaimed. Patrick smiled with satisfaction.

"Yeah, it's been ransacked. But they didn't get what they were looking for," he continued, picking up the bag and undoing the twist-tie, "because I hid it in a really good place." He slid a piece of frozen pita bread out of the stack in the bag. The edge of the pita had been slit open. He separated the sides and gingerly extracted a folded sheet of paper.

"Does this have something to do with your theory?" Lucy asked.

"I think you might say it proves it," Patrick laughed. He was still feeling delirious. Man oh man!

"Are you ready to tell me about it now?"

"Oh, maybe I will. Yeah, I think I will. Though I don't know why I should at this point. We're not exactly *close* any more, are we?"

Silence.

"Okay. Let me think how to organize this. There was the explosion at Lambert, right?"

"Yes."

"And Terry et al got put away for it, though, obviously, it was a set-up."

"They couldn't prove it."

"I know that, Lucy," Patrick said impatiently. "Just listen, all right?"

Silence.

"About a week before Gina and I went on that fucking doomed camping trip, I got a letter. An anonymous letter from a guy who was out there that day, working for Lambert. He said that he was standing twenty feet or so away from Jamie Clifford, smoking a cigarette, and that the Clifford kid called over to him that... Just a second." Patrick unfolded the letter and scanned the page. "The kid called out, 'Wiener alert!' and pointed over into the woods."

"'Wiener alert'?" Lucy repeated, with a tentative laugh. "What's that supposed to mean?"

"They called the management 'wieners,' he says. Anyway, before this guy could turn around, the explosion went off and everybody went crazy."

"Did this guy testify at the trial, Patrick?"

"He doesn't say. But he must've. He must have been a witness. There were about ten workers from Lambert at the site and they all testified. But they claimed that not one damn person from management was there."

"Why didn't this guy say anything?"

"Yeah. It would've been nice." Patrick swung his legs off the bed and sat up. "In the letter he basically says that he was too pissed off. That he wanted to see EES get screwed."

"And why is he telling you now?"

"Guilty conscience, the asshole."

"I bet you didn't tell the police about this, did you?" Lucy chastised.

"Christ, no. I've been trying to track the guy down. I looked up the newspaper reports of the trial but I couldn't find all the names of the witnesses. I was planning to check out the court records when Gina and I got back from up north. But that sort of got put off. Though not permanently, which is what they were hoping."

"*They*, Patrick? Who's *they?*"

"Lambert. They somehow found out what I knew and they tried to knock me off. That didn't work, so they came here looking for the letter."

"Why wouldn't they do it the other way around? It seems a bit more natural to try a smaller thing first, doesn't it?"

"Oh, Lucy, for chrissakes," Patrick said, irritably. The initial thrill was wearing off. He was starting to notice the wreckage. The glass sailboat he'd got out east was in pieces on the floor. "They probably didn't know about the letter at first. The guy may have let it slip that he'd been in touch with me. I don't know. It doesn't really matter."

"But what about him?" Lucy persisted. "If they tried to kill you, wouldn't they try to kill him, too? And what about the boy who was hurt? He's the one who could do the worst harm. He actually saw who was there. The 'wiener.'"

"Ha," Patrick said. "He can't do any harm. I talked to his mother before the inquest and she says he's completely paralysed and can't communicate. Lambert knows it, too. The fucking manager, Robitaille, calls there all the time to check."

"Really?" Lucy paused. "But there's still the guy who wrote the letter."

"Yeah, and I'm still trying to track him down. Assuming he's alive. I went out to see Terry in prison and he told me EES made lots of notes at the trial. They have everybody's names, he said, and where they were standing when."

"You went to see Terry Bantam?"

"Yeah. That's where I just came back from. I told him what was going on and he said he'd tell the kiddies at EES to let me see their files. Faster than going through court record shit."

"What did he think about it?"

"Oh, he was rattling the bars of his cell with excitement."

"You've got to tell the police, Patrick."

"I don't want to tell them yet. I want to find the guy first."

"Why?"

"Why? Christ, Lucy. I've taken shit from the cops for years. When have they ever helped me out?" Not at the Queen's Park protest where he was arrested for disturbing the peace, smack in the middle of the Toronto rush hour. And not up at the Shallow Bay logging site where they'd nabbed him on some trumped-up trespassing charge.

"But they're trying to help you out now, aren't they?"

"C'mon, Lucy," Patrick groaned. "Don't be so naive. That little gnome Eliot just wants a nice gold star for his forehead, like my grade three teacher gave out when you answered right."

"But if you tell them, then you'll really get your own back. You'll make them look bad about the EES thing plus you'll have found out before them who probably tried to kill you."

"*Probably!* Lucy! Doesn't it all fit together?" He heard Lucy take a deep breath. "You smoking in your office?" he asked.

"No, I'm not smoking. But I've got to get back to work. Tell the police, Patrick, okay? You were going to report the break-in, weren't you?"

"I hadn't really thought about it. I guess I might have to for the insurance or something."

"Did they wreck a lot of stuff?"

"Yeah. And my computer's been taken. Fax machine, answering machine, other shit."

"They *stole* things?"

"A blind."

"Well, tell the police," Lucy said, sceptically. "Someone's knocking at my door, Patrick. I've got to go." He heard Lucy call, "Come in."

"Milliken or Stanley?" Patrick asked.

"What?"

"Knocking at your door. 'Who's that knocking at my door, said the fair young maiden'?"

"Bye, Patrick."

"Yeah. Right."

Patrick put the receiver down and stared up at the ceiling. "Christ."

He shouldn't have called Lucy. She'd let him down, as usual, poking at his theory as if it were some kind of worm in her lab. How did he get involved with a woman who studied worms, anyway? Eyeless squirming things. Something kind of sick about being obsessed with worms.

He got up off the bed and started back towards the kitchen to find the broom so he could sweep up the broken glass. When he was halfway there, he realized he shouldn't be touching things, assuming he was going to call the cops. Did he really have to call the goddamned cops? He stood in the hallway, scratching his beard, neither here nor there. The doorbell rang.

When he opened the door it was to Francis Eliot.

"Good timing," Patrick said, frowning.

CHAPTER 20

Oh, give me land, lots of land, under starry skies above
Don't fence me in
Let me ride through the wide-open country that I love
Don't fence me in
Let me be by myself in the evening breeze
Listen to the murmur of the cottonwood trees
Send me off forever, but I ask you, please
Don't fence me in

Stan sang along with the Cole Porter tape, and wondered if Lucy would find this landscape too flat. The bus would be taking her through hillier country, up over the Niagara Escarpment, past expensive cedar shingled houses tastefully hidden by the right kind of trees. There'd be horses bowing gracefully and spring-fed ponds like Wedgwood blue saucers and a hawk circling above the hills exactly where you'd want one aesthetically.

Then the bus would descend to a less rolling country that got steadily flatter and barer. The horses would bow out to scraggy brown cattle, ponds would disorganize into swamps and the hawks would be far too common for art. There wouldn't be as many trees—certainly nothing you could call forest. The word used up here was "bush."

Not very scenic, he considered, as he headed south down the highway. And not very romantic. Except maybe for the stars in the wide sky at night and the stillness of being alone. He flicked off the tape.

He'd wanted to go down to get Lucy but she'd insisted on taking the bus. So he'd found out when there were buses to Barton, half an hour away, and she'd said she'd take the one that got in at eight. The last one went back to the city at eleven, but Stan had planned that she wouldn't be on it.

All afternoon, he'd been making Masala Dosai for dinner. Great big skinny pancakes wrapped around spicy potatoes with fresh coconut chutney and "gunpowder" sauce on the side. Lucy'd told him she liked Indian food. He hoped she liked it hot.

The last time he'd been out to the East Indian neighbourhood in Toronto, he'd stocked up on spices, and chilies for the freezer. The only thing he'd needed for the recipe was a coconut and he'd had a hell of a time finding one up here. Yesterday, he'd hit three towns and four supermarkets before he finally did.

"This is a coconut, eh?" the teenaged cashier had asked Stan at the checkout. "How do you get 'em open?"

"Well, I usually back over them with my truck." When it looked like she was willing to believe him he'd been mad at himself for being such a city-boy smart-aleck. "Just kidding," he'd told her. "I actually use a hammer."

After he and Lucy finished the Indian food they'd have English trifle for dessert. It didn't really go— this touch of the raj— but trifle was his favourite and he made it well. They could wait a while before they had it, maybe until after they'd finished the wine, or had another beer or two, whatever Lucy drank. Then he'd get a fire going and make some coffee and they could have dessert in front of the fire.

In the morning maybe they'd take the dogs for a walk across the fields. In the morning. Maybe. He smiled.

But first things first, he thought, mentally shaking himself, and the first thing tonight was dropping in on the Hoots. He hoped Lucy wouldn't be too bored.

Al Hoot was turning ninety and half of the township had been invited to his party. Stan really had to go, if only for an hour, partly because he liked the Hoots and partly because he owed them a lot. When he had first moved out here, Al and his son Brian had offered to help repair his cedar rail fence, and they'd worked like dray horses, even though Brian himself was almost seventy. Since then, they'd lent Stan tools and equipment, tilled his garden in spring and fall and ploughed his road in winter. Stan knew they considered him a nut for posting "No Hunting" signs and for being "one of them vegetarians." But they seemed to like him anyway.

They never read his column, as far as he knew. They probably wouldn't like him so much if they did. He'd once done a column defending "nuisance" animals— groundhogs, raccoons, porcupines— and just last week he'd mentioned pesticides. It was a complex world though, Stan thought. One of the nicest guys he knew ran the local slaughterhouse.

Stan drove past the stone clock tower in Barton, noting that it was five to eight. Now some small person did the soft-shoe and tipped its cap in his stomach.

He pulled in to the curb across from the bus station. He hoped he looked okay. He'd given his hair another trim but he wished he'd gotten to a barber shop. He was afraid the left side was shorter than the right. He was wearing his old green mock turtleneck and black wool cardigan, his faded black jeans and his new red Converse high-tops. The shoes should give the Hoots a laugh.

When the bus pulled in he climbed out of the truck and walked over to the station. Two white-haired women got off and then another woman with three little kids and then a long-haired guy and then Lucy.

She had on a man's overcoat from which her thin legs descended in black stockings. On her feet were old-style galoshes, the kind that buckled up. She was carrying her shoulder bag but no other luggage. Stan wondered if she had a toothbrush in her bag— it vaguely worried him that she'd brought so little.

"Lucy!" he called, when she didn't seem to see him. She turned, smiled slightly and walked towards him. He met her halfway.

"Hi," she said, the slight smile flickering on and off.

"Hi." He didn't kiss her. Her eyes didn't seem to be taking him in. They wandered, like her smile, and he felt it'd be trying to kiss a moving target.

"It's really mild," she said. "I thought it would be cold and wet. Snowing, maybe."

"You sound like an American," Stan said.

"An American?"

"Yeah. An American who's just crossed the Canadian border with his skis in July."

"Oh. I guess I do sound like that. I'm just so bad at dressing..." her voice trailed off.

Stan studied her face with uneasiness. Nearby a car backfired with a bang.

"I'm parked across the street," he said.

She followed him to the truck and got in. He'd cleared all the garbage out but had left her cigarette butts in the ashtray. He didn't know why. It was very silly. He slid into the driver's seat and looked across at her.

"Are you all right?" he asked.

She turned and smiled at him, focusing on his face for the first time.

"Sure," she said.

"Do you still want to do this?"

"Yes, Stan, I do. I really do. I'm okay. Really." She reached over and brushed his hand with her fingertips.

They drove back north with the sun slouched low under the bank of clouds on their left. Lucy gazed out at the fields and bush, glancing at Stan when he spoke to her, answering his questions quietly but asking few of her own. She smoked two cigarettes halfway through.

Stan was puzzled and anxious. He wondered if Lucy was having second thoughts. He wondered if she had been talking to Patrick. Fucking Patrick was probably still calling her.

"We're almost there," Stan said. "Another couple of miles. But we don't have to go to the party, if you don't want to. We could just go straight to my place."

"No. Let's go. I'd like to. It'll be fun." Lucy said this with as much enthusiasm as a convict being led to a lethal injection. Then she seemed to realize it and laughed a little. "I could use some cheering up."

"Hmm," Stan said. "You could." He made an attempt to sound mischievous. "I don't suppose you play euchre."

"Euchre? Not since I was in high school. We used to play in the cafeteria at lunch."

"Well, pretend you don't know how," Stan said, "or they'll never let you leave." He turned on to a dirt lane and pulled up beside the barn where a dozen trucks and cars were parked at a dozen different angles.

"Ready for fun?" Stan asked, turning off the ignition.

"All ready," Lucy answered quietly, smoothing out her hair.

"Well, now, here's Stan," a scrawny little woman with golden bracelets said. She was standing at the sink in the kitchen cutting open a bag of milk. On the counters to either side of her, Tupperware containers were stacked five high. The yellow form of a cake showed through the translucent plastic of one of them. "Warmin' up out there, Stan?"

"Yup," Stan answered. "It feels pretty good. Muriel," he said, turning to Lucy, "this is my friend, Lucy Shepherd, from Toronto.

Muriel is Al Hoot's daughter-in-law."

"Hi," Lucy said, putting out her hand. "I hope you don't mind that Stan brought me along."

"More the merrier," Muriel said, wiping her hand on her flowered apron before shaking Lucy's. "Glad to see he's got a lady friend visiting." Muriel looked slyly at Stan. "We got pretty worried about him last winter, all holed up like a bear. Needs somebody around to keep him up and taking nourishment."

Here we go, thought Stan. Let the ribbing begin.

When Cath had left him the news had travelled fast, tossed from farm to farm like a hot potato. He could always tell who knew about it by the way they didn't mention her, and didn't mention *anything* that had to do with women. For months, the conversations with his neighbours had been stilted, as if not being able to mention Cath had drained their resources of other topics. Except, of course, the weather. The good old die-hard weather. Stan couldn't count the number of times, during those months, someone had asked, "Cold enough for ya, Stan?"

He was almost relieved when, as if by plan, his neighbours had started joking around. The women would mention the names of local girls— Sandy at the insurance office, Helga at the library— who they figured were needing husbands. The men would stop their tractors when they saw him out gardening and say stuff like, "Them flowers are for the women. You better get one down here before you go soft."

Glancing at Lucy, Stan wondered whether he'd invited her here partly to show her off. The way Muriel was surreptitiously appraising her, from her boots to her balky hair, suggested there'd soon be talk. Probably with raised eyebrows. He imagined they'd find her strange.

"Yous go inside and make yourself comfortable," Muriel said. "Brian and his dad are in the living room. Brian'll get yous something to drink. Leave your coat on the couch there, Lucy."

Lucy slung off the overcoat. Underneath she was wearing a black pleated skirt and a man's oversized burgundy crew-neck sweater. She pulled off her galoshes. Her black shoes were flat-heeled and round-toed, with a strap across the top. She looked like a kid from a private school. Stan took her hand.

There were five card tables squeezed into the living room and four of them were filled with euchre players. Brian, twice the size of his wife, with a head like a block of pink granite, bellowed at them from across the room.

"C'mon in, Stan my man!"

Heads turned away from the cards and grinning faces took in Lucy. Stan nodded a general greeting and led Lucy over to the table where the still strapping Al Hoot was shuffling the deck with his large paw-like hands.

"Many happy returns, Al."

"Why thank ya, Stan," Al hoot said tranquilly, "Thank ya for comin'."

"I'd like you to meet my friend Lucy," Stan said, smiling at her.

"Happy birthday, Mr. Hoot," Lucy said.

"Al, sweetheart. I'm too old ta be formal."

"What can I get ya?" Brian hollered, standing up from his table and almost taking it with him. The other players held it down with their elbows.

"Lucy?" Stan asked. "Do you want something to drink?"

"Just some water, please." Lucy said, barely loud enough to be heard.

"Water, eh? Ya better be careful with that one, Stan. It's the ones that drinks water that ya gotta watch out for."

Lucy looked down at her feet. Stan wanted to kiss her but if he did she might not even notice. Everybody else sure would, though.

"I'll have a beer," he called to Brian. "Whatever you got."

"A beer. Yous sit down. D'ya play euchre, Lucy, or are ya like that old stick-in-the-mud friend of yers?"

"I haven't played in a long time," Lucy said. "I'm afraid I don't really remember how."

"Well, then yous two just relax." Brian barrelled out to the kitchen.

Stan looked around the room for a place to sit, not wanting to take a seat at a card table. There'd be other neighbours arriving over the next couple of hours, and some time about midnight "lunch" would be served. Salmon, ham, and egg salad sandwiches. Somebody's pickles and somebody's green jellied salad. The yellow cake would come out to "Happy Birthday" and then everyone would joke while Al opened his gifts. Stan was in on one of the presents, to the whistled tune of three dollars. Zane's wife, Shirley, had taken up the collection and had refused to accept a penny more.

"You can squeeze in over here," the same Shirley now called, gesturing to a sofa that had been pushed into the corner. "You're skinny enough to fit."

"Okay, Lucy?" Stan asked. Her eyes were slightly glazed and her hand felt cold and limp, though when he spoke to her she suddenly squeezed his, tight.

"Sure."

They sat with their legs pressed against the sofa, toes turned in, holding their drinks. Shirley passed them the bowl of pretzels from her table and chatted while she continued to play. Stan didn't really know the other players at the table, a woman with huge flabby arms and round dim eyes, and two old farmers, who had to be brothers, both with faces like fallow fields. Shirley's husband Zane was on the other side of the room.

"So what do you do with yourself, Lucy?" Shirley asked.

"I'm with the University of Toronto," Lucy replied.

"Secretary, are you?"

Stan laughed.

"She's a professor, Shirley. She gets called 'Doctor.'"

"Are you really? A professor," Shirley said blandly. "And how do you like that?"

Lucy took an uncomfortable sip of her water.

"I like the research. And the travelling," she answered quietly.

Stan waited for her to say more, but she just looked down at her lap.

"Lucy goes to a lot of conferences and things," Stan explained. "She travels all over the world."

"Do you, now?" Shirley said. "You should get that newspaper of yours to send you somewhere, Stan. Maybe down to Florida to look at the alligators. Get them to send you down in January."

"I wish they would," Stan said. "But they're not too generous that way. They are paying for me to go up to Shallow Bay, though."

"Up north?" Shirley asked.

"You're going up to Shallow Bay?" Lucy murmured, looking up at him.

"Yup. Strange, eh? Second time in a month. You remember that wildlife centre I told you about?" he asked Lucy. "My editor, Elizabeth, has decided she wants me to write a piece on it."

"Well, you make sure you take a compass, Stan. We don't want you getting lost in the woods," Shirley laughed, and then it was her turn to deal.

Stan looked at Lucy, who sat taking small desultory drinks of her water. She was pale, almost haggard, and her eyes looked lost. He decided to put an end to the torture, hers and, increasingly, his.

"Let's go, okay?" he said in an undertone.

"We just got here," she answered.

"It doesn't matter. C'mon."

CHAPTER 21

When they got outside, the sky overhead was lavender. A thin moon like a Muslim crescent was suspended in pink to the west. A nighthawk, too high up to see, called nasally for insects and a marmalade barn cat pounced in the grass.

Stan and Lucy walked silently to the truck. They got in and Stan took out his keys. Then he leaned back in his seat and closed his eyes.

"I'm so sorry," Lucy whispered.

"It's all right." He put his hands on the steering wheel and sighed. He heard Lucy rustling in her bag and figured she was looking for her cigarettes. But he didn't hear her light one. When he opened his eyes, she was staring straight ahead. Two tears were sliding down her cheeks and in her hand she was crushing a piece of Kleenex.

"Lucy," Stan said. She quickly wiped the tears away and looked at him. "Just tell me, okay? Just get it over with."

"I shouldn't have come," she said.

"It's Patrick, right?" Stan asked, practically tasting his bitterness. He looked away, out the windshield, focusing on the cat that was now slinking alongside the barn wall. Suddenly, Lucy laughed. A strange laugh almost like a cry.

He looked back at her, startled.

"Oh, God, Stan, is that what you've been thinking?" she said, distressed. "I'm so damn stupid and selfish. Patrick!"

"Then, is it me?" Stan asked, his thoughts scrambled with perplexity.

"No!" Lucy cried, her hand in her hair and her eyes anxious. "No," she repeated, "it's definitely not you."

"Sure?" Stan asked, going warm under her gaze. He would have liked to nab her then— out of sheer relief— but her troubled face put that out of the question.

"I'll tell you what it is," she began. "I guess I must have wanted to talk about it or I wouldn't have come." She took out her cigarettes and lit one up, rolling down her window. "I wouldn't have come and ruined your night."

"Lucy," Stan objected.

"I did, Stan, and I'm really sorry. Okay?"

"Okay, then," he conceded. "Tell me what's wrong."

Lucy took a long drag of her cigarette and blew out smoke. She took another drag and blew out more. Finally, she started to speak, calmly, as if she were telling a first-person story with fictional characters.

"I was talking to Robert today," she said. "He came into the lab."

"Robert?" Stan had to ask.

"Robert Milliken. You met him at the funeral, Stan."

"Oh, right. Sorry."

"He came in to tell me that he got the position on the National Science Commission. He'd just been notified."

"You told me a bit about that," Stan said, unconsciously shifting closer to her on the seat.

"Did I?" Lucy said mechanically. "Well, he told me he got it and I said congratulations. And then I said that I was glad that what had happened at the dinner didn't cause any problems for him."

"What happened at what dinner?"

"He went to a dinner of VIP-types in France. He got into an argument with a woman and she hit him, right in front of the Environment Minister, Geoffrey Stayner." Lucy leaned forward and blew smoke out the window, pausing for a second to watch it stream up out of sight. Stan could see her lips quivering. "Anyway," she continued, steadily losing her calm, "I'm such an idiot that I'd forgotten that he hadn't mentioned it to me himself and that I'd heard it from the head of our department. I felt really bad for saying anything."

"What was the argument about?" Stan had been staring at her mouth as she talked, and he was falling into a kind of dopey trance. He could hear the cat meowing outside the truck door.

Lucy looked at him unexpectedly and he snapped out of it.

"That's the thing," she said, her brows furrowed. "After she slapped him, this woman left and Robert told everybody that she was mad because he'd panned some of her research. So I asked him about it." She looked away and put out her cigarette, sliding the ashtray shut with a clap. "I asked him about her research and about what he had written. I said I'd be interested to read it."

She paused for so long that Stan thought he had missed something.

"Lucy?" he said.

Lucy continued, her voice so low it was almost a whisper.

"Then he asked me to go for a walk. He told me what *really* happened. He said that after they'd been introduced, she'd asked who, besides him, U of T had sent to the conference. He told her just Cecil Ho and me. Then she asked if I was the same person who'd presented at the last conference in Seattle and, if I was," Lucy's voice almost vanished, "why such a major university kept sending the same third-rate academics."

Stan felt a sudden nausea. His cheeks began to burn.

Lucy continued after a minute.

"She slapped him because he stood up for me. He told her that after he'd read *her* last paper he'd had it shredded for the cages in the rat lab." She laughed ruefully as the tears welled up and fell. Stan covered the foot of space between them and wrapped his arm around her.

"Oh, Lucy. Peach. It's okay." He kissed her cheek and tasted salt. He wanted to encircle her like a fire to keep away the wolves. To keep away people, who could be much worse.

"It's not very okay," she said, her voice breaking. "It's not very fucking okay."

"Who was she, Lucy? She's probably just jealous of your work."

Lucy sighed, the breath coming out tremulously

"I've never even heard of her. She's not in my field. She's a botanist. I don't know why she would say that about me if she didn't really think my work was shit. And I could tell from the way Robert told me that she isn't the only one. I seem to have a *reputation*..." She closed her eyes. "You've picked a real winner, Stan."

Stan tightened his arm around her, pissed off at everybody. Why did that jerk have to tell her about it?

"Robert knew I'd want to know," Lucy said slowly, although Stan hadn't asked the question aloud. "He was really nice about it. Plus, he took that slap. Defending my honour. God."

They sat in silence for the next little while as another car arrived for the party, its headlights coursing white across the barn. The marmalade cat outran the light and disappeared through a gap in the barn boards. The car doors slammed and laughing voices faded away towards the house.

"Lucy," Stan finally said, stroking her hair and feeling a bit of a fool, "I know probably nothing I say will make you feel any better, but I think you're pretty well superb. I'd like to dedicate sonnets to you and name a ship after you and stand under your balcony and pick you up and carry you around on my shoulders, okay?"

Lucy gave him a weak smile. Then she kissed him softly on the lips.

"Stan," she said quietly while he still held her tightly.

"Hmm," Stan answered, looking into her eyes.

"I think I need to go home now. I feel too worthless. I want so badly for it to be right."

Stan was pissed off at the whole wide world. He slid back over to the driver's side, started up the truck and threw it into reverse.

CHAPTER 22

"What a pile of shit," Freeman snarled, snapping an elastic between his fingers. He was balanced, with his jacket off and slung over his shoulder, on the edge of Eliot's desk. The station's heating system was still adjusted to winter temperatures and now, on a mild day like this one, the heat in the building was hard to take. The double-glazed windows didn't open and the air smelled stale and sweaty. Eliot dabbed his brow with his last clean handkerchief.

He'd decided that the best way to deal with Chris Freeman was to keep him thinking. Freeman, naturally, had more of the boring work and his hostility was rising with each new request. If they were going to get through this without a pre-emptive strike— Eliot's asking that Freeman be removed from the case— he had to keep feeding Freeman's brain. He wanted to hold on to Chris. His familiarity with the territory was worth the trouble. Plus, his suspicious mind-set acted as a kind of coarse sieve for new information. Nothing that sounded funny to Freeman would get past him without comment, at least nothing that was big and obvious. The subtleties Eliot could deal with himself.

He'd been telling Freeman about the break-in at Irving's and about the letter and Irving's theory. When Eliot himself had learned of Irving's concealment, he'd come as close as he ever came to sputtering. Irving had made Eliot stand in the hall while he teasingly fed him one tidbit at a time. Then he'd led him through the apartment, showing off the carnage, before shoving his famous letter in Eliot's flushed face.

"What a pile of shit," Freeman repeated. "Letter my ass. He probably wrote it to himself."

"It's a possibility," Eliot replied. A possibility he'd already entertained. The letter was typed on a computer, using the same kind of printer that was missing from Irving's. There was no envelope and so no postmark. Irving claimed that he'd picked up his mail that day when he'd gone out to do some shopping on Queen Street and that he'd tossed the envelope into a dumpster that he'd passed on the way home. He'd read the letter as he walked from the store, and had then run like hell back to the dumpster just in time to see it carted away down the road on the back of a truck. This all sounded very convenient, but there *was* a dumpster down the street from Irving's, in front of an apartment building that was being renovated.

"He probably wrecked up his own place, too," Freeman added.

"Perhaps," Eliot said, though this was less likely. Irving had indeed been to Kingston to see Terry Bantam, the prison records had verified that. Irving had visited Bantam twice, once on Wednesday and then again on Thursday morning, the day he'd returned to Toronto. Meanwhile, Eliot had called Irving four times in his absence. The first three times were on Wednesday evening and he'd gotten the machine. The fourth time was on Thursday morning and the phone had rung and rung. This was consistent with a break-in, and theft of the answering machine, some time late on Wednesday night. If Irving had set the whole thing up, he would have had to have an accomplice, or else have driven like a madman back from Kingston. And why, if the letter was a fake, would he have made that visit to the Cliffords'? Unless he got the idea for the letter *after* he'd been there and learned that Jamie couldn't talk.

But why, in the end, would Irving bother? It was ironic that they'd been spending time checking the movements of the victim in the case. Wasting time, probably. Eliot wondered how Irving would react to the news that there was some hope for Jamie, after all.

Eliot sighed stoically in the heat. He wished he was comfortable removing his jacket— or even unbuttoning it— but he wouldn't feel dressed if he did. Plus he was wearing his lucky suspenders, red ones with smiling blue brontosauruses that Jo had given him as a joke. The last person he wanted to see his suspenders was Freeman. He'd already removed the pink giraffe from his desk and had put it on the window sill, out of harm's way.

The Toronto police team that had gone over Irving's apartment believed that the break-in had the mark of the thieves who'd been working the Beaches over the previous few months. The kitchen window had been forced open with the same kind of tool and there was the same senseless damage done to articles of little value. There were no signs of a systematic search but plenty of signs of mindless mischief. The fingerprint report wasn't yet in.

In any case, Eliot thought, there was still the letter, and they had to work from the likelihood it was authentic. Irving's possession of the letter was certainly a motive for murder. Although, if he'd been killed, there was a good chance that the police would have found the letter in his apartment during the investigation. On the other hand, it was quite possible that there'd have been no investigation, at least nothing so extensive. It could well have been assumed that he'd simply poisoned himself by eating the wrong kind of mushrooms. Though if the Ferrara woman hadn't drowned, she might have cast some doubt on that.

"Hey, Francie," Freeman said, taking aim with his elastic. He shot it over towards the window and missed the giraffe by about four inches.

"Chris," Eliot said with a start. "Please. That was made for me by my daughter."

"Sorry," Freeman said, not sorry. "I was just wondering if you were all done being nice and loquacious."

"I was going to say, Chris, that I think we have to assume for now that the letter is authentic. We'll have to try to track down the person who wrote it. Go through the records of the Bantam trial. And we'll have to question George Robitaille again."

"Oh, we will, will we?" Freeman said unpleasantly. "You really gonna fall for this story?"

"I think it's the only thing we can do at the moment. Until we have some definite reason to dismiss it." He paused, puffing out his cheeks, while Freeman looked down at him sardonically. "This Laid-Off Hockey League has certainly narrowed down the search, hasn't it?" Eliot said.

"Huh," Freeman answered. "Yeah."

Eliot had learned of the LOHL while investigating the whereabouts of the ex-Lambert employees. Robitaille's secretary had faxed over a list of the twenty-two men who had lost their jobs. Four of them had moved from Shallow Bay— well before the attempted murder— eight had new jobs and were working the day Irving was poisoned, and the remaining ten were playing hockey up in Cochrane in the Laid-Off League playoffs.

The league had been formed in 1990, in the dark, lonely depths of a recession winter. Twelve northern Ontario towns were involved, all towns with cut-back industries and huge unemployment and men kicking around the streets with nothing to do but wait for their UI cheques and watch hockey on TV. The team rosters changed continually as some men found work and could no longer qualify, even if they could make the games, which were usually held in the afternoon. You had to be unemployed. New players would join the league wherever there was an opening, so often men from one town would play for another. They had to agree when they joined that they wouldn't go switching teams, even if an opening came up closer to home. At least not until the end of the season.

The season had just ended, with Sundridge winning the cup. The playoffs had been held in Cochrane with four games played on Monday, May fifth. All ten ex-Lambert employees had been there, either playing in games or watching them, and they could all vouch for one another.

"None of those guys coulda planned a poisoning anyway," Freeman now said. "Their brains have been too bashed up by high-sticking. You ever watch hockey, Francie?"

"No," said Eliot, "I'm not much of a sports fan. My wife watches wrestling sometimes," he added and then bit his tongue.

Freeman let out a derisive howl.

"Wrestling! Francie! You better mind your p's and q's. Someday she might knock you out with a sleeper and you'll wake up wearing an apron, up to your elbows in dirty dishes."

Eliot forced himself to chuckle and then picked up a paper from the file on his desk. It was a report on an interview with the contractor at the Muskoka cottage who'd backed up Ray Clifford's statement about the work that he'd done that day. The contractor thought that Clifford could have finished the work in fewer than ten hours. Maybe. But it would have taken him eight hours at least. So far, this was the only support Ray Clifford had for his alibi. The cottage was at the end of a long winding road, very private, with no close neighbours, and no one had seen Clifford either coming or going. The Cliffords themselves had had no luck finding the Canadian Tire receipt, but Eliot would look into it if the situation got serious enough. Right now, he was inclined to believe Ray Clifford's story.

He slipped the paper back in the file and took out another one with a list of names. Freeman, meanwhile, had picked up a pen which he was clicking rhythmically and sadistically with his thumb.

"These men who were laid off from Lambert's," Eliot said, trying to disregard the clicks. "Two of them testified at the Bantam trial. We need to talk to them. One of them has moved. We need to find out where to. If I were going to write a letter like that, I'd wait until I was away from the action."

"This an attempted murder investigation or a rehash of the Bantam shit?" Freeman asked. After waiting for a reaction that didn't happen, he went on. "You look like you're getting a bit jumpy, Francie. Worried ya missed something way back when?" Eliot now looked at Freeman, who was grinning with pleasure, scratching the tip of his pointy nose with the click end of the pen.

"You said in your report for the inquest that Irving claimed there was an opportunity for someone to have tampered with the mushrooms."

"Yeah," Freeman said, giving Eliot the stare.

"Did they leave the campsite together? Where did they go?"

"If Irving had told me that it woulda been in the report. He just said they were away for a while. Nobody was worried about him and his goddamn mushrooms then. I was supposed to be finding out where his lady friend had disappeared to. Remember?" Freeman dropped down from the edge of the desk and tossed the pen over towards Eliot. "Those mushrooms are your problem, Francie. All I know about mushrooms is they go good with steak."

Freeman turned at the door before leaving the office. He gave Eliot a two-fingered salute, laughed his monosyllabic laugh and disappeared down the hall.

Eliot took out his honey and dipped into it twice. He stood up, unbuttoned his jacket and flapped it around like a fat flustered pheasant. The perspiration was trickling down his sides and seeping into the waist of his pants. He wrinkled his nose in self-disgust. He did up his jacket and sat back down, reaching for the pen to make some notes about what to ask George Robitaille. And about what to ask Patrick Irving.

CHAPTER 23

Eliot got through to Irving on the first try.

"Detective Sergeant Eliot, Mr. Irving," he said in answer to Irving's abrupt "Yes."

"You find him yet?" Irving immediately demanded.

"Your letter writer? No, not yet," Eliot replied. "You'll have to try to be patient, Mr. Irving. We'll find him."

"Christ," Irving said. "I can tell you how to do it, if you need a few pointers. You check the trial records and, lo and behold, you find the name."

"Thank you, Mr. Irving," Eliot replied.

"You're welcome. How else can I help you? Would you like the time? A weather report? Or do you just need a little friendly encouragement?"

"I have a few questions for you. There are some gaps in the story that need filling in, if you'll be so kind."

"Gaps? What gaps? The only gap I can see is the one between our last conversation and the arrest of that bastard Robitaille. But I'm afraid you'll have to fill in that gap yourself. Unless you want to make me a deputy. Hey. That's not a bad idea, Eliot. As long as I get to wear a star."

Eliot raised his small eyes to heaven and wondered if Irving was related to Freeman.

"I'd like to remind you again, Mr. Irving," he said, "that the police are on your side. We're as eager as you are to find out who tried to kill you and I do wish you'd be a little more cooperative." That is, cut the crap, he added to himself.

"Yeah, right," Irving replied. "Anything you say."

"Good. Thank you. Now, I'd like to go over a few details with you and see if you have any ideas. I understand you're somewhat of an expert on mushrooms. Is that right?"

"I know more than most people," Irving said. "I'm mainly self-taught but I've been collecting them for years." Eliot thought he could sense caution in Irving's voice. He'd certainly come down a notch from the assured statement he'd made to Freeman.

"Do you have any theories about how the mushrooms you collected could have been tampered with?" Eliot had two reasons for asking Irving's opinion. The first was that his opinion was, in fact, well worth hearing, since his knowledge was considered to be first class. Eliot had that from a competent source, a mycologist from BC to whom he'd already spoken. And because the mycologist had made some suggestions herself, Eliot's other reason was really more to the point. Irving needed stroking if he was going to continue to talk. And Eliot wanted him to do that.

"Yeah, well," Irving was now saying, "I've obviously been thinking about it. I figure the first part is pretty basic. You could probably do it in your kitchen. Boil the false morels to extract the toxin. Distill the solution. Then, I don't know, maybe if you poured it on to the other mushrooms, the harmless ones, and let it soak in, or something, so it wouldn't rinse out when they were washed..." He paused, uncertainly.

"That might take some time," Eliot said.

"Yeah, I guess so," Irving replied. "I was going to try to test it out myself at some point. Use a dye solution, maybe. They sell morels in some of those rip-off specialty stores."

"Can you remember, Mr. Irving, just how many morels you ate that day?"

"How many? Christ, I don't know. Six. Maybe eight. Hardly any."

"Six? Or eight?"

"Christ, Eliot. I don't know. I wasn't doing piece-work. I didn't count." Irving was getting annoyed. Eliot changed tack.

"All right, Mr. Irving. Of course you didn't." No one would, Eliot reflected. Except maybe someone like Irving. However. "In your second interview with Detective Freeman, you told him that you and Ms. Ferrara left the campsite together at some point and left the mushrooms where someone could have got at them."

"Freeman. Yeah. He wasn't particularly interested, of course. He had it all worked out that I'd poisoned myself. You working with that creep?"

"Detective Freeman is helping with the case. Yes," Eliot said patiently.

"Tweak his little weaselly nose for me, then. Maybe it'll help improve his intelligence."

"Getting back to when you left the campsite," Eliot continued, dabbing at his hot brow.

"Yeah."

"How long were you away?"

Irving didn't reply for a moment and, when he did, he sounded reluctant.

"We didn't actually *leave* the campsite."

"Oh?" Eliot replied. "But you told Detective Freeman you did."

"I told him we weren't near the mushrooms the whole time. They were over with the rest of the food near the campfire and we were in the tent."

"You were in the tent?" Eliot mentally reviewed what he'd read about the campsite. He seemed to remember that the tent was about fifteen feet from the food and fire. "But you would have been quite close, then. You didn't hear anything?"

"Well, first of all, the Jack Falls are pretty loud. And second, if you really want to know," he added belligerently, "we were too busy screwing."

Eliot sat up in his chair. He felt a flush that wasn't the heat. Just then, Freeman passed by the window with one of the uniformed men and rapped with his knuckles on the pane. Eliot glanced at him briefly and frowned. Freeman made a tragic face.

Eliot remembered that Irving had said that his relationship with Ferrara was platonic. Eliot believed in platonic relationships— he'd had one with Jo for years before they'd married. But platonic meant platonic and precluded sex. Unless he was wrong about the meaning of the word.

"Mr. Irving," Eliot said. "Did you not tell Detective Freeman that your relationship with Ms. Ferrara was 'platonic?'"

"Yeah, well, Freeman was being an asshole. And it *was* Platonic until that day. Anyway, I couldn't really see why anyone needed to know about it. It just would've got into the goddamn papers. They love that kind of shit. Gina wouldn't have wanted anyone to know and I didn't either."

"Including your girlfriend?"

"My girlfriend?" Irving paused and then laughed unpleasantly. "I can see, Detective, or Sergeant, or Mister, or Sir, or whatever the hell I'm supposed to call you, that you've been nosing around. No, my girlfriend wouldn't have found out from the papers because I told her about it myself. Besides, she's not my girlfriend any more. Not that she ever was. She was my 'woman friend,' right? This is the nineties."

"You should have said something at the inquest."

"Strangely enough, nobody asked me about it."

Nobody asked. Eliot should have known he'd hear that from Irving. The classic end-of-argument response. He looked over at the pink giraffe. He'd have to give this some thought. He wiped the phone receiver with his handkerchief. It was sticky with perspiration.

"All right, then," Eliot said to Irving, finally. "Can you tell me how long you were... in the tent?"

"I don't know. Fifteen minutes. Twenty. And don't go asking me which: fifteen or twenty."

Fifteen minutes, Eliot thought, shaking his head at Irving's nonchalance. Fifteen minutes is not much time. Not much time for being romantic... or for attempting a murder.

"Well, Mr. Irving," Eliot sighed. "I don't know that I can thank you for this. You've been rather behindhand with your information. Is there anything else you haven't yet told me?"

"I had a hernia operation about two years ago."

"I'm sorry?"

"A hernia operation. Inguinal. You're the first person I've told. That's how much I trust you." Irving laughed.

"Shouldice?"

"What?"

"Did you go to the Shouldice Clinic? That's where I had mine done. Very good doctors and very good food."

"Yeah, so I hear. Christ, Eliot, you're a bit of a goof."

"Before I let you go, Mr. Irving, I think you'll be interested to know that the prognosis has changed for Jamie Clifford."

"Oh, yeah?" Irving said eagerly. "What's going on?"

"His doctors apparently believe he may develop an ability to communicate. He may regain some movement in his eyes."

"You're kidding!" Irving exclaimed, without hesitation. "That's fucking great!"

"Yes," Eliot agreed, "it is."

George Robitaille was just leaving for a meeting in Toronto when Eliot got him on the phone, but offered to stop by the station on his way out of town. Eliot met him at the front desk, holding a can of Mountain Dew that he'd bought from the pop machine down the hall. He led him into his barren office and then left him there while he went to get another chair.

When Eliot returned, puffing, Robitaille was near the airvent, feeling the heat that blew into the room.

"I've heard that police work is hell, Detective Sergeant, but I didn't realize that referred to the climate. Something wrong with your cooling system?"

"Yes, I think so. Would you like to sit down?" Eliot shuffled the chair over to the front of the desk and shuffled himself over to his own chair behind the desk.

"Thanks." Robitaille sat and glanced at his watch. "I hope you don't need me for too long. I was hoping to get down to Toronto by six."

"Of course," Eliot said affably. "I won't keep you long. In fact I was going to offer to wait until you got back from your trip. Thank you for coming in. And thank you for getting the list here so quickly."

"That's fine. No problem."

Eliot noticed his can of pop. It looked frosty cold and delicious.

"Can I get you something to drink?" he asked Robitaille, who had removed his glasses and was giving them a wipe.

"No, thanks." Robitaille replaced his glasses on his face.

"Well, then, we'll get right down to it." Eliot opened the Mountain Dew and took a long, thirsty quaff, covering a quiet burp as he finished. He glanced at Robitaille to see if he'd heard it. Robitaille was looking back impassively.

"You know, I was thinking over the EES trial, Mr. Robitaille, and I realized I never got your opinion of Bantam's claim that the explosion was set off by someone from your company."

Robitaille let out an easy laugh and relaxed back into his chair, crossing his legs.

"I wouldn't have thought you needed to ask. The idea was absurd. You remember where all my men were that day. There was no one that could have done it. It was a desperate move by Mr. Bantam and it probably ended up helping him out."

"Yes," said Eliot. "Perhaps it did."

"He and the other two should have been locked away for years. Until they turned green at the edges." Robitaille laughed again. "But then they're already green through and through, aren't they?"

Eliot smiled.

"And where were you again, Mr. Robitaille?"

"You mean where was I when the bomb went off? I was in my office, having lunch at my desk." He uncrossed his legs.

"How many people does Lambert employ under you at the management level? I should know, of course."

"You mean now or then?"

"Then."

"Then, we had four. But we had to let one go when things slowed down." Robitaille checked his watch again. "I'm not sure why you're asking about this now, Detective Sergeant. Does it have something to do with the Irving case?"

"In a very general way. I'm reviewing Irving's whole history up here. His involvement with EES, his departure, the bombing, the trial, the whole shebang."

"I see," Robitaille said doubtfully.

"But that wasn't the reason I wanted to talk to you." Eliot could see that Robitaille was getting hot and impatient. He looked like he was worried about sweating in his suit. Eliot could sympathize.

"No?" Robitaille asked.

"No. I wanted to ask you the question we've been asking everyone."

"And that is?"

"Where you were on Monday, May fifth."

Robitaille exhaled the breath that Eliot knew he'd been holding. Then he crossed his legs and chuckled.

"It's come to this then, has it? I've been added to the list of your suspects."

Eliot smiled serenely.

"Only the very long list, Mr. Robitaille. You can start losing sleep when you make the short one."

"Well, let me check my daytimer. I'm very good at keeping it up." Robitaille reached down and picked up his briefcase which he'd set on the floor beside his chair. "May I?" he asked before placing it on the desk.

Eliot smiled and finished off his pop. He thought about what he would have for supper. What he would really like was a liverwurst and onion sandwich but he'd probably have to settle for a sub. He hoped that tomorrow he could have supper at home. Maybe Jo would make him chicken and dumplings. He'd mention it when he phoned her that night.

Robitaille had found the page in his calendar.

"Yes," he said, adjusting his glasses. "I thought that was probably the day. I was over in Sudbury addressing the Rotary Club on 'The Future of Ontario Forestry.' That's a nasty one for you, Detective Sergeant. I must have had a hundred witnesses, including the mayor who had me home to dinner. Interesting man, the honourable Mayor Stewart. Was a Great Lakes freighter captain for over twenty years, then retired, moved inland and took up politics." He closed the day-timer and smiled. "So. That's where I was on May the fifth."

"Thank you, Mr. Robitaille. You do understand that I had to ask."

"Of course."

"Well, thank you. So many people take it badly. Oh," he added, as they both stood up, Robitaille closing his briefcase. "You operate a lab in your building, don't you?"

"We used to, Detective Sergeant, but it's another thing gone by the boards. It was a very small operation, in any case."

"Is it still set up? All the equipment intact?"

Robitaille looked at him quizzically.

"More or less," he said. "Why?"

Eliot went to the door and held it open for Robitaille to walk ahead of him.

"Not to worry," Eliot said.

They walked out together to the parking lot where Robitaille had left his Honda Accord. They shook hands and Robitaille got into his car. He rolled down the window to say goodbye.

"Thank you again, Mr. Robitaille," Eliot smiled a rosebud. "I almost forgot to ask if you've spoken to the Cliffords lately."

"Not in the last week or so, no," said Robitaille.

"Well then, you haven't heard the news about their son."

"Good news, I hope."

"Yes." And Eliot told him the news.

"Isn't that terrific," Robitaille replied. "It isn't a lot but it's a lot, relatively."

Eliot watched him drive away and gently flapped his jacket in the cooler air.

CHAPTER 24

The young raccoons trilled and squeaked from behind the wire mesh of their enclosure. Their short hunched-up bodies tapered in front to pointy-nosed faces, thinly disguised by black masks. They made Stan think of little kids who'd been invited at the last minute to a masquerade and whose mother hadn't had time to come up with costumes. She'd loaded them into the back of the station wagon and dashed over to the Shoppers Drug Mart, telling the kids to stay in the car. The kids had cried when they'd seen the masks because they'd wanted to be dinosaurs or axe-wielding psychos.

Stan had had his tour of the Shallow Bay Centre for Wildlife Rehab and was waiting out back for the director, Ian Smith. Stan and Ian had hit it off and Ian had offered him a bed for the night at his cabin up on the Speller. It was an invitation that Stan had eagerly accepted. It saved him from the Half Moon Motel, with its sign salaciously winking "Free Movies" and "Heated Water Beds," out near the highway on the way into town. He'd been wavering between the Half Moon Motel and the Comfort Inn and had decided, a little recklessly, to go for the one with character. But now that he'd been given a third alternative, he felt thankful and relieved.

Stan smiled as a small licorice nose poked through the mesh and sniffed. He left the raccoons and strolled over to look again at the male Northern Shoveler, a green-headed duck with a bill like a spatula. Northern Shovelers were rare in the east and this was the first one Stan had ever seen. The duck had been found snared in a fishing line. One leg was broken and it squatted miserably, not yet having touched either food or water, its head tucked under a ruffled wing.

Stan hadn't been prepared for Elizabeth's call on Wednesday afternoon. He'd been taking apart the fly-specked windows and was in a rush to get them cleaned and put back on before the mosquitoes started wafting in at dusk. He'd been short with Elizabeth on the phone, annoyed first because she was holding up his work on the windows and second, because he'd thought he'd been done with her for the week. He'd gotten his column in extra early— a light little piece on moles— and had intended to take the next few days off to get stuff done around the house. And then Elizabeth had told him that it was all set up. Ian Smith was expecting him Saturday.

Stan had felt unhappy about having to go but it was nothing to what he'd felt a few minutes later when he'd finally heard from Lucy.

After they'd left the Hoots', he'd got her down to the bus— the eleven o'clock bus back to the city. He hadn't even tried to take her home— she'd been too obviously desperate to be on her own. He'd left her at the station with a last sad kiss and had driven home to his ecstatic dogs and to the kitchen table set for two. On Monday morning, he'd tossed out the remains of the soupy trifle which he'd been eating with nausea all weekend long.

Five days had gone by without a word. Stan hadn't wanted to call Lucy first. He'd figured that when she was ready he'd hear. And then he did hear, on Wednesday.

Lucy'd told him that she was feeling better, "almost peppy" is the way she'd put it. It had helped a lot that she'd just been invited to give another paper, this time in Tokyo, in the early fall. So she must have *some* respectability, she'd said. Stan had never doubted it.

They talked for close to half an hour, Lucy doing her fair share. Stan forgot about the windows. She told him how she'd been interviewed by a Detective Eliot that morning, the one who was investigating Patrick's case. She said Patrick had christened the detective "the gnome" and she could see why, though he was really very nice. The detective had begged her pardon and asked about her relationship with Patrick, and then, almost as if he were walking on tiptoe, Eliot had asked how she felt about Gina.

Lucy had told him about their trip to the Speller and she'd seen that he was surprised. She gathered that Patrick had never mentioned it, and that would be like Patrick. He'd put off telling about the letter and probably wouldn't have mentioned the break-in, if there'd been any way to avoid it.

Stan hadn't known about any of this so Lucy filled him in. Stan was as sceptical about it as she was, thinking to himself that Patrick was a bonehead.

Lucy actually laughed a bit when she told Stan that the detective had asked for her alibi. She said she'd always wanted someone to ask her that "where-were-you-on?" question. It made her feel dark and dangerous, totally unlike the inoffensive academic she was. But on the day that the detective had asked about, she'd only been marking exams in her office. Nothing intriguing about that at all.

Stan now looked over towards the one-storey board and batten building where Ian Smith had his office. Out front, two student volunteers were hosing down a crate that had probably transported something large like a bear. They were spraying each other with water and laughing.

Lucy wanted to try again. She'd asked if she could visit Stan on Saturday night. She'd bring dinner, she'd added uncertainly, as if she had no idea how she was going to manage it. She couldn't make it any other day, not for at least another week.

Stan told her that he had to go up north and asked her if she wanted to come. She couldn't, of course. She had an experiment going that she just couldn't be away from. Stan had wanted to murder Elizabeth.

"Oh, Stan," Lucy had said, her voice low with disappointment, "I shouldn't have assumed you'd be free. I did, you know. But you've already seen how self-absorbed I am. I've already given you a real performance."

Stan joked, forcing his own frustration back.

"If you're really concerned about your personality, Lucy, then maybe you should be going into therapy. Checking out your inner child."

"I don't want to meet my inner child!" Lucy'd exclaimed. "I don't even like children."

Smiling to himself at the memory, Stan watched as Ian Smith walked towards him. Ian was a couple of years younger than Stan, more than a couple of inches taller and much heftier. His outstanding characteristic was hair. Hair on his face in a dark beard and mustache, hair like Samson's, thick and strong on his head, hair in tight curls on the back of his hands. Ian made Stan feel like a skinned rabbit.

"All set," Ian said. "You wanna just follow behind me? It's about twenty minutes, but I need to stop in town first. Beer." He smiled. "I hope you like spaghetti. I figure everybody does."

"That's great," Stan said, glad to have already established that Ian, too, was a vegetarian. Not the stereotype, that's for sure. Not scrawny and anaemic. "I'll buy the beer," Stan added.

"We'll see," Ian said.

The beer store was next to the Foodland at the end of the main shopping drag where it crossed an old metal bridge at the mouth of the Speller. The shallow bay of Shallow Bay spread out from here, widening eventually into the main body of water, Lake Gamenag, or Lake Gamey, as it was known by the locals. South along the bay was most of the town. To the north, there was a smattering of houses, a warehouse, a gas station and then trees.

Stan followed Ian's van as it swung into the beer-store parking lot, the two of them arriving just in time to nab the last of the available spaces. It was Saturday night in Shallow Bay and there'd be a run on Molson Canadian.

"Hockey playoffs," Ian explained as they joined the line in the crowded store. "Leafs against L.A. I hope you don't care, 'cause I don't have a TV."

"I don't care particularly," Stan replied. "I watch sometimes if I've got nothing else to do but I usually end up turning it off round about the twentieth car commercial."

There were half a dozen people in line ahead of them, all male, all between the ages of eighteen and thirty, except for the guy who was right in front of them, a middle-aged native man in a denim jacket. The line seemed to have hit a snag, and wasn't moving forward. A teenager at the front was arguing with the cashier.

"So," Ian said, after they'd watched the dispute in silence, "I guess you worked with Gina Ferrara, eh?"

"Yeah," Stan said. "We were actually pretty good friends."

"I never met her. I heard she used to come up here a lot. Used to do a lot of camping at that site where they found her. Or where they found Patrick Irving, anyway. I guess they found *her* quite a ways from there." He glanced at Stan and frowned. "Sorry. I shouldn't be talking about her like that. She was your friend."

"That's okay," Stan said. "Her death is still kind of unreal to me. I don't know if I've completely taken it in. She was so hale and hearty. She would've been disgusted with herself for drowning. She was a really good swimmer, a really good everything." Stan laughed. "You know, she used to sing that horrible Helen Reddy song sometimes as a joke... *I am strong, I am invincible, I am woman.* She'd bellow it out really sarcastically. But I think she actually believed it. And I believed it about her, too. She was tough. She made me feel like a ninety-eight-pound weakling."

The line finally began to edge forward. Stan continued to talk about Gina to this guy he hardly knew. He wondered afterward why he'd been so effusive. He thought it might be because of the hair. All that hair made it seem less personal. Talking to Ian was like talking to a rug.

"I feel bad for her mother," Stan said. "She's having a rough time. She never understood Gina when she was alive and now that Gina's dead, she's stuck with this blank that she has no hope of ever filling in. Mrs. Ferrara is Old World and Gina was very definitely New."

"I met Patrick Irving a couple of times," Ian said. "Is he a jerk or what?"

"Uh..." Stan began. He paused and thought of Lucy. "He's no

Mahatma Gandhi, I guess." He didn't know why he said that. Maybe Patrick was *a lot* like Gandhi. He didn't really know. Ian chuckled in any case, as if he'd got the joke.

"Well," he said, "jerk or no jerk, he's sure got this town having a conniption. Everybody you talk to has either been grilled by the cops or knows someone who was."

The man ahead of them picked up his twelve-pack of OV and edged around them, eyeing them as he did. They stepped up to the counter.

"Sleeman's Ale okay?" Ian asked Stan. Stan nodded. "Twelve," Ian said to the cashier.

"Twelve Slee Ale," the cashier boomed into the microphone, hitting the keys of the cash register as if he were bashing out a four-letter word. "$18.90."

"I've got it," Stan said, thrusting forward a twenty. He took the change as the beer came sliding through the hatch towards them along the metal rollers.

"You're sure?" Ian asked.

Stan smiled.

"Well, thanks."

When they got outside, there was a line of cars backed up right out to the road.

"God," Ian said. "Must be a big game." He gestured along the road where it headed north over the bridge and out of town. "Okay. We're going up that way about fifteen miles. Once we're out of town, we'll be crossing the river again. Then we'll pass a couple of paved roads to the right and then one to the left about five miles out."

"That's the one into the park," Stan said.

"Yeah. So you've been up here before?"

"Just once. A few weeks ago."

"Oh, yeah? Okay, then. Keep going past that road and you'll see a dirt road after it. That goes into the Gamenagi reserve. Don't take that one, take the next one, a few miles on. My place is at the end of it. I'll try to stay right ahead of you, but with all this traffic, we might get separated."

"Sounds pretty straightforward," Stan said. "I'll be fine."

"Okay. See you there." Ian carried the beer over to his truck and Stan headed off to his own. As he was taking out his key to unlock the door, he heard footsteps behind him and a low voice said, "Hey." Stan turned to see the native man who'd been ahead of them in the line.

The man had an impassive face, brown and deeply lined, and tired serious eyes. He stood with his hands squeezed into the pockets in the front of his jeans, and rocked slightly forward on the balls of his feet.

"I heard you talking in the beer store," the man said to Stan. "You were a frienda Gina Ferrara. You knew her pretty good." He said this as a statement, rather than a question.

"Yes," Stan said uncertainly.

"I got something you could give to her mother. Me and my nephews found that guy that day, that environmental guy."

"You found Patrick Irving?" The man was casting his eyes around him in a wide circle as he talked. Looking at him, Stan would say he was uneasy, even nervous, but his voice was slow and steady.

"Yeah," the man replied. "Then it turns out one of my nephews found her paddle. That real nice one she had. Hand-carved."

"Oh, right," Stan said. What he remembered was the column that Gina had written, a year or so before. "Ode to a Cherrywood Paddle," she'd called it, and she'd had a hell of a time getting it past Elizabeth, who'd bitched that no one would want to read about a hunk of wood. It was a great piece, though, Stan thought. One of Gina's best.

"I'll give it to you and you can give it to her mother," the man continued.

"Okay. Thanks. She'll appreciate that," Stan nodded. "How did you know it was hers?"

"Met her a coupla times. She used to come over to the fish fry we got. Sometimes by herself, sometimes with her family."

"Not with her mother," Stan said incredulously, trying to picture Mrs. Ferrara squatting around a campfire, dressed in mules and a flowered house dress.

The man pulled his hands from his pants pockets and then took a pack of Players cigarettes out of the pocket of his jacket. He opened the pack and held it out to Stan.

"No, thanks," Stan said.

"Never met her mother," the man said, lighting a match. "Blond lady and her husband. Sister, maybe." He cupped his hands around the lit match and then tossed the match away. "So, you staying up here somewhere? I can bring over the paddle. Got it out at my place." He blew smoke out of the corner of his mouth.

"I can come and get it, if you want. I'm driving right by there." Stan remembered Ian's description of the road into the reserve and then suddenly realized that maybe this guy didn't live there. He wanted to give himself a smack. But the man just looked back at him impassively.

"Road's too bad," he said. "You tell me where you are. I'll drop it off."

Stan passed on the end of Ian's instructions which the man took in without comment.

"I'm Stan O'Keefe, by the way," Stan tacked on at the end. The man gave a hint of a nod and, with one last sweep of his eyes, turned to walk away.

"Pender," he said, over his shoulder.

CHAPTER 25

When the alarm went off, Lucy jerked in her chair, her finger on the computer key trailing N's across the screen. She'd set the clock for one o'clock in the afternoon, to remind herself to eat.

She reached over the mess of paper on the desk and turned off the alarm. She didn't feel that hungry yet, so she lit another cigarette, glancing with dismay at the crushed butts in the ashtray, and then with even more dismay at the few cigarettes left in the pack. After she had lunch she'd have to go out to the store. She still had hours of work to do, Sunday or not.

She quickly read through what she'd done on the computer, sighed heavily and saved. She put her cigarette in the ashtray and laid her head down on her arms. "Put your head down," the teachers used to say, when they caught some kid being naughty. "Put your head down and keep it down." She made a wry face into her arms.

She was trying hard to keep on working. She was trying really hard. But sometimes dejection overcame her, like a cold wet wind moving in across the prairies, soaking her mind so sodden that tears came. Yesterday, she'd had to leave the lab when she'd felt a change in the weather and had told an over-curious Cheryl that she was going out to smoke.

The whole thing wouldn't be so bad if it hadn't come as such a surprise, hadn't turned her world head over heels. She knew that in general she was really a mess. Her life was like some sloppy experiment that she could never step back from far enough to fix. But her work— she'd thought that was something else.

She'd figured she was good at what she did, she'd thought so without really thinking. She'd published steadily over the past few years— the important years that preceded tenure— and she'd been asked to attend so many conferences that she'd had to fit her lab work in sideways. She'd assumed she was a credit to her department and school, when all along there'd been whispering, as far away as Israel. If she hadn't been so damned complacent, she probably would have heard it.

It didn't help that she had to see Robert. But she did have to see him— he was always around. This past week, he'd been working as much as she had— he was trying to tie things up before taking his appointment in July. His lab was just next to hers and they often met in the hallway, because he paced up and down there when he was thinking out a problem.

Not that when they met, Robert ever referred to the "incident." He only smiled at Lucy kindly while she felt her face going red. And, really, it was the smile that did it. For though she saw no trace of pity there, she saw something else— something that had to do with the closeness of a shared secret. A shared secret about her inadequacy, though that was apparently anything but "just between the two of them."

Despite the smiles, she no longer suspected that Robert was interested in her. He might have been but he wasn't any more. His conversation was always friendly but formal and he hadn't again asked her out. If Lucy wanted to be uncharitable she'd say it was his ambition. His public image wouldn't gain much sparkle if his private life included her... an intellectual deadbeat. Lucy felt the low-pressure system that preceded tears and stood up fast before they could fall.

"I just wish to hell that he'd hurry up and go," she said as she crossed over to the kitchen. She took a swipe at the smoky filaments that floated in the room like cirrus.

Lucy lived in a bachelor apartment, one of six carved out of a Parkdale mansion and drywalled into self-containment. The design was inspired by a size ten shoe box— a white, perfect rectangle with a snug-fitting lid. Somewhere under the wallboards there was probably a fireplace, above the dropped ceiling, plaster rosettes, and under the grey carpet, hardwood floors. It had cost someone some effort to hood the history, to stifle the rambling Edwardian. It cost Lucy very little, though she sometimes wanted to swing a sledgehammer at the walls.

She went to the window and slid open the slider. The wind shoved in like a boor. The Saturday *Post* on the kitchen table snapped its pages and blew apart. Across the room near the couch, the Japanese paper lamp that Patrick had given her fell over on its side. "Shit," she said and quickly pushed the window closed.

Lucy went and straightened the lamp and then came back, stepping past the large green garbage bag that she'd missed getting out at the end of the week. She opened the fridge and stared in at three oranges, six bottles of tonic water, four jars of tartar sauce and a brown paper package that she thought might be hamburger. She stared a bit longer and then opened the freezer.

The freezer was jammed with two kinds of food— frozen vegetables and vanilla ice cream. She took out a bag of vegetables and some tartar sauce from the fridge and slammed the doors closed with her forearm. She put the food on the counter and then looked over at the sink.

She owned three pots and they all were dirty, and had been, for several days. She almost decided to forget about eating. It seemed too complicated. She remembered Dr. Drake, a microbiology professor in her department, who'd claimed to have discovered the ideal meal. It was nutritionally balanced to perfection and had something to do with fish sticks, broccoli, and a scrambled egg. Every Saturday, he'd cook it up in quantity and wrap it into individual servings, enough to last him through the week. He'd been a wan and hollow-eyed man who retired early. But at least he'd been organized, Lucy thought.

She ran both of her hands through her hair and then rolled up the sleeves of her floppy sweater. She scrubbed a pot and a fork, her sleeves unrolling into the suds. She half-filled the pot with hot water and put it on the stove.

She walked back to the computer and got her cigarettes and then came and sat down at the kitchen table and sorted out the windblown newspaper. When she'd got each page more or less back into place, she scanned the headlines and stopped part way down. She coughed. There was an article about Patrick and the police investigation.

"The police are dragging their heels and I don't know why," Patrick was quoted as saying. "But maybe their hearts aren't really in it. Maybe they don't really care."

"Oh, Patrick," Lucy groaned, leaning forward on her elbows and peering down at the page. It had barely been two weeks since the inquest and nobody could reasonably expect results. But Patrick was Patrick and anything but reasonable. She almost wouldn't blame the police if they *did* decide to throw up their hands. Must be hard to have the job of hunting down someone you're coming to regard with a certain fellow-feeling.

The water on the stove came to a boil and she went over to the counter. She picked up the bag of frozen vegetables and dropped it on the counter with a thud. Then she ripped open the end with her teeth and rattled the icy chunks into the boiling water. She came back to the table, lit a cigarette and sat.

On the third page of Section C her eyes found the name, Stan O'Keefe.

"Here's a short story about a mole," she read, "that found a place in history. In 1702, King William of Orange died from a fall when his horse tripped on a molehill. The Jacobites, who had fought King William, drank to the health of the mole that dug it, raising their glasses high with the words, 'To the little gentleman in black velvet.'"

Lucy looked up from the page and smiled. Maybe Stan was back now from Shallow Bay. He'd wanted her to come with him to the wildlife centre and she'd badly wanted to go. But she'd had to be in the lab yesterday to check her specimens for evidence of auxinic hormonal secretion, evidence she'd been testing for for ten months. Because auxinic hormones stimulate plant growth, it would be a real coup to prove that earthworms secreted them into the soil.

Lucy could use a coup right now. A coup would do much for her self-respect. She wished that she could be more like Stan, who seemed to glide through sharp criticism without being cut, or at least, without bleeding to death from something superficial. Lucy was ashamed of her performance when she'd gone up to see him.

Stan, she thought, Stan. She could have hid herself in his arms that night and God knows she'd been tempted to. She could have let him comfort her, soothe her into insensibility with his quiet voice and earnest eyes. She could have... But she couldn't. It wouldn't have been fair. She didn't want him having to prop her up like a weak and spindly plant. She didn't want him having to tend her.

If she was going to carry a torch for him— and the torch was lit and waiting— she wanted to pick it up firmly and carry it about without a care. She wanted to see Stan's face all bright, with no subtle shadowing of sad compassion, no sign of him feeling sorry for her. That would only happen if she steadied her hands. Made herself sturdy. Absolutely unfrail.

"Am I a nut or what?" she asked aloud, touching Stan's name on the newsprint with her finger and standing up. She went to the stove and took the pot off the burner, holding the lid at an angle over the top and draining the water into the sink. She lost half the peas and carrots in the process. "Shit shit shit," she said. She put the pot on the counter and opened the jar of tartar sauce, stuck in the fork and scooped out a large dollop which she stirred into the vegetables. She looked down at the result with distaste.

Lucy thought about a plate and decided not to bother. She carried the pot back to the table, put out the cigarette burning in the ashtray, sat down and began to eat, looking over the pot at the paper. She read the rest of what Stan had written about moles, how they burrow, how they bite, how they mate.

"During mating season, the males and females maintain a brief truce. But it has nothing to do with a change of heart. Moles mate sneeringly. There are no kind words or loving caresses."

Lucy put down her fork and considered. She didn't know if she could wait till she was the Rock of Gibraltar. She wanted to see Stan now. If she kept at her work for the rest of the day and got into the lab first thing in the morning, she might be able to swing it. Take that bus to Barton and be with him. Get back to Toronto by Tuesday noon. If Stan was free. If he wanted her.

She lit the last cigarette in the pack and went over to the phone. Her good head for numbers remembered his. She heard three rings and then got his machine.

"This is Stan. Leave a message. Please," Stan's voice said, and then a dog barked before the beep.

"It's Lucy," she began, screwing up her eyes. "How was your trip? I was wondering what you're doing tomorrow night. Can I invite myself again? Um," she paused, thinking of what else to say, "I'm just reading about moles. Call me please." Another pause. "Oh, it's Sunday. I made myself a vegetarian lunch. It's delicious."

She hung up the phone and looked over at her lunch. Then she went to the computer and got back down to work.

CHAPTER 26

"Folly!" Stan yelled. "Drop that!"

The old black retriever stood and wagged at him, a brown stalk of last year's burdock clenched in her mouth. She held it horizontally like a trapeze walker's balance pole, though one end was heavier, branching out in tufts of burrs.

"Drop it!" Stan repeated.

Folly shook the burdock out of her mouth and then sat on the grass with her tongue hanging out.

"Good dog," Stan said, jamming his garden fork into the ground, "but you're gonna drive me right up the wall. You're gonna have burrs spread all over." He picked up the burdock and carefully put it back in the wheelbarrow. Folly had snatched it from there when he wasn't looking. It was the retrieving instinct that made her stick-crazy. She wasn't happy without one in her mouth.

"Go find another stick," Stan said, patting her. The old dog trotted off on stiff arthritic legs. Some burrs had somehow stuck to her tail and waved about triumphantly.

Stan was doing some cleaning up— digging out weeds and mowing the lawn, the wide sweep of lawn that he'd intended to be meadow. When he and Cath had first moved to the farm, they'd had grand ideas of naturalizing the yard, planting wildflowers and indigenous shrubs. Stan had brought his push-mower from the city which he'd pictured himself using maybe once a month. Just to maintain a path through the meadow, a meandering swath through the poppies and cornflowers, from the road to the door of the house.

That first summer, the meadow had simply looked neglected, as if they couldn't be bothered to keep it neat. The Hoots had ingenuously offered to cut it, saying they knew Stan and Cath didn't have the equipment. The second year had been better— it had looked like a pasture— and the thoughtful Hoots had offered to send over some cows.

Stan had then started mowing a small circle around each of the shrubs, persuading himself that they needed more room. But the circles had slowly gotten bigger and bigger until finally the "meadow" grew in irregular patches, isolated between intersecting circles of lawn. It had looked stupid and Stan had given up, after having sweated a small sea's worth of Sunday salt water. He'd finally said to hell with it, and bought a tractor-mower. Cath had been angry and said he should have waited.

Stan dumped the wheelbarrow on top of the weed heap, a burgeoning mountain of burdock and twitch. Folly trotted back to him with a toothpick-sized stick.

"You've got to be kidding," Stan said as she dropped it. "That's a very poor excuse for a stick. A stickette." He reached down and tossed the stick as far as it would go— about three feet— and Folly lunged after it. He winced at her rigidity. She was getting really old. He left the wheelbarrow beside the weed heap and started towards the house. "C'mon. Let's go inside," he said. "Slim!" He whistled.

The skinny messy second dog came charging toward them from around the side of the house, his long ears flapping like laundry. He dashed between Stan and Folly, did a grass-gouging turn, and rushed up behind them, nosing Stan in the bum.

"Slim!" Stan said, angrily. "No goosing! You do that to Lucy tonight and I'll kill you."

He swung open the squeaky screen door and let the dogs go into the mudroom ahead of him. As he followed them in, he picked up Gina's paddle from where he'd leaned it just inside the door. The man called Pender had kept his promise and had dropped off the paddle while Stan and Ian were at dinner.

Stan's phone rang and he hurried into the living room, still holding Gina's paddle. It was Elizabeth, as he should have known.

"I tried to get you twice this morning, Stan. Where have you been?"

In analysis, Stan wanted to say. What the hell's it to ya?

"Outside," he said.

"Oh," she replied. "Outside." She said it as if the concept were new to her. Her office didn't have any windows. "Well, I just wanted to find out how it went. Anything interesting?"

"Sure," Stan said. "All kinds of stuff."

"Good." Elizabeth paused. "Where did you stay?"

"At Ian Smith's."

"The director's place? So you didn't have to pay for a hotel, then."

"No," Stan answered, rolling his eyes. "And I didn't have to pay for dinner or breakfast, either. You got off real cheap this time, Elizabeth."

"Well, do your gas receipts and anything else. And fax in your column as soon as you can, okay?"

"The one on butterflies. Yeah, I've already started working on it."

"No, Stan. We wanted the Wildlife Centre this week."

Stan sat down in his grandmother's chair, propping the paddle against his knee.

"You're kidding," he said. "You didn't tell me that, Elizabeth."

"Yes, I did."

No, you damn well didn't, Stan thought. His notes from the weekend were still in the truck and he hadn't even glanced at them yet. He was well ahead on his column on butterflies so he'd been feeling in good shape for the coming week. He'd thought that he'd be free for the next couple of days, at least.

When he'd got home on Sunday, he'd heard Lucy's message and he'd called her back right away. Yes, he'd said, of course she could come. No, on Monday he didn't have other plans. He couldn't help grinning, despite last week's disaster, when she'd then said that she had to be back on Tuesday. In a giddy game that had lasted pretty well all his life, hope and disappointment had lobbed his brain between them. He was almost used to it now— the joyful, painful back and forth, the thonk at either end.

He'd told Lucy he'd drive her back down Tuesday morning. He had some things to do in town.

When they'd said goodbye, he'd called Mrs. Ferrara to tell her he'd drop by the paddle. Mrs. Ferrara sounded bewildered, but said, nonetheless, "Thank you, Stanley. You are such a nice young man."

Finally, Stan had phoned his friend, Peter-the-Doctor, and arranged to meet for a movie at seven Tuesday evening. So he'd made his plans and was determined to stick to them. But he'd have to start thinking about that column right away.

"Elizabeth," Stan finally said to her, "can you try not to spring things on me for a while? If I get this done for you will you promise to stick to the schedule?"

"I don't know about springing things. Nobody is springing things. One change is all we made. And you did know about that, Stan."

"Okay," Stan conceded, wanting to get the conversation over with. "Maybe I forgot."

"Thursday, please? First thing Friday at the very latest?"

"Yeah. See ya."

Stan hung up the phone and looked at Slim and Folly, who were lying in front of him, panting pink tongues.

"You lucky dogs," he said to them. He stood up and took the paddle over to the corner behind the living room door. He leaned it up against the wall, swung the door back over it and then walked into the kitchen. He had to do a few things for dinner but nothing fancy this time around. Soup and salad and brownies with ice cream.

The brownies would only take a few minutes to make.

The house was in pretty good shape. He'd do a quick vacuum to pick up the dog hair. The weather was so mild they could sit on the porch.

"Stop making plans," he chastised himself. He shook his head and then headed outside to the truck. He'd better take a look at those Wildlife Centre notes right now.

CHAPTER 27

"Can I?" Stan asked Lucy who was raising her lighter to the cigarette in her mouth. They were sitting on the screened porch, watching the dusk fall and the bats flicker, the gas lamp on the table throwing an ever more distinct circle of light as the night pitched darker around it.

"Can you what?" Lucy said, taking the cigarette from her mouth.

"Light this?"

"Yeah. I never smoked but I always liked the lighting bit. Although matches are more fun than lighters. Wooden matches are the best. They give such a good whoosh."

Lucy passed her cigarette and lighter to Stan and smiled at his grave concentration as he lit it. He puffed at the cigarette shallowly, without inhaling, and then handed it back to her.

"Disgusting," he said.

Lucy inhaled deeply and then threw back her head and slowly blew smoke up towards the rafters. "Ambrosial," she sighed. She looked across the table at Stan who was now watching her with a small mischievous smile. "What?" she asked.

"I was talking to Al Hoot the other day," Stan said. "He asked me how old you were. I think he thought I was robbing the cradle, you looked so young that night." Lucy raised her eyebrows. "I told him I didn't know," Stan continued, "but that you didn't have your driver's licence yet." Lucy laughed and took a sip of her espresso, into which she'd already stirred three spoonfuls of sugar.

"I'm thirty-two going on Triassic," she told him. "At least that's how I feel these days." She sipped at her coffee again. "This is really good, Stan. The whole dinner was great. I've been eating so pathetically lately."

"You said on your message you'd made a vegetarian lunch."

"I don't want to talk about it," Lucy replied.

From somewhere in the distance, around the back of the house, a dog started barking and then another dog joined it. Their voices were muffled. Stan groaned.

"Dog duet," he said. "They've gone and locked themselves in the barn. The door to the hay mow opens in but it's kind of wonky. They can shove their way in there, but then the door closes behind them and they can't get out. I forget to put on the latch. It happens all the time."

"Are you going to go let them out?" Lucy asked. She'd been introduced to the dogs when she first arrived and was immediately on intimate terms with Slim. Stan had had to drag him away, lecturing him as he did so. Meanwhile, Folly had done a wiggling shuffle around Lucy's legs, almost knocking her over with the long piece of two-by-four she held clamped in her mouth.

"They'll be okay for a while," Stan said. "They always bark for a minute when they realize they're stuck. Then they get all caught up in the mouse action. I'll go let them out later on." He put his hands on the table and leaned forward towards Lucy. "Would you like a brandy, maybe?"

"Sure," Lucy smiled.

"I'll be right back," Stan said. He pushed up off the table and went into the dark house, through the mudroom and into the kitchen where he switched on a light. Lucy's "overnight bag" was looped around a kitchen chair, a large sagging duffel with a tiny bulge at the bottom. She'd taken it into work that morning so she could go straight from there to the bus. She'd been pleased with herself for having been so organized. Stan guessed from her embarrassed pride in this accomplishment that she was using what she could to shore up her self-confidence. It was probably unconscious but that didn't matter. It seemed to be working. Tonight she was assured and relaxed. A peach.

Stan now opened a cupboard in the wooden hutch and took out the brandy and two glasses with the words "49th Parallel" painted on them in blue. "Classy," he said to himself, at the same time thinking that Lucy would like them. She'd liked the whirligig in the shape of a blimp and the beat-up mailbox where he kept the bread. He could tell by her eyebrows, the way they went up.

He took the bottle and glasses and headed back out, switching off the light as he left the kitchen. The glow from the porch looked soft and friendly. Lucy was watching the night.

"The dogs have stopped barking," she said to Stan. "There's some sort of animal out there, though. I can hear it scratching around."

"Oh, yeah? Could be a raccoon. They hang out around the compost." Stan poured the brandy and handed one to Lucy. She took a sip and smiled at him. Stan went over to the old green sofa that he'd moved out to the porch for the summer. He sat down and leaned forward with his elbow on his knee, the glass of brandy cool against his cheek. "How about coming over here?" he said quietly.

Lucy stood up without a word and slipped across to the sofa. She sat down next to him and pushed her shoes off her feet with her toes. It was a warmish night and her legs were bare. She drew them up under her so that now she was facing him, one arm resting on the back of the sofa. She ran her hand through her hair, glanced at him quickly, smiled again and sipped at her drink. A large moth, attracted by the lamp, thrilled for a moment against the screen.

Stan tasted his own brandy and then put his glass down on the floor. He sat back in the sofa and examined Lucy intently.

"You've got amazing hair," he said, reaching out to touch it.

"Hmm, right," she replied. "Amazing."

"No, I like it. You always look like you just got out of bed."

"I don't know if that's exactly the image I want to project," Lucy smiled.

"Maybe not always," Stan said, gently taking the glass from her hand, "but it's fine now." He put the glass on the floor next to his own and then, keeping his eyes on her face, he lifted her hand and kissed the inside of her wrist. "You're here," he said, "and I feel like I'm sixteen years old."

"I sort of do, too," Lucy answered. "But I think that's okay." She drifted towards him with both her arms and he gathered her up like a net. She thought of her dreams of breathing underwater. He thought of the flying fish that leap above it. But they both thought of these things only briefly.

Lucy's legs unfolded along the sofa and Stan kicked off his shoes and settled in beside her. As he kissed her, he ran a hand down her smooth bare leg.

"You're cold," he whispered. Her hands wandered up under his sweatshirt and across his back. He couldn't help but flinch. "Shit, you're freezing," he said.

"Sorry," she laughed. "I'll warm up in a minute." Stan reached over her, pulled down the striped afghan that was folded across the back of the sofa and tucked it more or less around them. When he turned again to look at her, a moment later, she was lying absolutely still, staring up at the ceiling.

"What's the matter?" he asked, with sudden apprehension. Lucy's eyes came back to him, as if she'd been away somewhere.

"Nothing," she said, as her fingers began softly tracing his shoulder blades. "I thought I smelled smoke for a second." She gently pressed him down towards her. Her hands, already warmer, stole further and further down his back. Stan closed his eyes with her kiss, begging himself to give up what he knew he knew— that the smoke *he'd* been smelling was not from her cigarettes. He almost succeeded. He felt his mind raising a white flag to Lucy.

Slim started to howl and the flag snapped down. Stan opened his eyes and drew back. Lucy went still and she locked eyes with Stan as they both listened to the dog, whose howls began to alternate with high-pitched barks. Stan gave Lucy a despairing look. He could smell the smoke plainly now.

"I'd better go check," he said. "It's probably just someone burning brush." He kissed her on the lips, sighing deeply as he pulled away. "Shit," he said. They unravelled themselves from one another and Stan swung himself off the sofa. Lucy sat up slowly and reached for her glass of brandy. Stan watched her as she swallowed some. Her eyes were bright and beamy like the moon through new leaves. Her pale cheeks were flushed. Shit.

"Do you want me to come with you?" she asked.

"No," Stan said, bending down to pull on his shoes. "Whatever you do, please don't move. Don't move from that couch physically or mentally. I'll be right back."

He went out the porch door and down the wooden steps. He went through the grass around the corner of the porch.

Grey smoke was slung low in the darkening air, caught by the hollow between the barn and house. Smoke seeped through the boards on the walls of the barn and down into the centre of the hollow. The overflow wandered vaguely up until it was scattered by a wind near the shingled roof. Stan could see yellow light flickering through the window in the ground floor manger. Slim was howling. Stan started to run.

He scrambled up the bank that led to the hay mow and shoved open the door. Slim shot out of the darkness past him, followed by a surging cloud of smoke. Stan backed off from the door, coughing, and the door swung to. A mouse fled over his foot. He took a deep breath, pushed the door open again and yelled inside for Folly.

Only smoke came out, and Stan couldn't see past it. He could hear a low crackle, like a dangerous idea. He yelled for Folly and yelled again.

"She's still in there?" Lucy had come up behind him, breathing fast, her hand gripping his arm.

"Fuck," Stan said, "I can't see anything! I can't see a fucking thing! Folly!" he cried. He was beginning to lose it, he could feel it happening, as if he were a terrified deer or rabbit. His body was freezing with indecision, starting at his feet.

Inside the barn, a long thin flame flashed up from the floorboards. It lit up the hay mow. It was terse and effective. A dozen bales of hay were now on fire.

With the shock of the light, Stan's brain grasped that Lucy had gone past him through the door. Through the thick smoke he could barely see her, silhouetted by the flaming bales.

"Lucy!" he cried and his feet started running. She was coughing and dragging at the body of Folly. Darting snakes of burning hay scintillated the air around her.

"I've got her, Lucy. Go!" Stan heaved the large black dog into his arms as another lick of flame shot up from below. He stumbled through the smoke with the dog, behind Lucy, who reached the door and pushed at it, first with her hands and then with her shoulder.

"I can't get it open, Stan! It won't open!" She looked back at him aghast, her eyes streaming.

"Pull!"

When they got to the bottom of the bank they stopped. Stan dropped Folly on her side in the grass and quickly knelt down beside her. Fire had now spread to the roof of the barn and waved above it in fitful bright tendrils.

"Is she alive?" Lucy asked, squatting beside him. She reached out and put her hand on Folly's head.

Stan put his ear against the dog's chest and listened. He coughed and looked at Lucy. Tears left meandering tracks down the grit on her cheeks. His own eyes felt like they'd been through hell.

"I think her heart's still going," he said quietly. "Lucy, go and call the fire department, okay? Nine-one-one. The directions to the house are right by the phone." He put his palms on Folly's chest, pushed and released.

Lucy jumped up and started running to the porch. Part way there, she turned and yelled, "Where's the phone?"

"In the living room!" Stan yelled back, continuing to pump Folly's chest. He noticed for the first time that Lucy was barefoot.

Lucy never made it to the phone. She ran through the porch into the pitch black mudroom, where she stubbed her toe on something and swore. As she was cautiously trying to feel her way forward, she was hit on the head by something hard that dropped her down drastically into an even darker dark.

CHAPTER 28

When he examined his face in the mirror, Eliot saw that he'd missed a spot. He sloshed his safety razor through the water and carefully shaved below his left nostril, looked again, and pulled the plug out of the sink. He turned on the hot tap and wetted a washcloth. He scrubbed his face with the washcloth until it shone like an apple.

He went out of the bathroom and over to the closet where he'd neatly hung up his shirts and suits. He chose his clothes deliberately— white shirt and navy suit, tie with horizontal stripes, brontosaurus suspenders. He chose the suspenders because he needed a lift.

The case was going nowhere and there'd been noise from Headquarters. They were talking about sending up a replacement for Freeman. But, thought Eliot, it wasn't Chris Freeman's fault. If you keep hitting dead ends you can only back up, and the person to blame is the one giving directions. And that was him, D.S. Francis Eliot.

It seemed as if a requirement for working for Lambert's was that you have a good alibi for Monday, May fifth. All Lambert's employees, either present or past, at every level, including management, had been doing something that day with others, had been seen by friends, co-workers or families. It was so darn tight it would almost make you think conspiracy if it didn't also make you think that you could be totally wrong.

Eliot tied his tie and put on his suit jacket. He picked up his briefcase and left the hotel room, smiling good morning to the desk clerk as he trundled through the lobby. He went out to the parking lot and got into his car. He headed through town to the Donut World.

They'd found the letter writer, Alex Dockstader. He'd been living for the past six months in B.C., working for a small truck-rental firm. He wasn't at all surprised to hear from the police. He'd figured he would sooner or later. Eliot had passed over the futile question as to Dockstader's silence at the trial and instead had asked him why he hadn't contacted them first. And why had he written to Patrick Irving? If not to the police, why not to Terry Bantam?

"I don't know," Dockstader had answered. "The first person I thought of was Patrick Irving. He's such a stubborn bastard and everybody knows him. I figured he'd get something done. I figured he wouldn't give up."

Eliot had asked him who else knew about his letter and Dockstader had let out a shout.

"Nobody knew! Are you kidding? You think I'd go blabbing anything around after what happened to Jamie? Nobody worried about blowing him up. You think they're going to let me get away with squealing? No way, man. I waited until I was far away from Lambert."

"You're sure now," Eliot had persisted. "You're absolutely sure that no one knew that you wrote to Irving."

"I didn't tell nobody," Dockstader had said, and so Eliot had clunked into another dead end. No good motive and no opportunity. It was time to back up from Lambert and try a different route.

He parked the car and went into the Donut World, pausing to glance at the newspaper headlines in the *Toronto Post* box by the door. At least the case hadn't made the headlines today. At least not the ones he could see. He shrugged uncomfortably and went up to the counter.

"I bet you wanna honey cruller," the young woman with the pony tail said to him, smiling. "And a small coffee, double double." The badge on her uniform said "Sheila."

"Yes, please, Sheila," Eliot answered, wishing that life was always so simple. If only everyone wore their names on their shirt-fronts, as well as their lies and their secrets. But then, of course, he'd be out of a job. And what would he do instead, he wondered? Maybe become a magician— he'd always liked tricks, especially the sawing in half. But magic was illusion and illusion was lies, so that job would disappear, too. He started to consider other lines of work.

"Did you want something else today?" Sheila asked, nudging the coffee and doughnut towards him.

Eliot snapped to and smiled her a rose. He paid and went out to the car, keeping the coffee at arm's length so he'd be sure not to spill it on himself. He put it on the hood of the car until he got the door open, then picked up the cardboard cup and slowly lowered himself into the seat, holding the coffee out the door as he did.

A different route, he said to himself. Well, we tried the one to Ray Clifford.

Clifford was off the hook. A canoeist had been found who'd seen Clifford going in and out of the cottage where he'd claimed he was working on Monday afternoon. They'd also tracked down his purchase through the Canadian Tire computer. Clifford had found his receipt, and the computer had verified that he'd bought brake pads and spark plugs and a bag of barbecue chips in Huntsville at 8:23 p.m. That was one hundred kilometres from the Speller River.

Eliot was relieved that Ray Clifford was in the clear. His father's heart sympathized with the Cliffords' troubles. He'd often wondered over the past few weeks how he and Jo would handle the same situation— if something devastating happened to one of their girls. He liked to think they would pull together, not worry at their marriage until it frayed apart.

On Sunday, when Eliot had made it home for dinner— corned beef and cabbage with scalloped potatoes— Jo had broken the news to him that Annie had been caught smoking at school. They'd held a conference after the girls left the table and had agreed on what to tell Annie— that they were confident she'd soon make her mind up to quit, she was too clever to do anything else. Annie had rolled her eyes as they talked, but they'd both thought afterwards that she'd been taking it in.

Not, of course, that there was any comparison to the terrible situation at the Cliffords'. But he and Jo *did* seem to work things out. Eliot pulled slowly into the parking lot and rolled towards his space. A cruiser was parked beyond its line so that he had to shift back and forth to squeeze his car in. The coffee on the dashboard slopped around and a thin pool formed on the top of the lid. Eliot watched it anxiously out of the corner of his eye.

Freeman was leaning against the bulletin board in the front reception area laughing at a notice with P.C. de Freitas. He saw Eliot come in and gave him a salute. Eliot said, "Good morning, Chris, de Freitas," and asked Freeman to join him in his office. Freeman made a show of getting himself going, pushing himself off the wall as if he were weak and unsteady. Constable de Freitas gave him a slap on the arm.

"Time to change tack, Chris," Eliot said after swallowing some cruller. Freeman was lodged on the edge of Eliot's desk, ignoring the second chair. "We're not having much luck with our Shallow Bay suspects."

Freeman folded his arms and looked out the window.

"Oh, I don't know about that, Francie. There's about three hundred here we haven't even touched. We could get through 'em all by Christmas."

"Yes," Eliot said. He pulled loose a bite-sized morsel of cruller, catching the crumbs in the palm of his hand. He popped the piece into his mouth and brushed the crumbs into the waste basket beside the desk. He sipped at his coffee and looked up at Freeman. "I've been thinking about the woman, Gina Ferrara."

"Huh," Freeman said. "Irving's 'platonic' babe. The stupid goddamn bastard." Freeman had been ready to throttle Irving when he found out he'd been lied to. Eliot had seen boiled-down poison in Freeman's close-set eyes.

"She certainly had the best opportunity," Eliot said, "but we don't yet have a motive. We don't know much about her relationship with Irving except that she'd been chasing him. From what he says."

"Yeah, right. Chasing him. Makes you sick. And screwing him. From what he says." Freeman looked at Eliot, sardonically.

"Yes. It's hard to know exactly what to believe when Irving has been so dissembling."

"Dissembling. Yeah, right." Freeman looked back out the window. "It somehow makes me feel all sunny inside thinking Ferrara maybe tried to kill Irving. Easier to stomach than the idea that she was after him for *love*." Freeman choked out this last word as if it were a chunk of bad meat. Eliot sipped his coffee and gazed at the giraffe.

"She could have really been going to get help," he began, "assuming he'd be dead by the time she got back. If she *had* got back and he *had* been dead then she could have been a witness to what he had eaten. She could have described the poisonous mushrooms."

"Yeah, but what about if he hadn't been dead?"

"She was probably sure he would be. She wasn't a chemist, of course. She made a mistake with the dose. She gave him a lot, but not quite enough."

"Goddamn lucky bastard."

"I'd like you and de Freitas to go down to Toronto today and take a look through Ferrara's apartment. Talk to her family and friends as well. Find out what you can about her and Irving. Get their history, and so on."

Freeman took the deep audible breath of a long, long-suffering man.

"You mean I gotta talk to her mother again?"

"Why?" Eliot asked. "What's wrong with her mother?"

"It's like she just got off the goddamn boat," Freeman said.

With a small, perplexed frown, Eliot studied Freeman as if he were a freak of nature. He wondered what Freeman's history was. He wasn't married.

"Chris," he couldn't resist asking, "is there anyone you actually *like?*"

"Daryl Hannah," Freeman snapped. "And you, Francie, of course."

Eliot sighed and pulled over a file. Freeman watched him as he opened it.

"So what are *you* gonna do?" Freeman asked him.

"I'm going to call Patrick Irving."

"You get all the fun stuff," Freeman complained. He jumped down from the desk and went to the door. He opened it and turned.

"So we say sayonara to Lambert, eh?"

Eliot looked up to see Freeman smiling like a crocodile, his mouth barely curved from a thin straight line.

"Yes, Chris. I think it's time to move on."

"And we say sayonara to Freeman, I hear. I mean, since he took so damn long to move on. Since he got all caught up in explosions and letters and B and E's down in Toronto."

"I'd like to keep you on the case, Chris. I'll see what I can do."

"Sure," Freeman said, smirking.

CHAPTER 29

Stan came out of the drug store with a bottle of aspirin and twisted the lid off as he walked to the truck. He pulled loose the cotton ball and jiggled out three pills, popping them into his mouth one at a time and throwing his head back with each swallow. He hadn't had much sleep and his head was killing him.

Reaching the truck, he climbed inside, and leaned his forehead on the steering wheel. He should really call Peter and cancel their movie. If only the city had cots you could rent to lie down on for half an hour.

Stan could have gone back to Lucy's, but she wanted to work and, anyway, she was in worse shape than he was. She'd been treated for a concussion as well as minor burns to her feet. She'd lightly grilled her bare soles on the floor of the barn.

"It's not that bad, Stan," she'd insisted, seeing him grimace with her every step from the emergency ward back to the truck. She'd refused to take a wheelchair and had her arm around Stan's neck. "It's kind of like I stood on my head too long at the beach." She'd gingerly felt the back of her head. "Yow."

When she hadn't come back out to him from the house after ten minutes— ten minutes of blazing heat from the fire— he'd hurried back into the house with Folly. He'd found Lucy lying on the mudroom floor. With trembling hands, he'd set down the dog and felt for a pulse in Lucy's neck. Then he'd run to the living room and made the call. He'd cradled Lucy's head in his lap, stroking her hair, until the ambulance and the fire trucks had come wailing down the sideroad. With the crescendo of sirens, Lucy's eyes had opened and Stan had touched her cheek in almost painful relief.

"The ambulance is here, peach. You're going to be okay."

Lucy had tried to lift her head. Then she'd winced and closed her eyes.

"It's all right," Stan had said. "Just stay still."

"I thought I was defending my thesis," she'd whispered. "And there were four leeches there taking notes. Land leeches, I think. *Haemadipsae.*" Stan had smiled, despite himself.

"You've been unconscious, Lucy. Out cold."

"Oh, that explains it. There you go."

Stan now raised his pounding head and started the truck. He maneuvered from the parking lot out on to College Street and headed east to Mrs. Ferrara's house.

By the time he and Lucy got back from the hospital, the fire had been pretty well drowned. All that was left of the century-old barn was a charred skeleton of steaming timbers and the rubble-stone walls of the foundation. The lights of the fire trucks had flashed at them luridly, the radios had cackled and bleeped. Stan had mourned the young barn swallows, burned in their nests.

A fireman had ambled over to Stan's truck, his face as red as if it had been roasted, his upper lip beaded with sweat. He'd stuck his hand in through the window to Stan. He was at least six-foot-three and built like a water tank and his name was Kevin Dewson. He was the fireman who was married to Cath.

"Sorry about the barn there, Stan. Too bad we didn't get the call sooner." He'd peered past Stan at Lucy and had eyed her openly. Stan had imagined him preparing an at-home report. "Well, I guess we're going to get going now. Take it easy, Stan, eh?"

"Yeah, okay, Kevin. Thanks," Stan had said. "Say hi to Cathy," he'd added mechanically.

Stan had set Lucy up on the fainting couch— the "Freud couch," as he liked to call it. He'd brought ice for her head, pillows for her feet, a woollen blanket for her chill and an ashtray. Squatting beside her, he'd watched her trying to stay awake. She'd winced and smiled as she covered her yawns. They'd said very little while they waited.

The police had arrived after two in the morning and Stan let them in. When they got to the living room, Lucy was sitting up sleepily, trying to comb some order into her hair with her fingers. A shock angled up at the back like an outcrop.

Stan had sat beside her as she'd lit a cigarette and told the two cops her story. Such as her story was... it had been too dark to see. The only thing she could say for sure was that she hadn't hit her head on anything. Something had hit *her* on the head. The cops had nodded and then had turned to Stan.

Nothing seemed to be missing, Stan had told them, nothing that he'd noticed so far. Not that he had much of value anyway, except his computer, and that was still there. And so was his TV, an ancient black-and-white, and his turntable and old Sony receiver. He certainly hadn't seen anyone but then he wouldn't have, anyway. He'd been all caught up with Folly and the fire.

The fire. About the fire. Did he think it could have started by accident? Stan had replied that he couldn't see how. The weather had been wet. He never kept gas or solvents in the barn. In fact, the building wasn't even wired. The electrical system had been needing an overhaul and he'd had it disconnected until he had the money.

On their way out, the cops had looked around the mudroom, checking for anything hard at head level. They'd asked Stan if anything was out of place. Nothing was. They'd gone. At three in the morning Stan had been dead on his feet.

Stan now turned the corner on to Mrs. Ferrara's street and got a parking spot right in front of the house. He sat for a moment and closed his eyes, seeing Lucy's pale sleeping face in the waving blue light and Slim sprawled on his back on the floor, his body twisted and legs awry, as if he were dancing to the drumbeat in Stan's percussive head. He saw Folly lying on her side, breathing shallowly and twitching with dreams. The fish on the lamp swam round and round, the shark chasing the grouper, the lobster after the shark.

Stan took a long breath and climbed out of the truck. He grabbed Gina's paddle from the back and went up the walk to the house. The door opened before he reached it. Mrs. Ferrara had seen him coming.

"Hi, Mrs. Ferrara," he said.

"Stanley," she said distractedly, looking over his shoulder towards the street.

Stan turned and saw two young men coming quickly along the sidewalk. They started up the walk and paused to look at Stan tentatively. One was wearing a suit and the other had on sunglasses and shorts.

"Yes, yes," Mrs. Ferrara nodded at them. "You come to see the apartment."

"Do you want me to come back?" Stan asked her as she gave the men the once over and then the twice. She glanced at Stan and took his arm.

"No, Stanley. You come in. You go in the living room. I show these boys the apartment upstair." She pulled Stan through the door and left him standing in the living room. He could hear her chattering to the young men as she led them up to the second floor.

Stan looked for a place to put the paddle and settled it up against the wall by the door. He went and sat on the cream and gold sofa and covered his eyes with his hands. The only thing he saw now was his headache. He put his hands on his lap and looked around. No flowers any more.

He gazed at the photos on the wood veneer table. He tried to find Gina in the correct little communion girl and wasn't able do it. He had better luck, though, with the bridal picture of Linda. There was Gina's wry mocking look in Linda's eyes and the hair was the same dark brown. But Gina would never have worn blue eye shadow and she'd have choked at the thought of ringlets.

Gina had kept her hair cut short and she hadn't worn much make-up. Stan had never seen her in a dress— she'd worn jeans and big suit jackets and sometimes a baseball cap. She'd worked out regularly at the downtown "Y" where she'd sometimes get the come-on from admiring gay women. She'd tell Stan about it, smirking, at the same time seeming rather pleased.

"Gina," Stan sighed, "Gina." Stan leaned back on the couch. He wished he could just stretch himself out and give in to the pain. His head was getting worse instead of better. The aspirin hadn't done a thing.

Rattling footsteps came down the stairs and the two young men rushed by the living room door. There was a bang as the front door slammed that ricocheted off Stan's brain. Soft slippered footsteps followed and then Mrs. Ferrara appeared in the room.

"Are they going to take the apartment?" Stan heard himself asking, his hand on his temple, trying to steady his head.

"These boys?" said Mrs. Ferrara, worriedly. "These boys I don't know." She sat on the edge of the La-Z-Boy and fiddled with the hem of her dress. "I think these are homosexual boys. In the paper I ask for a couple."

A couple of gays? Stan vaguely asked himself. "Hmm," he said to Mrs. Ferrara.

"This apartment is empty many weeks," Mrs. Ferrara said, now looking out the window. "I think that maybe if nobody take it then I move Gina's things to there. Linda and Manny and Robby, they go to Gina's last week and start putting her things in boxes. We must move them because soon it's the end of the month. Robby thinks we should have a company. But it's so expensive, Stanley." She looked at him for agreement.

"Yes, it is," Stan nodded. Robby, he thought, must be Robert Milliken. He wondered how Milliken liked her calling him Robby. Dr. Robby, VIP.

"You will have coffee, Stanley?"

"No, thanks, Mrs. Ferrara. I'm not feeling too well. I think I'd better get going back home."

"Oh, I'm sorry for you, Stanley. You have flu?"

"Just a headache. Anyway, I brought you the paddle."

"Yes," Mrs. Ferrara looked at the paddle and then back at Stan. "Is funny. You call about the paddle on Sunday and yesterday two people call me about the paddle. First one man and then one lady. They want to buy the paddle."

"Is that right?" Stan said, getting up with a grimace. "How did they know about it?"

"They both say they read in the paper what Gina write. This article she write. The man tell me he is a collector and he know Gina has this beautiful paddle. The lady say she has a paddle made by the same man and she would like another. I tell them I don't have the paddle. I tell them I have it soon but I don't know if I will sell it. I tell them Gina's friend Stanley will bring it to me today and I will decide. They can phone me another time."

Stan stood and stared at Mrs. Ferrara. Through the throb in his head he suddenly saw an idea. A great big fat quivering idea.

"You told them *I* had it, Mrs. Ferrara? You mentioned my name?"

Mrs. Ferrara looked alarmed. Stan was staring at her something fierce. He couldn't help it— he was prepossessed, and his idea was painfully having children.

"I'm very sorry, Stanley. I think I say 'her friend Stanley, from the newspaper.' I'm sorry. I should not say your name." She looked as if she were going to cry.

Stan tore his gaze away from Mrs. Ferrara and his mind from the gibbering ideas. He went over to her and took her hand. "It's okay, Mrs. Ferrara," he forced himself to say calmly. "Don't worry about it at all. It's okay that you mentioned my name. It's just my headache. I'd better get going."

She followed him to the door and stood in the doorway as he got in the truck, calling "Thank you, Stanley!" as he drove away.

Stan parked in the glare on College Street and walked back to the corner where he'd seen a phone booth outside a variety store. He dialled Lucy's number and then leaned his forehead against the glass wall, squinting down through the pain at his All Stars.

"Hello?" Lucy said.

"Lucy. It's Stan."

"Hello."

"How are you feeling?"

"Kind of better, I guess. I've been working with my feet up on my desk and the keyboard in my lap. I've got a fan blowing on my feet."

"Sounds comfortable as all get out."

"Hmm."

"Lucy, I was wondering if you could call Patrick."

"Oh."

"I want you to ask him something for me." Stan focused on a blob of flat grey gum that was stuck to the floor near his feet.

"Okay. I guess so," Lucy said. "What is it?"

"Ask him," Stan said to her, his voice starting to clang in his head like a bell, "where the police said they found his paddle."

CHAPTER 30

"Lucy? I can't believe it," Patrick said. "This must be the first time you've ever called me."

"Patrick," Lucy replied. "No, it isn't."

"Name me another time."

"I called when you were in the hospital. I called you a couple of times."

"That doesn't count. You only called me then to be civilized. Because you would have been a shit if you hadn't. Besides, it took you days to get around to it."

"That's because I didn't know, Patrick. I called you as soon as I found out."

"Uh-huh," said Patrick, sarcastically.

Lucy sat on the floor by the "telephone table"— two blue plastic milk crates stacked one on the other— and forced herself not to get drawn further in. She looked for her cigarettes and found them by her leg but she couldn't see her lighter.

"Anyway," she said, peering around, "I'm calling you now, okay?"

"Yeah. Right. I ask myself why."

Lucy spied her lighter on the kitchen table and pushed herself up off the floor. Her feet were still tender but walkable on. The back of her head was sore and lumpy.

"Just a second, okay, Patrick?" she said.

"I ask myself why not."

Lucy tiptoed across to the lighter and then tiptoed back and sat down. She lit her cigarette and took a few puffs before she picked up the phone. Patrick was humming on the other end.

"Sorry," Lucy said. The humming stopped. Patrick put on a nasally voice.

"Thank you for calling Patrick Irving. Our operators are all busy at the moment but please stand by and someone will be with you shortly." He started to hum again.

"You're in a strange mood," Lucy said. The humming stopped. "I've been trying to get you since yesterday. What happened to your answering machine?"

"It got all worn out waiting to record your voice so it went on vacation to recharge."

Lucy smiled. "Home to Japan?"

"Home is in Oshawa. I buy Canadian-made. It got stolen, Lucy. Remember?" He paused. "So you wanna go to a movie?"

"I don't think so, Patrick," Lucy said.

"Right," Patrick said shortly. "Just checking."

"How are you, anyway?"

"You really wanna know or are you just being civilized?"

"I really want to know."

"Lousy."

"Oh."

"I got a call the other day from the gnome. He starts asking me again about Gina, all this shit about our sleeping together. He wants to know 'the history' of our relationship, like we were Lewis and Clark or something. Then he asks me if there was any time when Gina was alone at the campsite."

"When Gina was alone?"

"Yeah. Alone with the mushrooms. Turns out now they're thinking that Gina tried to kill me. Can you fucking believe it? They've given up on getting Lambert. Robitaille spun them some tale about how he was in Sudbury boring a bunch of Shriners and the gnome says everybody else is covered. So who's left? Look around. Gina Ferrara. Woman on the spot."

Lucy stubbed out her cigarette and examined her hand. Her fingernails were dirty. She needed a shower. Why would Gina want to kill Patrick?

"Gina was in love with me, for chrissakes," he continued. "As if I couldn't tell that. And as if I wouldn't have noticed anything when we were fooling around. I think if I'd been about to poison someone I was in the middle of screwing, I might seem a little preoccupied. Gina wasn't preoccupied. She was all there. Anyway," Patrick snorted, "I don't know why I'm even talking about it. It's a fucking farce."

Lucy lodged the phone between her shoulder and ear and began to clean the fingernails on her left hand with the thumbnail on her right. She wondered briefly how "all there" she'd ever been with Patrick. And how many times he had *thought* she was "all there." She felt a twinge of guilt.

"It does sound pretty weird," she said to him.

"No kidding," Patrick said.

Lucy coughed and got another cigarette. She put it into her mouth and then took it out while she said quietly to Patrick, "Stan's got a theory."

"Oh, Stan does, does he?" Patrick scoffed. "I bet it involves a little bird or a bunny."

Lucy lit her cigarette and ignored his last snipe.

"You'll like this theory, Patrick. You'll like it better than the one about Gina."

"Seeing a lot of Stanley these days, are we?"

"Patrick, will you please listen? I need to ask you a question."

"Your question or Stanley's?"

"Both."

"Uh-huh."

"Do you remember if when the police brought your things to the hospital they said anything about where they found your paddle?"

"No."

"No, they didn't say anything?"

"No, I don't remember."

Lucy sighed and looked at her nails. She bit one that was ragged. Stan was going to be disappointed. He'd been starting to get all caught up.

"Okay, I'll bite," Patrick said after a moment. "Why do you want to know?"

"Well, Stan was up in Shallow Bay on the weekend..."

"How nice for him. Was he catching butterflies?"

"Stan was up in Shallow Bay," Lucy repeated, a little louder and with a touch of ire, "and he ran into the man who found you."

"Ye-es?" Patrick said.

"Well, one of his kids found Gina's paddle, somewhere on the trail, Stan thinks. This man had met Gina before and she'd shown it to him so he knew it was hers. He gave it to Stan."

"Huh," Patrick said, his interest sparked. "Does Stan want it? I wouldn't mind having it. It's really great."

"Patrick," Lucy chastised him. "Stan gave it to Gina's mother." Lucy made a face. Patrick could be so obtuse. "Anyway, Stan thinks that if your paddle was with your stuff on the bank and if this kid found Gina's on the bank, then that means Gina didn't have one with her in the canoe."

"Lucy," Patrick in turn chastised, "she would've taken her paddle. What else would she have used? Her hands?"

"Patrick," Lucy began.

"That would have been a really good way to get herself drowned. If she forgot to take a paddle she deserved it. Christ."

"Stan doesn't think *she* forgot, Patrick. He thinks that whoever *killed* her forgot."

There was silence on the other end.

"Are you still there?" she asked.

Lucy crossed her legs, trying to get more comfortable. A motorcycle buzzed down the street, the noise rolling in through the open slider. A teenage boy's voice yelled, "Dougie!"

"What about the cops?" Patrick was saying. "They must have searched out there right after they found me. Why didn't they find it then?"

"Stan thinks the kid found it before the police got there. He doesn't think they even know about it yet. He got the feeling that the father was mad. That he was worried his kid would end up getting into trouble."

"So," Patrick began, testing the waters before he jumped in. "So, Gina must've run into the guy who poisoned me when she left. And he killed her so she couldn't talk. He stuck her in the canoe," Patrick jumped in and started laughing, "but he forgot to put in a goddamn paddle! What a jerk!"

"So you think they *did* find your paddle with your stuff," Lucy said.

Patrick stopped laughing.

"Shit. I don't know. They didn't say they didn't. I don't know. I wasn't really paying attention."

"I guess we'll have to ask them then," Lucy said. Patrick couldn't help but laugh again.

"Man! They'll be thrilled if this turns out right! It totally fucks their theory! It brings them right back to Lambert! Man!"

Lucy unwrapped her legs and stood up. She could picture Patrick moving his feet and arms, splashing round his bedroom with excitement. She squished her cigarette in the ashtray.

"Okay, then, Patrick. We'll see what happens."

"Yeah," he replied, "I'll call them tomorrow."

"I think," Lucy said, a bit uncertainly, "you should let Stan call them. After all, it was his idea."

"Give me a break," Patrick said.

"Gina was his friend."

"Christ, Lucy, she was my friend, too."

"But he'll have to explain to them how he got the paddle."

There was a long pause in which Lucy saw Patrick scratching his beard as he searched for a response. She didn't know if it was worth an argument but she found herself feeling stubborn for Stan's sake. Gina had been his friend.

"Tell him I hope he enjoys himself, then," Patrick said. "I hope he enjoys his little triumph."

Lucy hung up the phone and glanced at the clock, a spiky gold wall clock that had come from her parents and could have been made by a white trash Aztec. It was quarter to nine so Stan was still out. He'd gone to a neighbour's and would be back at ten.

She remembered distressfully that she'd invited Stan for dinner on Saturday and she had no idea what she was going to feed him. If only she'd had a mother who knew how to cook more than Tuna Noodle Casserole and Busy Day Stew. Tomorrow, on her way to school, she would stop and buy a cookbook.

CHAPTER 31

Walking did not come naturally to Francis Eliot and his feet were moving under protest. The air conditioning at the station was on the fritz again and all he could think of when he looked at the giraffe was high summer on the Serengeti. He loved to watch nature shows with his girls in the evening.

Eliot needed to think while he waited for Freeman, so he'd come outside into the crisp morning air. He plodded through the weeds at the edge of the highway, away from the station about thirty feet and then back again and beyond it another thirty feet, knowing he must look insane. If Eliot hadn't been who he was, he would have been picked up by now. He knew that they were watching him from the station windows.

He'd been called by Toronto's 18th Division before he left his office the previous night. They'd raided a garage in the suburban west end and had seized a large stockpile of stolen goods. Among them were items belonging to Patrick Irving. They'd arrested four men on suspicion.

So that was that as far as that went, though, of course, the tie between Lambert and the Irving robbery had always seemed rather tenuous. And Irving was sure to take it badly, despite the preparation he'd had two days before.

Eliot had tried to break the news to Irving gently. There was not enough evidence to support a connection between the explosion, Dockstader's letter, and the attempt on Mr. Irving's life. He'd then told Irving about the Lambert alibis.

Irving had surprised him by immediately laughing and when Eliot had told him about the Rotary meeting, he'd even made a joke— a rather strange joke about Robitaille in a fez. It wasn't until Eliot had brought up Ferrara that Irving had become his old abusive self. He'd scorned their suspicions in no uncertain terms.

Eliot had had to work long and hard to haul Irving's history with Gina Ferrara out of him. Omitting Irving's captious comments, what it came down to was this: Irving had met Ferrara at a Christmas party and she had asked him for his number. He went out for drinks with her twice. She seemed fascinated by his activism, and especially by the fact he'd been arrested. She started coming to the meetings of the group he was forming and started to phone him more and more. Irving decided it was getting out of hand, so he told her about his girlfriend.

Gina didn't seem to take this seriously. In fact, she acted almost as if it made the whole thing more fun, more of a challenge. She kept coming to meetings and asking him out. He had dinner with her once, he just couldn't keep saying no.

And then, when Irving hadn't heard from Gina for a while, he thought she'd given up, had maybe met someone else. Until, one day, out of the blue, she called him about the trip to the Speller. She said she was doing a series on camping for the paper and thought maybe he could help her with the first article on collecting and cooking wild foods. She said she could use the company of an expert. Would he go?

Irving didn't want to. She had an ulterior motive— having him to herself, alone. He knew she thought that when she got him there he'd probably end up giving in. So he told her no, he wouldn't go.

Then on Saturday, her column appeared, announcing to the world that he was going. So he went, grudgingly, and it turned out he was right. She started coming on to him almost before they pitched the tent. And, as it turned out, she was right, too. He gave in to her advances.

"The End," Irving had said. "You know the rest."

Eliot had then asked him about opportunity and, after protests of bad memory, Irving had finally admitted, "I went into the woods to piss at one point. I don't know about you, but it takes me two minutes. Gina made some crack when I came back about me being so modest."

So, Eliot thought, trudging along his fourth tour of the highway, we now have resentment at being rejected and maybe jealousy as well. Both possible motives for someone obsessed.

We have opportunity, too, he thought, though, sadly, a very brief one. If the B.C. mycologist was right, however, there might have been enough time. Most of the preparation would have been done long before— boiling the false morels in eighty per cent ethanol, reducing the solution to a toxic powder, dissolving the powder in water, injecting the tasteless solution into a true morel— or filling a syringe to inject one of Irving's own mushrooms on site— all that would have been done earlier.

As Eliot passed the entrance to the station parking lot, he met a car slowing down to make the turn. The driver was de Freitas and he rolled down the window. Freeman called over from the passenger side, grinning like a demon.

"Getting a little exercise, eh? Getting those juices flowing up to the brain?"

"I was just coming in."

"Well, you better. We got something here that'll tickle Francie's fancy."

Eliot waited by the door while de Freitas parked. Freeman came capering, almost dancing, up to him, grinning and twirling his briefcase. Eliot had never seen Freeman so... enthused.

"Just you wait, Francie. Just you wait." He made an exaggerated bow towards the door and Eliot led the way into the building.

As they walked in, the desk sergeant called Eliot over and handed him a note.

"Message for you, sir, while you were out. I didn't want to disturb you."

"Thank you, Sergeant," Eliot replied. He glanced at the note and saw the name "Stan O'Keefe" and a long distance number below. The sergeant had added, "Re: Ferrara."

"That's a friend of hers." Eliot felt Freeman's breath on his neck. He folded the note exactly in half.

"Her mother told us about that guy but we didn't get around to seeing him. Lives outa the city somewhere or other. We figured what we got here is more important right now." Freeman whacked the side of his briefcase.

"Come into my office, Chris," Eliot said.

"So we get to her apartment and it's half packed up. It's a real dump. Boxes all over the place. We start looking around. There's all these lesbo-feminist books lying in piles, clothes and shit. I see this box with a photo album sticking out the top so I pick it up and open it and look what falls out."

Freeman tossed over some papers, stapled at the top. They were photocopies. The top page had the title, "Neurological Consequences of Exposure to Low Dosage Monomethylhydrazine in Rats." Below was written, "Sally M. Braithwaite, Ph.D. Anatomy & Alicia L. Lerner, Ph.D. Botany." Eliot smoothed out the pages and then looked at his palms. He wiped them with his hankie.

"Well done, Chris," he said to Freeman.

"Most of it's gobbledygook. But that's the drug, right? Mono whatever it is. That's what the toxicologist said got Irving." Freeman was staring down at the papers covetously, as if he wanted to snatch them back up.

"We'll take a look and see if we can decipher this. See what it says about mushrooms. We can get some help if we find we need it. Look up these women who wrote it." Eliot smiled at Freeman, his pearly teeth showing briefly between his pink lips. "Well done," he said again. He leaned back in his chair and folded his hands on his stomach. The heat didn't feel as debilitating now— they must have had in a repairman.

"Now, Chris," Eliot said, "who did you see when you were in Toronto? Did you learn anything of interest?"

Freeman raised his eyes from the desk to Eliot. He lifted his lip and said, "Tch."

"What's the matter?" Eliot asked him. The sneer on Freeman's face was appalling.

"That's all you're gonna say about it, eh, Francie? You gonna keep it to yourself or maybe pass it on?"

"Pass it on?" Eliot then realized that Freeman wanted the credit. He wanted assurance that Headquarters would know it was he, Freeman, who had made the connection. "Of course, Chris. I'll certainly pass it on."

"Huh," Freeman said, but his face relaxed. "We talked to the mother, sister, and husband of sister, cousin, and a couple of people she worked with at the *Post*. Nobody could tell us nothing about her and Irving. Nobody even knew they were involved. The most we got was from her brother-in-law. He said Ferrara seemed not all there the last time he saw her, preoccupied. But then her sister said no, she seemed fine."

"I see," Eliot said. "And her mother told you that you should talk to this," he picked up the folded note and unfolded it, "Stan O'Keefe?"

"From what I could figure out, he was Ferrara's only friend. Mama Ferrara thinks 'he's such a nice man.' She musta said that a hundred times."

"Well, Chris," Eliot said, "Let's call Mr. O'Keefe and see what he has on his mind."

The voice on the phone was hushed but eager, as if the speaker were in a sickroom or library. It reminded Eliot of the way Jo used to sound when she was reading a storybook to the drowsy girls, back when they were small. But rather than putting Eliot to sleep, Stan O'Keefe's story braced him like a bucket of water. A bucket of water poured over his head while he'd been sitting with his feet up, enjoying.

O'Keefe's story was about paddles and Penders and phone calls and break-ins and fires. Eliot silently swallowed it down. His mind plumped up while his complacency shrank. Freeman, meanwhile, began to crowd Eliot, edging across the desk, repeating, "What?" while Eliot shook his head at him, distracted and frowning.

"Well, Mr. O'Keefe," Eliot sighed, finally. The story had ended without dessert, leaving Eliot's mind grumbling with dissatisfaction. "Thank you very much for this. You've been very helpful indeed. I think I'd like to come out to see you in person. Some time in the next few days. But I will call you beforehand, of course."

"Yes, okay, fine," the voice said and then paused. It began again, hesitatingly. "Can you tell me, though, if I was right about Patrick's paddle? Was I right to be suspicious? It's been keeping me awake, wondering."

"Yes, Mr. O'Keefe, you were right. Mr. Irving's paddle was found on the bank."

"Hmm. Thanks."

"Thank you... I'll be in touch, then. Goodbye."

"What, for chrissakes?" Freeman almost roared when Eliot put down the phone. Eliot sighed again and reached down to the drawer where he kept his honey. He didn't care any more if Freeman saw him. He wouldn't even care if it made the headlines. He dipped two fingers into the jar and sucked at them, raising his face to Freeman's drill-like eyes.

"Dear, oh dear, Chris," he said to him, finally. "We haven't been kind to the memory of our Gina Ferrara. We've doubted her morals and her affections. I myself have doubted her sanity. We've almost accused her of attempted murder." He smiled wearily and apologetically. "But worse than that, Chris, worse than that... we've left her up the river without a paddle."

CHAPTER 32

Stan was watching Gina as she paddled up Bay Street, her hair blond like a Valkyrie's and down to her waist. He was looking down at her from a great height above. He was an eagle— with an eagle's eyes— perched on the top of a bank tower. He could see bruises on Gina's head, the blank look in her eyes. Her mouth was opened in an "O" like a megaphone.

And then there were cockroaches scrambling over her feet and up her white dress in thin rusty rivers. "Stan, you peabrain," her voice came harshly. But her lips didn't move from the Edvard Munch "O."

Stan awoke from his dream into a strange, thick light. The bedroom was dim and translucent in the grey dawn, almost as if, during the night, the mist from outside had crept in through the windows. The air was moist and sullen and thunder rumbled far off. "Angels bowling," Stan said narcotically, and then rolled over, hoping unreasonably to get another hour's sleep.

But the dogs had been waiting for his slightest sound or movement and clambered out from under the bed, Folly trembling with the approaching storm, Slim trying to lick whatever part of Stan was within the reach of his tongue and managing an ankle. Stan groaned and then reached out and patted them both. Folly's trembling increased with Stan's touch.

"You crazy dog," Stan murmured and pushed himself up into a sitting position. With his foot, he picked up the T-shirt that he had torn off in the night and pulled it on. He tugged up his striped boxer shorts. Then he sat for a moment, rubbing his eyes.

"Gina," he thought, "I'm sorry," though he wasn't sure exactly what for.

He stood up unsteadily and went out of the room and down the stairs, the dogs tumbling after him. In the kitchen, he turned on the stove and then opened the freezer and took out the coffee. He filled the espresso pot with enough to serve six and put the pot on the now-warm burner. Then he went into the mudroom and let out the dogs.

They barked into the darkening morning. It was as if the dawn had gone into reverse. Stan stood yawning and watched it darken. He chastised himself, as Gina had in his dream.

How *could* he have believed that she had drowned by accident? He should have known that Patrick's illness wouldn't have thrown her off. She'd probably gone down that stretch of the Speller a dozen times. She wouldn't have lost her cool. She was the kind of person who could watch the approach of an avalanche and appraise it for thrill factor as she clamped on her skis. She could ride out anything, if she saw it coming.

If she saw it coming, Stan thought, ruefully. Someone must have got her from behind. Just like they got Lucy. He sighed and went inside.

Up in the bathroom, he stared at his reflection and thought through the whole thing, again.

"Okay," he said, wearily. "So he'd just killed Gina or knocked her out. He wouldn't have been too composed. He might have put her in the canoe and then just got out of there and not remembered about the paddle till later. When he finally did remember he would've freaked right out. By then, time would've gone by and nothing would've happened. He would've started to wonder why the police hadn't clicked." Stan took a minute to brush his teeth. He rinsed his mouth and then swallowed a vitamin.

"Then it came to him that the paddle *hadn't* been found. At least not by the police. And that would've driven him even crazier. He would've wanted to know where it was. He would've started checking— maybe first up by the campsite or with Gina's mother."

"So he calls her up and pretends he's a collector and she tells him she doesn't have it. She tells him *I* have it. He figures he'd better try and grab it before it makes it back to her. Who knows, he worries, what'll happen to it then? The fewer people who see it the better. So he decides he'll try and get to it first. He comes to my house to steal it... Shit." Stan doused his face in hot water and rubbed it hard with a towel.

Stan had been trying to sneak past the same old problem and once again it tripped him up. The man who'd killed Gina— or, yeah, maybe the woman— had to know where Stan lived.

It wasn't as if Stan actually had an address— RR 2 Barton wouldn't have got anyone far. To find Stan's place, a person would've needed directions and there weren't many people to give them. There were his neighbours, but none of them had been asked. A couple of friends in Toronto, but how would this guy know who they were? If Lucy had talked to anyone, she would have told Stan. He'd already run all this by her.

So, maybe there wasn't a connection after all. Maybe the break-in, the fire, and Lucy's concussion were all the work of some local creep.

"It doesn't really matter that much, anyway," Stan sighed.

He went back down to the spluttering coffee and slid it off the stove. Then he scooped out the dogs' breakfasts from the huge lidded container in the corner, knowing Folly's storm neurosis wouldn't allow her to eat and that Slim would take the first opportunity to get a second share. So he put Slim's bowl outside with Slim and brought Folly in to stare, her teeth chattering like Chiclets in a box, at her own. Then Stan went and got his coffee, emptying the pot into a large black mug. He stood and sipped for a minute as the trees outside began to waver and reel.

What a mess Gina's murderer had made of it all, Stan thought. He poisoned Patrick but not well enough, then hung around for two hours to get seen by Gina. Why the hell would he do that? You'd think that he'd have got out of there fast.

Stan carried his coffee out to the porch. Slim flew by, chasing some noisy sparrows. The sky was getting dark as loam.

"Unless," Stan murmured, sitting down at the table and cradling his coffee between his hands. His eyes narrowed in concentration. Folly trembled up to his knees and pressed against him. He put a hand on her head, unconsciously. "Shit!"

Slim flew by in the other direction. Stan suddenly rose and stared at Folly.

"Shit!" he repeated. "The whole investigation was centred on Patrick as the victim. The cops had their hands full with all their own theories plus all of the ones that were provided by Patrick. Gina was completely forgotten." Stan closed his eyes. "Even by me."

The wind began to twist at the leaves of the silver maples that bordered the vegetable garden and Stan suddenly felt sick of himself, deathly sick. His shallow disregard for his friendship with Gina made him feel dizzily ill. He hadn't even mourned for her, he hadn't shed a tear. And he was maybe her closest friend.

"I'm so sorry, Gina," Stan said again. He sat down and put his head in his hands. The whirligig on the roof began to rattle in the wind. A heavy rain began to drop, hard and loud.

It was fucking Patrick Irving who had thrown him off, Stan now thought. Patrick and his self-important theories. The only thing that *he* had got right was the initial fact of the poisoning. The rest was just rank egotism.

God, Stan fretted, how could Gina have liked that guy? But for that matter, how could Lucy? For the fortieth time, Stan briefly pondered that latter mystery and got nowhere. Then he returned to Gina.

He just couldn't see strong, self-sufficient Gina chasing anyone, going after Patrick the way he'd described. But probably Patrick had exaggerated that part— after all, the only word they had for what happened was his. The only word they had for *anything* was his... Stan drank some coffee and thought about that some more.

"Shit!" He jumped up so quickly that Folly let out a bark. "Patrick."

"Patrick," he repeated. He began to walk erratically around the porch like Slim gone wild on a scent. "He knows all about mushrooms. He could've poisoned himself to throw off suspicion. Made sure the poison was not enough to kill him but *was* enough to make it look like somebody had tried. Then he followed Gina back down the trail and hit her before she got in the canoe. He went back and played dead until somebody found him!"

"Yeah," he muttered, "yeah. And then later, when he remembered about the paddle, he rigged up this vague excuse that he wanted to go back and check. But he didn't say anything about it to the police. Just like he didn't say anything about the sex thing with Gina. At least, not until after the inquest concluded that her death was accidental. *Then* he told them— when he needed to give them a time for someone to have got at the mushrooms. Shit! Gina probably didn't drag *him* up there, he probably dragged up *Gina!* Oh, that bastard! Gina!"

Thunder grumbled over the fields and Folly trembled into a corner. Stan repeated his wild tour as he went through his theory again. But this time he stopped part way around and caught himself against the wall. His mind had caught the thought of Lucy.

"Oh, Lucy," he moaned.

If Stan was right, and he *had* to be right, Lucy was going to be shattered. For though she might have sometimes doubted Patrick's reasoning, she'd never doubted his sincerity. She'd never doubted his word. Stan had been jealous of it— of her faith in Patrick, of her loyalty even after their break-up.

And now Stan would have to tell her that Patrick was a murderer.

"No," he said firmly, "I won't. She doesn't need to hear it from me." But then he had another thought. About the police.

If *he* had figured out about Patrick, the police were bound to have figured it out, too. Any day now they'd be calling Lucy, and Eliot would discreetly question her about Patrick's behaviour. Maybe Stan should prepare her for it so she could get over the shock. Maybe he should tell her the next night when he saw her.

Stan looked out anxiously at the rackety rain and then grabbed for the rest of his coffee. The wind was picking up, slanting the rain towards the house.

He didn't know what to do— tell her tomorrow, or let things take their course? Goddamned bastard murdering Patrick. Murdered Gina. Why?

Thunder suddenly cracked like a thousand pistols. A thick sheet of water like the Jack Falls sideways was thrown by the wind through the windows of porch, soaking Stan in his underwear, and Folly. Stan ran to the door and yelled out to Slim. The dog slid like an otter across the lawn, skitted in through the door, and the three of them dashed drenched inside.

CHAPTER 33

The rainy sky made it feel hours later than it really was. It was Saturday evening, going on seven, and Stan was at Lucy's for dinner. As he stood at the counter and poured red wine into pink juice glasses, she came up behind him and kissed him under the ear. He jumped and spilled the wine.

"Shit," he laughed.

Lucy twirled a short strand of his hair between her fingers and murmured into his ear. "Tonight's going to be a good one, Stan. I can feel it."

Stan turned and wrapped his arms around her.

"We needed a change of venue," he said.

"Yes. From the O'Keefe Centre to the Brown Derby."

"The Brown Derby?"

"I think it was a strip joint on Yonge Street."

"A strip joint, eh? Hmm." They kissed.

He handed her some wine and they clacked glasses and went together to sit down at the table. Stan still hadn't decided what to say about Patrick or whether to say anything at all. He felt unbalanced at her place, in this sparse, white apartment like a hermit's cell. The lines were so regular that they should have made things straightforward. Instead they made him feel tipsy and strange. Lucy lit a cigarette and looked at the clock.

"It should be here soon," she said. She propped her elbow on the table and her chin in her hand and fastened her eyes on Stan. Then she slowly smiled, her eyes going soft and deep. Stan blushed under her look and then blushed even redder— he was head over heels. Lucy laughed suddenly and picked up her cigarette, which had been trickling up blue smoke between them. "Now I'm staring at *you*," she said. She took a drag and asked, "How's Folly?"

Stan's soaring mind plunked itself down. He wet his dry mouth with some wine.

"She's pretty good, I guess. She's been sleeping a lot."

"You never told me how she got her name."

"Oh." Stan smiled. "Well, I found her on a highway when I went away one weekend. I think someone had dumped her. I took her home to my apartment– I was living in Toronto then, in an apartment about half the size of this one– and I advertised. Nobody ever claimed her. So I either had to take her to the pound, or keep her, and I couldn't take her to the pound. So, my folly." He shrugged. "It's also the name of a dog in a Jane Austen novel. I used to read a lot of nineteenth-century literature."

Lucy nodded.

"Cecil Ho, my department head, is always reading Victorian stuff. Whenever he travels he packs some thousand-page tome." Lucy looked at Stan thoughtfully. "You know, Stan, I was talking to Cecil today, and he told me he thought I'd be getting my tenure. He thinks I've been doing really good work."

"Great!" Stan exclaimed.

"Yes, it is." She narrowed her eyes. "But now I'm really confused about what that woman said. The woman from Israel who slagged me to Robert. She must have something against me, though I can't imagine what."

"Hmm." He considered, trying to see this clearly. But he couldn't. He made a suggestion. "You know what I'd do, Lucy? I'd call her up."

"Call her?"

"Yeah. Find out what her problem is." He hesitated. "I don't know. Maybe it's a stupid idea."

"Hmm," Lucy mused, frowning, sipping her wine. "She's at Tel Aviv University."

Stan watched her gaze wander up to the ceiling where it hovered for a minute near the white globe light. Then it fell suddenly back to his face. "So," Lucy said. "I guess you would've told me by now if you'd found anything out about the fire."

"Yeah," Stan answered, "no one's got back to me. I went and talked to some of my neighbours to see if anyone saw anything and the police had been there first. No one did see anything, though. I haven't heard from Eliot, either."

"Hmm. I wonder what they're up to. I wonder if they're thinking the same thing as Patrick. That Gina was murdered because she saw something."

This was Stan's chance, if he wanted to take it. A buzzer buzzed feebly like a dying bee.

"That'll be dinner," Lucy said, rising. She took her wallet and went to the door and Stan watched her dress swing around her knees. It was the colour of a December five o'clock sky, a deep, deep blue– almost black. And her feet were bare again tonight.

"Jeez, you're soaked," Lucy said to the delivery man.

"It's pissin' out, mon," came a West Indian voice. "Twenty-won-fifty."

Stan looked at the window while Lucy was scratching for bills. The grey pane glittered with rain– the same rain that had chased him into the house, yesterday when he was wild.

"Thanks," Lucy said and pushed closed the door with her shoulder. She displayed the pizza box with a self-effacing smile.

"I'm really embarrassed about this, Stan. Some dinner for you to drive all this way for."

"No, it's good, Lucy. I don't eat much pizza at home and I sure can't get it delivered. This makes me feel like I'm in the city– pizza and nowhere to park."

Lucy doled out the pizza and the iceberg salad with its pale tomato wedges the colour of red dye number three. She got up once to get the salt and pepper and then again to get some forks. Then she settled into her chair and looked quizzically at Stan.

"What's the matter?" she asked.

Stan had been gritting his teeth. He realized he must have looked pretty weird.

"Nothing," he said, blushing, and assailed his pizza. He thought, c'mon O'Keefe, you've got to make up your mind. Clam up or tell, you dope. He knew if he told it would put the kibosh on the night, and that would be the third night running. What would it matter if he waited till morning?

Lucy picked at her pizza with her long slim fingers and Stan watched her as he chewed. She picked at it delicately, her fingers fine probes, her eyes focused and intent as a microscope.

"Lucy, don't you like green pepper?" he asked.

"I'm not crazy about it," she smiled.

"I assumed you liked it, 'cause you asked me if I wanted it on the pizza. I can't stand it either."

Lucy laughed her odd laugh and mussed up her hair.

"I guess we both must be trying too hard," she said and reached across to take his hand. Stan thought, Yeah, Patrick the murderer can wait until morning.

The evening aged into sagacious night while the rain pattered on the windows like mice. Stan felt everything spinning— dimming, receding into darkness— everything but Lucy, who approached him with smiling, sure-footed resolve.

At first, Stan found himself listening for the sure-thing disaster— Patrick breaking down the door, or an air-raid siren. But soon he only heard the beat of Lucy's heart as he laid his head on her breast.

Stan opened his eyes as his body shivered from a soft tickling touch on his neck. He was lying on his stomach with his arms pinned under him. He rolled himself over and saw Lucy in the darkness, kneeling beside the bed. He reached out drowsily to stroke her white shoulder and she dipped down towards him like a nocturnal bird silently visiting a pond.

"I'm sorry," she whispered. "I didn't want to wake you. You should try to get back to sleep."

"What time is it?" he whispered drowsily back. His hand traced out the shadows that obscured her body.

"It's just after three." She caught his hand and kissed it. "I'm going to stay up for a while."

Stan yawned and stretched himself. He gently pulled her to him as his body relaxed, and held her for a moment, kissing her. Then sleep slowly lowered him into a well and he felt Lucy's hands disentangling and then the slight roughness of blanket moving over him.

When Stan next awoke it was to Lucy's murmuring voice. A line of light shone at the base of the bedroom door. He propped himself up and reached for his watch on the table beside the bed. The luminous dial showed twenty to four.

Lucy's voice was desultory— on and off— until finally Stan heard nothing. He got up out of bed and went to the door.

Lucy had her overcoat over her shoulders and her hair was pushed back from her forehead. She sat slumped on the floor beside the telephone, her hand holding a cigarette that she wasn't smoking, her eyes staring at something that she didn't see.

"Lucy?" Stan took a step toward her. She swung her eyes over to him. Lucy was crying. "Peach, what's the matter?"

Lucy's voice came out weak and tired and forlorn. "I just called Barbara Strasbourg in Tel Aviv, Stan. She told me something about Robert."

CHAPTER 34

It was understandable. When the second paddle wasn't found, it was perfectly understandable that they had assumed it had disappeared down river. Eliot couldn't fault Freeman. If only the Pender boy had left Ferrara's paddle where it was.

Towards the Pender boy, Eliot had felt both anger and sympathy, the former giving way to the latter in the course of his interview with him the day before. Paul was a sullen, resentful boy who would probably come to no good, like dozens of teenagers Eliot had met over the years. Paul did things stupidly, to impress his friends, and later in life, when he didn't have any friends, he would do things stupidly because he was bitter. Paul was the kind of kid Eliot wished he could reason with and knew he couldn't touch. Paul Pender was not like his girls.

Paul's silent uncle had brought him into the station, gripping him by the shoulder and propelling him forward. From the hands of his uncle— out of the frying pan— Paul was taken by Freeman and pushed into the chair. Freeman had battered him with hard anger until Eliot had intervened, the boy's sullen yet nervous face eliciting the compassion that Freeman had later derided.

"Goddamn little bastard," Freeman had said. "He's just gonna go home and tell all his friends how he sucked us in." Unfortunately, Freeman was probably right.

Paul Pender had found the paddle on the trail, up where it curved around a big piece of rock with a small cave at its base that Freeman had remembered checking during the search. The cave was plenty big enough for a person, Freeman had said. Someone could have been in there when Ferrara came by.

Eliot had had the paddle picked up from Ferrara's mother and sent to Forensics. He expected to have the report back soon. In the meantime, he was waiting for some Toronto visitors— Lucy Shepherd and Stanley O'Keefe. He'd been called by the station early that morning, while he was still in his pyjamas at the hotel. The message was that Shepherd and O'Keefe needed to talk to him right away and wanted to see him in person.

Eliot wondered if it was about Patrick Irving. Ms. Shepherd had been Irving's girlfriend until very recently and both she and O'Keefe had gone with Irving to the Speller the day he'd been released from the hospital. Eliot had been having some honeyed thoughts about Irving, but they'd been anything but sweet.

Eliot's desk phone rang and he picked it up.

"Stan O'Keefe and Lucy Shepherd are here."

"Thank you. I'm coming right out. Please tell Detective Freeman to come to my office."

Eliot hastily buttoned his suit jacket and bustled out to reception. Lucy Shepherd was sitting over in the corner next to a dark-haired man, Stan O'Keefe. They were holding hands but let go rather self-consciously as Eliot crossed over towards them. They stood up and Eliot briefly took in that Lucy Shepherd was slightly taller and that Stan O'Keefe needed a shave. Eliot smiled and shook their hands.

"We can talk in my office. Would you like some coffee?"

"Oh, yes. Please," Stan said, while Lucy nodded. They both had circles under their eyes.

Eliot passed on their orders for coffee to a P.C. and led them through the corridor. The station had the hushed, careful feel that came with a Sunday morning.

Freeman was sitting by the giraffe on the window sill, looking hung over. He'd brought another chair in but not one for himself.

Eliot made the introductions and they all sat down. Stan turned to Lucy and said to her quietly, "Maybe you want to start."

"Yes," she said, glancing at him. "If I could just figure out where."

"Maybe you could start with the conference."

"Yes."

She told them about going to a conference in France with her colleague Robert Milliken, the man who'd been married to Gina Ferrara's cousin. Robert's wife, Kelly, had died of cancer the previous winter.

"I talked to Milliken last week," Freeman growled. "An uptight bastard."

"Yes, Chris, thank you," Eliot said. Lucy Shepherd continued.

She told them how she'd heard about an incident at a VIP dinner in which Robert Milliken had been slapped by an academic from Israel. She told them about the explanation that Milliken had given her— how he'd insulted the woman after the woman had insulted *her*, Lucy's, academic reputation. She told them how upset she'd been with what Milliken had hinted— that her own work was looked down on by the scientific world in general— but then came to be perplexed when she received strong evidence to the contrary. Stan— Mr. O'Keefe— had suggested she call this woman and ask for an explanation. And so she had, late last night.

"When I told Barbara Strasbourg who I was, she didn't say anything for a minute and then she acted as if my name had just rung a bell. She said, 'Oh yes, you were in Bordeaux at the conference, weren't you? I'm sorry I missed your talk.' That made me really angry. I thought she was being sarcastic. I said, 'Dr. Strasbourg, please don't give me that shit. Robert Milliken told me what you said.'

"She said, 'I'm sorry, Dr. Shepherd, I don't know what you

mean. The subject of my conversation with Dr. Milliken was not something he'd be likely to repeat.' So I told her what Robert had told me. I was getting really annoyed."

Lucy opened the large bag she held on her lap and put her hand into it. Then she paused, with furrowed brows. Stan, who was watching her, said, "Is it okay to smoke?"

"Yes," Eliot said, glancing at Freeman.

"Give her your coffee cup," Freeman said. Eliot removed the lid from his styrofoam cup. There was an inch of cold coffee inside. The thought of the coffee mixed with ashes filled him with distaste.

"Maybe you could track down an ashtray, Chris."

"That's okay. Thanks," said Lucy, reaching for the cup and lighting a cigarette. "Thanks for letting me smoke." She took a puff. Eliot wanted to run a brush through her hair. She looked like she needed a mother. "Sorry," she said, continuing.

"When I told Dr. Strasbourg the story that Robert had given me she let out a really weird laugh. And then she said, 'Dr. Shepherd, you're putting me in a rather uncomfortable position. You're forcing me to divulge a secret that I've kept for three years. But I'm very glad you're doing it.' And then she told me about Alicia Lerner."

"Alicia Lerner," Freeman interrupted. "Wasn't that the name of one of those broads, Francie? One of those two mono-whatsit broads?"

"Yes, Chris," Eliot said, rubbing his hands together and then folding them demurely before him on the desk. He was interested. "We have an article here co-authored by an Alicia L. Lerner, a Ph.D. in Botany. The subject seems to be the toxin that was found in Patrick Irving's system after he was poisoned."

"That would be the same person," Lucy said, eagerly. "She did a post-doc in my department."

"And in Robert Milliken's department," added Stan. Eliot glanced at him. He had his chin in his hand and his elbow on his knee. He was looking down at the floor. When the coffee was brought in he took it gratefully, as if it were first aid.

"Please go on, Dr. Shepherd," Eliot said.

"Yes. Well, Alicia Lerner left the department just after I got there. She'd got an assistanceship at Tel Aviv University and that's where Barbara Strasbourg met her. They apparently became very good friends, very close. Alicia Lerner told Barbara Strasbourg about something that had happened to her before she left U of T. Something that Robert Milliken had done." Lucy paused and looked anxiously at Stan, who nodded almost imperceptibly.

"Dr. Strasbourg told me that one night while Alicia was working late in the lab, Robert came in. She'd apparently had the feeling for some time that he was interested in her but she hadn't let it get anywhere. Anyway, when Robert found Alicia alone, he started coming on to her and when she tried to put him off, he got angry." Lucy puffed on her cigarette and closed her eyes. "Robert raped her," she sighed, mournfully. She took a moment before continuing, then opened her eyes straight at Eliot. It almost threw him off.

"I was stunned. I asked her why Alicia didn't do anything, tell anyone. She told me that Alicia knew that she was leaving and that she just wanted to put it behind her. She also thought that no one would believe it of Robert Milliken. She was probably right. *I* didn't at first."

"And where is Alicia Lerner now?" Eliot asked. Freeman began tapping his fingernails on the sill, softly, as if it were a muffled snare drum.

"She's dead. She died in a car accident last year."

"I see," Eliot said, glancing at Freeman, who upped the tempo of his drumming. "And she never told anyone about this rape? Other than Barbara Strasbourg?"

"That's the whole thing," Lucy replied, looking again at Stan. "Alicia told Barbara Strasbourg that she'd got some revenge by writing to Robert's wife..."

"Who's also dead," Freeman said.

"Yes."

"And so Barbara Strasbourg confronted Milliken with this at the conference?" Eliot asked.

"Yes. He laughed at her, so she slapped him."

"And he lied to you about it afterward."

"Yes."

The drumming stopped and Freeman clicked his tongue impatiently.

"Nobody could've touched him," Freeman said. "An alleged rape, dead victim, no witnesses, it wouldn't have mattered who she told. There wouldn't be a case."

Eliot had to agree.

"Lucy," said Stan quietly, "tell them what Milliken's up to now."

"Yes. Robert's just been made director of the National Science Commission. He'd been in the running for the past few months and was shortlisted a week before Gina's death."

"Gina Ferrara," Eliot said. "The cousin of Milliken's wife."

Lucy nodded and then looked at Stan, who put his coffee down on the desk. He scratched his nose and then started to speak.

"Gina was a pretty good friend of mine. She was close to her cousin, Kelly. I got the feeling Kelly was the only one in her family that Gina could relate to. I remember Gina saying once that she wished Kelly would dump her husband— 'the lord and master,' I think she called him. I think Gina tried to put up with him for Kelly's sake. Anyway," Stan sighed, "Mrs. Ferrara told me a while ago that when Kelly was in the hospital dying, Gina visited her every day." He glanced at Lucy and then looked at Eliot. "Lucy and I have been thinking that Kelly might have told Gina about the rape."

Eliot sat back in his chair.

"Gina would have had a fit if she heard about it," Stan continued. "She would have gone right up the wall. Maybe Kelly asked Gina to do something about it or maybe she asked her to keep quiet. In any case, maybe when Milliken was shortlisted for this big prestigious job, Gina couldn't stand it any more. Maybe she confronted him– I can see Gina doing it. Maybe she threatened to expose him so he wouldn't get the job."

"You think the scandal could have been enough to affect Milliken's bid for the post," Eliot said.

Lucy Shepherd nodded. "These days, yes."

"You said you're in the same department, Dr. Shepherd. How well do you know Robert Milliken?"

Lucy dropped her cigarette into the styrofoam cup. She'd smoked it almost down to her fingers.

"I thought I knew him fairly well. But he's always been distant and formal."

"And did you notice any change in his behaviour, before Ms. Ferrara's death, or after?"

"In his behaviour to *me* there was a change after her death. He was friendlier, more intimate. I thought for a while he was attracted to me." Eliot saw her shudder. "Now, though, I think he may have been trying to get information."

"Information?" Freeman said. "What kind of information?"

Lucy looked at Chris Freeman and pushed her hand through her hair. Her eyes narrowed in thought.

"Robert knew about me and Patrick Irving and he always kept himself up-to-date on how the investigation was going."

"He would've. Anyone would've," Freeman retorted. "But *he* would've, for sure."

"Yes," she said, "I know. But when we were in France together,

Robert took me to dinner. I told him about our trip up north, about how we canoed up to the site. He was cooler afterwards, almost distracted. I'm wondering now if that's when he remembered about Gina's paddle." Lucy lit another cigarette. "Patrick gave us a ride back from the airport and he told us about the inquest. Robert asked if the police had any idea about how the poisoning was done."

"What's his field of study?" Eliot asked.

"He's an entomologist."

"What's that?" Freeman said.

"He studies insects."

"Huh," Freeman said. "Not mushrooms." Then Stan swore softly and Eliot looked towards him.

"I think that Milliken might have been to the Speller before. I just thought of it now. He might have gone there with Gina." Stan hesitated and everybody waited, Lucy eyeing him questioningly. "The guy who gave me Gina's paddle, Pender? He told me he'd met some of Gina's relatives before, up on the Speller. He thought one of them was her sister." Stan looked at Lucy. "I never met Kelly, Lucy. Did she have blond hair?"

"Yes," she answered, "very blond."

"Then it could have been her. He said a blond woman and her husband. Gina's sister's hair is dark brown, like Gina's."

"Goddamn fucking natives," growled Freeman.

"Detective Freeman," Eliot said sternly. "That will be enough." But Freeman was talking under his breath and didn't pay any attention. There was an uncomfortable silence which Eliot broke, turning to Stan O'Keefe.

"Does Robert Milliken know where you live?"

"I don't know how he could. I don't exactly have an address that you can look up in a phone book," Lucy interrupted. She looked worried.

"He might have known you live near Barton, Stan. I may have told him. The day that he told me the lies about Barbara Strasbourg and I was so upset, I think he asked me if I would be okay and I told him yes, that I would be fine, I was going to your house, out in the country. I may have said near Barton. I'm sorry," she ended, "I can't remember."

"It's okay, peach." *Peach?* thought Eliot. "It probably doesn't matter. My place is a good thirty miles from Barton, anyway. He couldn't have found it from there." Stan smiled at his peach. Freeman yawned.

"So, that's what we came here to tell you." Stan swallowed the dregs of his coffee. "We kind of thought it all fit together." He shrugged.

"It's an interesting scenario," Eliot mused. "Poisoning Irving would have served two purposes. It would have got Ferrara on her own where Milliken could get at her, and it would have thrown us off track by making us look for someone who wanted to kill Irving. It did both, certainly."

"Huh," said Freeman, "there's too many 'if's. What happened to Ferrara poisoning Irving?"

"Gina poisoning Patrick?" Stan interjected. "You've got to be kidding! *I* thought..." He looked quickly at Lucy, who was swirling the contents of the styrofoam cup and looking at him inquisitively.

"You thought, Mr. O'Keefe?" Eliot looked at him, smiling, with small curious eyes.

"Gina wouldn't have tried to kill Patrick," Stan murmured, looking like he wanted to hang himself. Everyone sat in silence.

"Well," Eliot said, finally. "Will the two of you be going back to Toronto now? Can I reach you somewhere if I need to?"

"Stan," Lucy said quietly, still swirling the cup, "would you mind if I came to your house? I don't know if I can handle going to school and seeing Robert. I'd like to take a few days off."

Eliot watched Stan break into a smile. It opened across his face like a Christmas present.

"Sure, Lucy, of course."

Eliot rocked himself back in his chair. "Well, Chris," he said, "what do you think?"

"Talk to Milliken and then I'll tell you. He's probably got a goddamn alibi."

Freeman jumped down from the window sill, taking the pink giraffe with him. Two legs and the neck snapped off.

CHAPTER 35

"It's unusual for me to be at home on a weekday, Detective Sergeant. But I've got rather a lot to organize."

Dr. Robert Milliken sat on the green leather sofa in his pale grey living room crowded with art. Except for a few ceramics scattered here and there, the art took the form of black and white photographs and, except for a huge fuzzy abstract of something that looked to Eliot like a urinal, the photographs were all of women. Eliot delicately raised a stubby finger and pointed towards one of the pictures.

"Marlene Dietrich?" he asked.

"Yes," Milliken replied, crossing his legs and folding his arms. "It's a Steichen. Quite a famous shot."

"I thought it looked familiar." Eliot looked around the room again and wondered how Jo would like sharing her house with so many other women. He wondered how Milliken's wife had liked it. "This is a remarkable gallery."

"Thank you. I think it is. I've been collecting for about twenty years. It all started when my wife and I dropped in on an auction. We hadn't intended to bid on anything, but then I saw this," Milliken gestured to a photo of a pale young woman in white standing demurely with her hands clasped before her, "and I couldn't resist. In twenty years I've built up quite a collection. All images of women looking straight at the camera."

Eliot looked again at the pictures. It was true— the women were all gazing back.

"I love them for their intimacy," Milliken continued. "I almost feel they are looking at *me*." He smiled with what looked like practised self-consciousness. "I'm afraid, Detective Sergeant, that I must sound rather vain."

Eliot tried to smile his disagreement but his mouth puckered stiffly in protest. He reached for his cup of chamomile tea and sipped it to hide how he felt. Milliken had offered him a cup of tea and Eliot had expected orange pekoe. Instead he'd been given this flowery green tisane, which wouldn't be so bad if it had some honey in it. But Milliken hadn't even offered sugar. Eliot gingerly replaced the cup on the saucer. It was a paper-thin cup with a tiny handle that made even his small hands feel big and clumsy. He didn't think he liked Dr. Robert Milliken.

"Dr. Milliken, when was the last time you saw your wife's cousin?" Eliot quietly asked. Milliken crossed his legs.

"Gina, you mean, or Linda?"

"Gina Ferrara, yes. I'm sorry."

"About two weeks before her death. We met for lunch, as I told your colleague last week."

"Did you do that often? Meet Gina for lunch?"

"Every now and then," Milliken replied. "When my wife was

alive we used to see each other often. My wife and Gina were very
close. But I only saw Gina twice— perhaps three times— after my
wife's death." Milliken reached for his own tea and picked it up,
then looked at it thoughtfully before drinking. "Three times, yes.
Once for lunch and twice for dinner at her mother's house." He
drank some tea and smiled conspiratorially. "I've never had much
in common with the Ferrara family, as you can imagine. However."
He balanced his cup and saucer on his knee. "I don't have any family
of my own and they made it their mission to save me from my
solitude."

"They're looking after you," Eliot said.

"Yes. Especially the talkative Mrs. Ferrara. It's a funny thing,
though, Detective Sergeant. Solitude is the human animal's idea of
hell but I, unfortunately, rather enjoy it."

"Unfortunately?" Eliot asked.

"Unfortunately because I have so few opportunities, and now,
with the Science Commission, I'll have fewer than ever. That's why
I value a day like today when I can work on my own at home."
Milliken reached forward and set down his cup of tea on the table,
a long wooden oblong with legs of black metal. "The last time I had
a day at home was back at the beginning of May." He looked at
Eliot, grimly. "It was the day that Gina died, in fact. Monday, the
fifth of May."

Eliot waited suspiciously for him to continue. He'd been
planning to stroll to this subject casually, but the professor had
yanked him there by the hand. Eliot's small eyes watched Milliken
like dark glass beads, emptied of anything that would give an
impression.

"Yes," Milliken said, after a moment, during which he
smoothed his grey slacks, the colour of Lake Simcoe on a cloudy
day. "I was preparing my talk for a conference the following week
and I made certain that I wouldn't be disturbed. I turned off all of

the phones and let the answering machine take my calls. Luckily, I didn't do that today or you wouldn't have been able to reach me."

"That's your usual practice, is it?" Eliot asked.

"Yes. I turn off the phones and don't answer the door. My neighbour from across the road was rather annoyed because I didn't answer when he knocked that day. Extremely rude of me, of course. But he *will* drop by uninvited."

Eliot looked out the plate glass window past birch trees and a winding gravel road. Just at the edge of his field of vision he could see part of a cedar house. Someone in the cedar house could see Robert Milliken's. He took another sip of his tea.

"It's interesting you should mention May the fifth, Dr. Milliken. I was planning to ask where you were that day."

Milliken looked at him with surprise. Or a good imitation of surprise, anyway.

"Where *I* was?" he asked.

"Yes," Eliot repeated, "where *you* were. But it seems that you were here."

"I don't think I understand, Detective Sergeant. You suspect that I may have tried to murder Patrick Irving?" He smiled at Eliot with a curve that implied that the absurdity of the idea was self-evident. Eliot was getting a little fed up. Milliken was too disingenuous.

"It's not Patrick Irving that we're concerned with," he said, with more impatience than he'd really have liked.

Milliken leaned back on the sofa and folded his arms across his chest. An expression crossed his face like a false dawning idea, and with it came and went a slight flush.

"You aren't reconsidering Gina's death? You aren't thinking there was foul play?"

"We *know* there was foul play, Dr. Milliken." Eliot put down his cup quickly, so it rattled. "Now, you said you were here on

Monday, May fifth. Is there anyone at all who can confirm that?"

Milliken stared at him, trying to think. Or trying to look like he was trying to think. Eliot wasn't sure which.

"Perhaps my neighbour saw my car. He's retired and usually at home. My car would have been in the driveway. I only park it in the garage in the winter. But really," Milliken added, with a sudden movement of his hand, as if he were batting away a gnat, "if you're thinking I was involved, the idea is ridiculous. Gina and I weren't always on the best of terms, but we liked each other. At least, I liked *her*, Detective Sergeant, as any of her family could tell you."

Eliot rubbed his hands together and noticed they were dry. He'd pick up some Jergens on his way back north. But there'd be no time for dinner at home.

"I'd like you to stay where we can be in touch, Dr. Milliken. You don't have any conferences coming up? You aren't planning to leave the country?"

Milliken now stared at him with a brand new look— one that was, this time, authentic. Eliot could read in it Milliken's realization that he wasn't just one suspect out of several. Milliken was *the* suspect and he didn't know why. Milliken slowly shook his head.

"Nothing until the end of next month," he said.

Eliot urged himself out of his chair and Milliken stood up, too. Eliot felt the women watching from the walls. Watching and waiting. He sighed and looked up at the tall professor, who towered solidly and maddeningly above his own five feet four.

"Have you ever been up at the Speller River?" Eliot asked him. "Perhaps with your wife and Ms. Ferrara?"

"Six or seven years ago, yes." Milliken's mouth was set like a trap. No unnecessary word would get past it now.

"What did you and Ms. Ferrara talk about the day you had lunch?"

"Family, mainly. Our work. The food."

"Not about Alicia Lerner?" There was a very long pause, during which Eliot imagined he saw Milliken teeter slightly, like a building in a high wind.

"I'm sorry," Milliken finally said. "I don't know what you mean." He smiled slowly and then almost seemed to suppress a yawn.

Eliot didn't like Dr. Milliken.

Across the road, Milliken's neighbour was lying in a hammock on his large front porch. Eliot hailed him from the foot of the driveway so as not to startle him by appearing up close, and then trundled toward him, holding out his I.D.

The neighbour, Bill Scofield, was a small wiry seventy-year-old with sunglasses and a silver beard. He swung himself out of the hammock with enviable ease and gestured towards two Adirondack chairs. They both sat down, facing the road and Milliken's tasteful blue-grey house. The birch trees showed the house only in glimpses but the view of the driveway and Milliken's burgundy Acura Integra was completely clear. Eliot asked Scofield if he remembered the day.

"Early last month. It was a rainy Monday. You knocked on Dr. Milliken's door, thinking he was home, but he didn't answer."

Mr. Scofield laughed heartily.

"Yup. I remember. I wanted to return the step ladder I borrowed. I tried to phone him first but he had his galldarn machine on so I figured I'd run across. I knew he was in there, his car was home. But he must have not wanted to see me. Can you imagine that? A charmer like me?" He laughed again and then started to cough, caught his breath and laughed. Eliot smiled at him, thinking, too many cigarettes.

"Do you remember what time of day that was?"

"Around five or six o'clock. I waited till then, thinking he might come out to get his mail."

"And his car was there all day."

"Yup. Didn't move."

"When did you next see him?"

"Next morning. Then he did come out to get his mail. I hollered to him about the step ladder but he asked me to drop it off some other time. He said he had the flu and was going to bed. He skedaddled back into the house."

Eliot pursed his lips as he gazed at the car. The Milliken homestead was ten clicks from Barrie. He turned to Scofield who was swinging one leg that he'd crossed over the other.

"If your car broke down and you had to get into town, how would you do it? I assume there's a taxi service that would come out here."

"You got me," Scofield replied. "I've never had to try it. If I was in that situation, I'd call my grandson to come pick me up. But, if you were young and nimble you could probably walk it in a couple of hours. Nice walk, too. Take some short cuts through the woods."

"Yes," Eliot mused. "If you left at six or so in the morning, you'd reach Barrie just when the stores were opening." He beaded in on Scofield. "Are you an early riser, Mr. Scofield?"

"Me? Not a chance. I stay up to watch the late show." He laughed. "Great one on last night. *River of No Return* with Marilyn Monroe and Robert Mitchum. You've never seen such nonsense."

"I've seen it," Eliot said. "Rory Calhoun's in it, too."

"Yup," Scofield laughed, "good memory."

"Tell me, Mr. Scofield. How well did you know Kelly Milliken?"

Scofield suddenly sobered up.

"Kelly Hanlan. She kept her last name." He stopped his leg from swinging. "I knew her to chit-chat but not really well. They only moved out here a couple of years ago and they were never much for socializing. She liked to garden, though, and was always complaining about too much shade. You can see the tulips she planted by the house. Funny how they still come up when she's gone."

Eliot peered across the road at the smudges of white and pink. He hadn't noticed them before. He looked back at Scofield.

"What was your impression of their marriage? Was it a good one?" Scofield coughed and stood up, turning away from Eliot.

"I'm not what you'd call an expert on that. It took me thirty-five years to see my own marriage was a mess. To me, theirs looked normal. But Kelly used to seem pretty worn out and a couple of times she looked liked she'd been crying." Scofield turned and frowned with a small wave of his hand. "But then, her husband was the least of her problems."

CHAPTER 36

Lucy stood staring at the edge of the vegetable garden like a Bedouin who had stumbled on a jungle. She wore an extra-large white T-shirt that came down to her knees and an old fishing hat of Stan's that he'd never worn fishing. He had never fished in his life. The leaping trout on the front of the hat was leaping over Lucy's left ear. She shaded her eyes with her hand.

"What can I do?" she called to Stan, who was squatting among the carrots, thinning them carefully. Stan grinned.

"Great outfit," he said.

"I should've gone home to get some clothes. Your stuff makes me look like a goof."

"Yeah," Stan said, "I know the problem." He stood up and looked around him. "I don't know, Lucy, you like bugs. Why don't you check the tomatoes for beetles."

"Who says I like bugs? I *don't* like bugs. I only like things with no legs."

"Ugh," said Stan approvingly, "you're quite a gal."

"Stan," Lucy hesitated, sitting down on the grass, "I think I need to get back to the lab. I love being here with you but I've got so damn much work. I'm just going to have to face Robert."

Stan stepped over the carrots, the beans and potatoes and came and sat down beside her. He wasn't surprised to hear this. She'd been using his computer to make some notes from memory while he researched his column on wolves. But he'd seen her increasing chagrin.

It was the days that were difficult, the long, dull days. The nights weren't a problem at all. Their love-making melted away her frustration, and melted away his worry, until they were simply a soup of sighs. It was the days. He took her hand.

"I wish I knew what was going on," Lucy said. "Robert may not even be at school. He might have been arrested by now."

"I doubt it," Stan said. "Not unless they've been able to place him up on the Speller. And I imagine he wouldn't have made that too easy."

"No," Lucy agreed. "He wouldn't have." She paused. "You know, I understand why he lied to me, Stan, but why did he have to use *that* lie? He purposely made me think that I wasn't worth shit."

"He did it because he's a bastard, peach. Plus, it was pretty clever. He wanted to nip your curiosity in the bud, or at least to throw you off."

"And he figured I was too gutless to follow it up. And he was right. I wouldn't have, if you hadn't been so reasonable."

Stan frowned. He thought, Yeah, reasonable. As reasonable as my theory about Patrick. Stan was glad that he had put off mentioning it.

Lucy sighed. "So, when's the gnome supposed to be here?"

"He should be here now. He said ten o'clock." Stan kissed her and stood up. "I'll drive you down to Toronto whenever you say. Just let me know, okay?"

Beyond her Stan spotted a dark-suited figure, short and round with a shiny head, creeping toward them from the direction of the house. A slow-moving June bug. The gnome.

"Here he is," he said to Lucy, who quickly stood up.

Eliot came toward them and was tackled and twirled by the dogs. Stan grabbed them both by their collars.

"Let's go sit on the porch, Detective Sergeant. I can leave the dogs out here."

Eliot looked relieved and wiped his head with a handkerchief.

"That'll be fine," he said.

"Can you tell us what's going on?" Stan asked. "Are you getting anywhere with Milliken?"

"We're making some progress," Eliot said vaguely, "but we still have a long way to go."

"Did he say where he was that day?" Stan persisted. "Could he have been at the Speller?"

"He says he was at home, preparing work for a conference. We know that his car didn't leave."

"Robert lives near Barrie, doesn't he?" Lucy asked. "Somewhere outside of town."

"Yes," Eliot said, "about ten kilometres."

"So, you're trying to figure out how he could've got up north and out to the river without the use of his car. Is that right? Am I warm?" Stan asked.

Eliot smiled but didn't reply. Stan took it as a yes.

"I guess he didn't borrow anyone's car."

Eliot just smiled.

"If he got into Barrie, he could have rented one. But I guess you've checked that out." Eliot was smiling and Stan was annoyed. He never liked playing twenty questions. He thought that Eliot should be more forthcoming. He thought that he and Lucy deserved it. "You've checked out the car rentals, I imagine, haven't you?" Stan repeated with fake nonchalance. Lucy laughed.

Eliot crossed his short, plump legs and rested his hands on his stomach.

"Computers can be very helpful, Mr. O'Keefe. They keep such thorough records. Credit cards, for instance. Dr. Milliken hasn't rented a car in Ontario since 1989."

"Uh-huh," Stan said, "but aren't there lots of little companies that don't have computers?"

"Not in Barrie, Mr. O'Keefe."

"Oh," Stan said, defeated.

"Now," Eliot said, "I have some questions for each of you and since we've been discussing transportation— Dr. Shepherd, I'll start with you."

"Okay," Lucy said, straightening herself up and looking alert.

"The evening you came out here to visit Mr. O'Keefe, the evening of the fire, June ninth?"

"Yes."

"How did you get here?"

"By bus. I took the bus to Barton and Stan picked me up at the station."

"And did you leave from home or from work?"

"I left from work. From the school."

"Do you remember seeing Dr. Milliken that day? Did you speak to him before you left?"

"Um," Lucy said, "I may have seen him in the hall or something. But I don't think I spoke to him."

"So he wouldn't have known you were coming here, then."

"Well," Lucy said. "I had my bag. If he saw me with it he might have assumed I was coming here."

"And what time did you leave for the bus?"

"Five-thirty, quarter to six."

Stan looked back and forth between them, following closely. He thought he had the gist.

"If Milliken figured you were coming to my house, Lucy, and he knew that I lived near Barton, he could have driven there and waited for the bus and then followed my car to the house." He looked at Eliot. "Right?"

Eliot looked at Stan with surprise.

"Well done, Mr. O'Keefe. Dr. Milliken left his lab at quarter to six, telling a student he was spending the evening in the library. But he left his car in the reserved lot. He took it out again at eleven-thirty."

"Shit," Stan said. "And he didn't rent one. And I don't suppose he was on the bus with you, Lucy." She made a face. "The timing sure is right, though, isn't it?"

"Yes," Eliot agreed. "Indeed it is." His little mouth smiled at Lucy. "Thank you, Dr. Shepherd." He smiled at Stan. "Now. Mr. O'Keefe."

Stan felt nervous all of a sudden, the way he did when he was crossing the U.S. border. He'd be perfectly innocent of any wrongdoing, but would still turn red like a kid caught in a lie. It was a wonder he and his truck had never been strip-searched. But then maybe his behaviour was considered normal. Maybe it was the blasé ones that ended up getting grabbed. He waited for Eliot and tried not to seem blasé.

"About your friend, Gina Ferrara. You both worked for the *Post*, did you not?"

"Yes," Stan replied. "I still work there."

"What can you tell me about her work habits? Was she one to spend a lot of time researching her assignments?"

"Researching her assignments?" Stan smiled, no longer nervous but amused. "She didn't usually write stuff that required much research. She usually just had to go out and do things and then write about what she did. She always waited till the last moment, too, though she used to put on a show for our editor, Elizabeth Atkins. Gina was really good at making Elizabeth believe that she had her column done and was only neglecting to send it, even though she wouldn't touch it until the night before the deadline. But Gina was such a great writer that she always pulled it off," Stan ended admiringly.

"I see," said Eliot. "Then you can't visualize Ms. Ferrara preparing for her last column by reading up on poisonous mushrooms in scientific journals."

"Ha!" Stan laughed, "You've got to be kidding!" then realized that he'd sounded rude. "Sorry, Detective Sergeant, but no. I'm so far from being able to visualize that that I might as well be on the moon. Gina wouldn't read scientific journals to research her column. No."

"It may be a small matter," Eliot said. "Mere speculation. But you may remember that we have a copy of an article co-authored by Alicia Lerner, found in Ms. Ferrara's apartment."

"Hmm," Stan said, glancing at Lucy, who was blowing a slow, steady stream of smoke into the air. "Weird." He felt Eliot's eyes on him. Eliot seemed to be waiting expectantly.

"We have two theories," Eliot prompted.

"Uh, yeah," Stan said, resuming concentration. "Yeah." He suddenly had it. "Gina got interested in Alicia Lerner so she tried to find out more about her. She looked up stuff she'd written. Why else would she be interested? She'd heard about the rape. The article in her apartment," Stan concluded with satisfaction, "would prove she'd heard about it. Right?"

"'Prove' is a strong word," Eliot smiled. He paused. "But we have another theory as well."

This was beginning to remind Stan of some sort of Platonic dialogue. He'd always found Socrates exasperating. There's only so much you can take of a know-it-all. Especially one who's always smiling. Stan sighed.

"Robert might have planted the article." This all of a sudden from Lucy. "Maybe he put it there so you'd think that Gina poisoned Patrick."

Eliot tapped his fingertips together with a pleased and contented smile. His eyes seemed to twinkle like the Little Dipper.

"Well done, Dr. Shepherd. Very well done, in fact." Stan felt a ridiculous rush of pride which must have shown on his face, because Lucy rolled her eyes at him.

"Perhaps, Mr. O'Keefe, you would show me your garden. My wife has been after me to put in some vegetables but I never seem to have the time."

They stood overlooking the foot-tall corn plants and Stan tried to picture the plump detective wrestling with a rototiller.

"You're married, are you, Detective Sergeant? Do you have any kids?" Eliot reddened at Lucy's question and Stan was surprised at her interest.

"Yes, I do. Triplet girls, Emily, Charlotte, and Anne."

Stan laughed.

"You're not a Brontë fan, are you, by any chance?"

Eliot slightly squirmed.

DEADLY BY NATURE

"My wife's a great reader. I wish I had the time."

"And what's your wife's name?" Stan grinned. "Not George?"

"Not George," Eliot sighed. "But still a man's name. Her name is Jo. Jo Olychuk."

"It's amazing, really," Lucy began, staring out over the fields, "how many women keep their names when they marry. I mean, women you wouldn't expect. Even Robert Milliken's wife, Kelly. I thought she was really conservative. She kept her last name, Hanlan."

"That could be a man's name, too," Stan said. Lucy looked at him quickly.

"Stan," she said, "I've never rented a car. What do you need? A credit card?" Lucy's intensity startled him.

"A credit card and a licence, peach. You don't have either."

"But what happens to that stuff when you die? Does somebody have to notify somebody to get you struck from the records?"

"I guess so," Stan said vaguely but he felt a small twinge. He shifted his eyes to Eliot.

Eliot seemed to have been taken by a tremble, starting down at his feet. He vibrated. It looked, any second, like he might start to bounce. His voice, when it came, was almost a squawk.

"Oh, *very* well done," Eliot said.

CHAPTER 37

"The prosecuting attorney began his summation today in the trial of Robert Milliken, newly appointed Director of the National Science Commission. Milliken has been charged with first-degree murder in connection with the death of Gina Ferrara, former

233

columnist for the *Toronto Post*, as well as the attempted murder of Patrick Irving, environmental activist.

"Ms. Ferrara drowned last May while seeking help for Patrick Irving with whom she was camping at the time of her death. Irving had become seriously ill after ingesting poisoned mushrooms.

"While the defendant listened with a bemused expression, the prosecutor, Marco Zanetti, reiterated the key points of evidence which, he stated, 'amount in total to a volume the size of Gibbon's *Decline and Fall.*' Edward Gibbon wrote the *Decline and Fall of the Roman Empire* in the late eighteenth century. It ran to nearly a million words."

"Yeah, yeah," Ray Clifford commented and then continued his reading aloud.

"Zanetti recounted the testimony of expert witness Dr. Elaine MacMillan, a mycologist from the University of British Columbia. Mycology is the study of fungi. MacMillan had suggested several methods by which the poisoning of Irving could have been accomplished.

"She indicated that the most likely scenario was that a single non-poisonous mushroom of the same variety as that collected by Irving— widely available at upscale specialty stores— could have been tampered with in advance and then added to those that Irving had found himself. She said this would require a familiarity with the area and a knowledge of what mushrooms Irving would be likely to find there in early May. It would also require a certain degree of scientific expertise, as the toxin would have had to be extracted and distilled from the poisonous variety of mushroom in which it naturally occurs.

"Milliken admitted visiting the Shallow Bay area six years ago with the victim, Gina Ferrara, who was his wife's cousin. He is a professor of entomology— the study of insects— at the University of Toronto. In Milliken's defense, his lawyer, Carlton Fay, had provided contrary expert opinion to suggest that the poisoning could have been carried out by anyone with a rudimentary knowledge of chemistry.

"As to the alleged murder of Ferrara, Zanetti repeated the testimony of the first pathologist who had examined Ms. Ferrara's body. The pathologist indicated that the wounds to her head were consistent with a blow from a heavy object. A smooth rock or a metal boat anchor were two possibilities he'd admitted.

"Zanetti then recounted 'the most damning evidence of all'— that brought forward by Detective Sergeant Francis Eliot of the Orillia OPP. It involved the discovery of four transactions made with a credit card belonging to Milliken's deceased wife, Kelly Hanlan.

"Early on the morning of the day of Ferrara's death, Hanlan's MasterCard was used to rent a car from a Hertz office in Barrie. Four hours later, the card was used again in Cochrane, an hour's drive from the alleged crime site, to purchase an inflatable kayak, a small anchor and a four-horsepower motor. An employee at the sports store identified Robert Milliken as the purchaser.

"Again, late that evening, gas was purchased at a service station on Highway 11, using Kelly Hanlan's MasterCard. The card was used the fourth and final time, a month later, to rent a car from a Budget office in Toronto, a ten-minute walk from the university where Milliken worked. The significance of this final transaction, Zanetti indicated, would be explained in what was to follow.

"In the case of the car rentals, Hanlan's driver's licence had been presented as well. D.S. Eliot suggested that the licence had been altered by Milliken and that, given his respectable appearance, it was unlikely that it would have been examined closely by the car rental employees.

"In his own defence, Milliken claimed that his wife's identification had gone missing several months before from her room in the Princess Margaret Hospital when she was being treated for cancer. He stated that he had been too distraught over his wife's condition to report the theft and that, after her death, it had slipped his mind. With regard to his positive identification by the sports store employee, Milliken simply claimed that she must have been mistaken."

"Clever comeback," Ray said and went on.

"Throughout the trial, Milliken has insisted that he never left his home on the day the murder was committed.

"Zanetti then began a discussion of the defendant's possible motive. He reiterated the statement of..."

"Ray!" Susan interrupted, standing in her nurse's uniform in the doorway. "Why do you have to read him that? You know how I feel about it."

"Christ, Susan," Ray said angrily. "Why don't you go to work? What am I supposed to read him? Garbage about the goddamn constitution?"

"There are lots of other things in that paper. You just zero in on whatever's most morbid."

"You don't think Jamie would be interested in this? You don't think he wants to hear it?"

He looked at his son, who lay in the bed, stiff, still, pale, and expressionless.

"What do you say there, kid? Tell your mother what you want. Do you want me to read this or not?"

Jamie's face didn't change, except for his eyes, which flew up in an emphatic "yes."

"Where d'ya think you're going?"

Angus Pender sat in the stern of the loaded canoe and stared up at his nephew, Paul, who was standing on the dock.

"To the fucking fish fry, what d'ya think?" Paul put his hand on the gunnel and prepared to get in.

"Not with me, you ain't," Angus said and pushed him back

with the blade of his paddle. "I ain't havin' no useless mutt hangin' off my coat-tails this year. You wanna go chase girls, you find your own ride. You come with me, you gotta work."

Paul looked at Angus balefully and spat in the water. Then he stepped down into the canoe. Angus pushed off from the dock into the streaming Speller.

CHAPTER 38

A late September breeze rustled across the field, strumming the golden rod and Queen Anne's lace. A small V of Canada geese flew in from the north and disappeared, honking impatiently, over the trees to the south. Beyond the trees, the oats and barley swayed buff and ecru and a pair of deer took some of their last placid steps before hunting season had them running scared.

Stan lay propped up on his elbows on an old plaid blanket, scratching out his column on a yellow lined pad. Lucy lay on her back, reading from one of the stack of books she'd brought out from the city, a can of Coke on the ground beside her. The dogs were asleep in the tall grass and flowers.

Stan read over what he'd written so far: "The chipmunks are desperate. With each shorter, cooler day you can watch their anxiety increase. They jerk and scurry like so many White Rabbits, their cheeks bulging with the seed they've filched from the feeders. They keep their heads down, and their bodies flat, as they hustle from the feeders to their nests in the woods. Between food and shelter is an open field commanded by circling hawks."

Stan put a stroke through the word "desperate." He replaced it with "frantic" and stared at the page. Then he smiled ironically and stroked out the entire paragraph. The shadow of a cloud slid across his back as he chewed on the end of his pen.

"Stan," Lucy said.

"Hmm?" Stan looked at her. She had put down her book and was gazing up at the sky.

"Sorry to interrupt, but I want to ask you something. I was thinking about when we were at Gina's funeral. You remember how Robert was sick?"

"He had a cold or something, right? He probably got it when he was out in the rain."

"Yes," Lucy said, "but there was something else. He looked really strange, kind of tanned and pale at the same time."

"I remember thinking he looked weird, but that was the first time I'd met him. I figured he always looked like that."

"I was wondering if he was wearing make-up."

"Make-up?" Stan laughed.

"Yes. He probably got badly bitten by black flies. Maybe he was covering up the marks."

"Huh," Stan mused. "Yeah."

"And you know what else I was thinking?"

"What?"

"That maybe Robert never *intended* to kill Patrick. That he only wanted to make him really sick so that Gina would have to go off on her own to get help. Having Patrick alive to tell the story afterwards was better for Robert, right? It backed up the whole accident idea and focused the investigation on Patrick."

"Shit, yeah. Maybe you're right." Stan said. "Pretty clever."

"Do you think he'll win his appeal?" Lucy asked.

"God," Stan answered, "I can't see how."

"No," Lucy said. "Neither can I." She picked up her book. Stan turned back to his pad.

"Chipmunks," he wrote after a moment, "are cheeky. Especially this time of year." He crossed this out immediately. He scanned the trees and thought he saw a flash of yellow. Perhaps it was an evening grosbeak.

"Stan."

He looked at Lucy.

"Yup."

"Patrick..."

"I don't really want to talk about Patrick, Lucy. Patrick is *persona non grata* out here on the farm."

"I was just going to say he must be happy. I mean, that they're re-opening the EES investigation and everything."

"He must be pleased as punch, I'm sure."

"Sorry. Go back to work."

Stan tore the top page from the pad and stared for five minutes at the smooth new blank one. He started writing, "Simon. Theodore. Alvin."

"Uh, Stan," Lucy said, tentatively.

Stan scratched out the chipmunks and turned toward her with an expression that showed his vexation.

"What?"

"I'm sorry, Stan. I'm driving you crazy. But I want to say one last thing. Then I'll go in the house and leave you alone."

"Oh," Stan said, not too sure he liked that idea. Lucy sat up and crossed her legs. She lit a cigarette and smiled a little.

"I have a confession to make," she said.

"Yeah?" Stan said, and sat up, too.

"I've been wanting to tell you about this for ages but I was afraid that I'd sound like a creep. A creep or an airhead. Or both. It's about..." she hesitated, "the *persona non grata*."

"Oh," Stan said.

"I thought for a while that maybe *he* killed Gina. I mean, the idea crossed my mind."

Stan stared at her in disbelief.

"You're kidding," he finally said.

"I know. It's disgusting, isn't it? But I thought that he'd maybe set the whole thing up."

"When did you think it?"

"As soon as you asked me to call him about the paddle. When you told me that you thought Gina'd been murdered."

"As soon as that," Stan said quietly.

"I knew almost immediately that I was wrong. Patrick wouldn't kill anyone. He couldn't." Lucy looked at Stan beseechingly before she continued. "I wasn't sure I should tell you about it, but then I thought that you ought to know what I'm capable of. You shouldn't trust me, Stan."

Stan took the cigarette from her hand and dropped it sizzling into the can of Coke. He eyed her as he made his own confession.

"But *you* thought it because you're so damn intelligent, Lucy. I thought it because I was jealous. I thought the same thing, peach."

Lucy eyebrows went up and then she slowly smiled, her eyes shining slightly mad.

"You did, Stan? Well, there you go."

Stan grinned suddenly and bowled her over. He trapped her between his arms.

Everything, meanwhile, lilted.